MIAMI NIGHTS 2

VICTOR L. MARTIN

MIAMI NIGHTS 2

A Novel by

Victor L. Martin

Wahida Clark Presents Publishing
60 Evergreen Place
Suite 904
East Orange, New Jersey 07018
973-678-9982
PO Box 383
Fairburn, Georgia 30213
www.wclarkpublishing.com

Miami Nights 2 by Victor Martin
978-1-954161-43-6 Paperback
978-1-954161-44-3 eBook
Library of Congress Cataloging-In-Publication Data:
LCCN 2021916350

1. Porn Industry, 2. Coconut Grove, Florida 3. Modeling, 4. Street Lit, 5. Miami, Florida 6. African American Fiction 7. Urban
Cover design and layout by Nuance Art.*.
Book design by Nuance Art.*.
Proofreader Rosalind Hamilton
Sr. Editor Linda Wilson

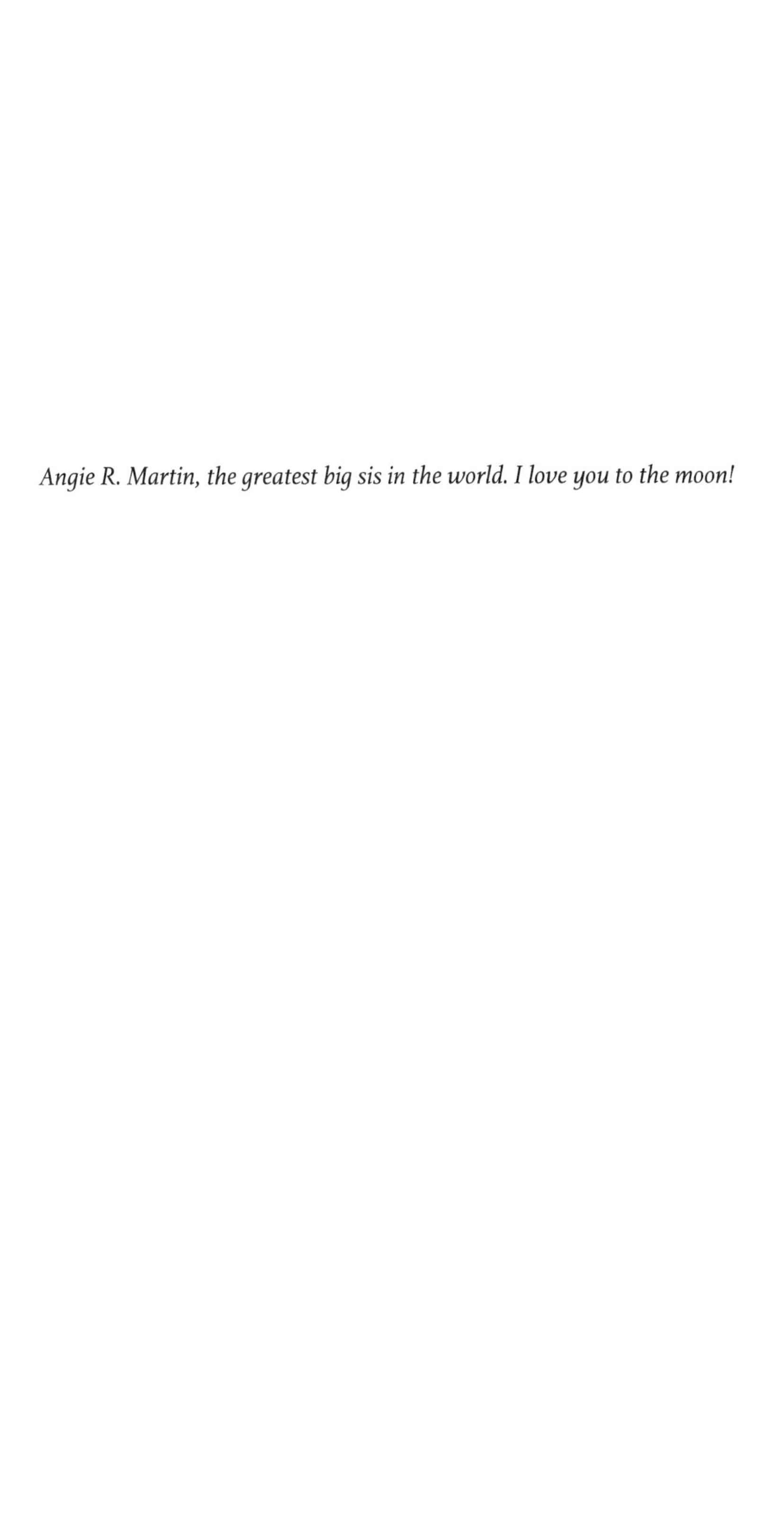

Angie R. Martin, the greatest big sis in the world. I love you to the moon!

ACKNOWLEDGMENTS

First and foremost, I have to recognize the truth. I am blessed to have this talent to write, and my thanks is given to God. Here I am, giving y'all *Miami Nights 2* and again I have to show my sincere appreciation to Wahida Clark and the entire WCP team. Thank y'all for never giving up on me and I'll be ready to get on my grind when I join y'all on the daily hustle. And yes, I intend to add screenwriter and producer to my list of achievements when I touch down in Atlanta. WCP...we still Hittin'!

I have to give a major plug to Yung Joc, Shawty Shawty and Mz. Shyneka. Y'all keep me SMH and tuned in with y'all on the *Streets Morning Takeover*.

Nuance, just when I thought you did your best with the old cover art for *Nude Awakening 1&2*, you of course proved me wrong with these superlative covers for *Miami Nights 1,2,3*! Thank you, and you will have your chance to top these on my next project with WCP.

To all my readers that enjoyed NUDE I, I wanna thank y'all for riding with me and accepting the vivid, erotic style of my writing. This *Miami Nights* trilogy is sex on paper. It is good from start to end!

I'll go ahead and share the news about my aspirations to turn the *Miami Nights* trilogy into a film. I am going to write the screenplay and to let y'all in on my vision, here is my dream cast.

Trevon Harrison = Gucci Mane

LaToria aka Kandi =?
Jurnee Cruz = LaLa Anthony or Dascha Polanco
Kendra Paige = Jazmine Sullivan or Niecy Nash
Swagga = ?

Honestly, I left Kandi undecided because it's impossible for me to envision the perfect Queen to portray Kandi when the following are squeeze into my head; Nicki Minaj, Cardi B, Amara Lanegra, Anansa Sims, Kash Doll, Dream Doll, Thicky Minaj, Asian Doll, Saweetie...see my issue?

Now Swagga, the antagonist. Hmmm? Who would y'all like to see portray him? Oh, yeah...here's my open pitch to Gucci Mane. I will be fortunate if you stepped in and take the lead role. If you're open to this venture, we'll create a classic film. So, I'll go ahead and speak it into existence.

MIAMI NIGHTS

Starring Gucci Mane

Screenplay & Produced by Victor L. Martin

I HAVE TO BELIEVE IT...TO ACHIEVE IT.

To my behind the scenes supporters, I have to show my appreciation to TaTaNisha L. McKenzie once again. Thank you for typing my next project and for posting my words and pictures on social media that I have to send via snail mail.

Lalonie Willhite, I am pleased to know you and I'll never forget how you held me down in my greatest time of need back in 2018. And now you are an author! Congrats on that!

Miami, yes, Liberty City was my home in the past. Much love to 65th Street, Holmes Elementary, Brownsville Jr High. And how can I speak about my old hood and not mention Uncle Luke, Trick Daddy, Trina, Rick Ross, City Girls, Liberty Square Park, Pork & Beans Projects, USA Flea Market, and everyone that's reppin' 305, including Pitt Bull and DJ Khaled.

As it is known to my longtime fans, I write with humility.

However, I need to speak about myself. As an author = a writer of a book, I want to let it be known that what you've read or will read with my name on it, I wrote it. I don't invest in fronting, no need for me to get someone else to write for me…I'm just that good. If I've stepped on some toes, move your feet.

KEEP YOUR EYES DRY & YOUR HEART EASY
-Victor L. Martin

Author Info
Web: VictorLMartin.com
Facebook: Victor L. Martin-Author
IG & Twitter: @VictorlMartin_

THEME SONG
BRS KASH FEATURING DABABY, CITY GIRLS

"Throat Baby"

Black Lives Matter

1

—————

AIN'T NO FUTURE RIGHT FOR ME

January 20
Friday, 3:10 P.M. – Miami, Florida

"This some real live bullshit!" Trevon muttered behind the wheel of his brand-new damson metallic Audi A8. "I knew they was gonna find that bitch ass homo thug not guilty!"

Seated next to Trevon, LaToria aka Kandi, settled back into the black leather seat with her arms crossed. "Swagga isn't worth the stress," she muttered.

"I know," Trevon replied, staring at the courthouse up the busy street. "I just can't get over what he did to you . . . or what he did to us!" he expressed, punching the bottom of the steering wheel.

LaToria sighed. "We have to move on from this."

"It ain't easy," Trevon said, slumping back into the seat.

"You got too much to lose. For real, I'm not trying to raise this baby by myself, Smooth."

"I wouldn't dare risk my freedom for that bitch ass coward!"

"Well, we both need to move past this and focus on us and our baby." She laid a hand on his knee. "Ain't trying to lose you."

Trevon looked at her belly. In the month of June, she would

bare his firstborn, and it was a moment that he was looking forward to. "What we gonna do about this film?"

LaToria shrugged. "I don't think anyone will really care about Swagga fucking that tranny. With our luck, he'll find some way to make it blow up in our faces. Besides, with Chyna dead, I don't see nobody giving a damn, and that's just how I feel."

Her words fell hard on Trevon. In truth, he had too much at stake to focus on any type of revenge toward Swagga. Money proved stronger than truth, and it had set Swagga free. Not guilty was the verdict of the kidnapping charge against Swagga. His high-powered team of attorneys argued heavily that no one could firmly prove that Swagga had actually kidnapped LaToria and taken her aboard his yacht. They turned their focus on Swagga's former bodyguard, Yaffa.

Trevon had to accept the reality and remember his own chance of freedom he was given behind killing Yaffa in that warehouse. Even still, he was having trouble letting shit ride behind his beef with LaToria's ex. As she had just mentioned, they were still in possession of the video clips of Swagga and Chyna. LaToria leaned toward the idea of moving up to Atlanta with Trevon, leaving Swagga and the stress and past behind. Exposing Swagga's homosexual tastes would only bring drama back into their lives.

"I wanna go home," LaToria said

"You ain't going to Amatory with me?"

"Nah." She shook her head. "I'm tired, and plus my feet hurt."

"Told you not to wear them heels so—"

"Look," she interrupted. "He's coming out!"

Trevon sat up the moment Swagga made his exit from the building. A roar of cheers went up from the mass of spectators that awaited Swagga's appearance. Trevon's jaws flexed at the sight of Swagga standing on the top step with his skinny arms raised triumphantly. He was surrounded by his legal team and entourage. The bright sun danced off the pricey diamonds that filled his mouth.

Trevon took it all in with silence. He saw Swagga taking a pose on the steps in front of a group of photographers while the crowd worked itself into a frenzy.

LaToria turned her head, forcing herself to let go of her anger. All that mattered in her life was the baby and loving Trevon.

Trevon steered the bluish black A8 from the curb. He didn't speak until he reached the first stoplight on Biscayne Boulevard.

"You thought about what we spoke on last night?"

LaToria sighed. "Don't make a big deal of it. You signed the contract, and it's business, so I'm okay with it."

Trevon glanced at her, trying to understand how she was so at ease with him going forward with his contract with Amatory Erotic Films. He was willing to opt out of the contract for the strength of his relationship with her. She told him she saw no wrong with him doing nine more films.

"You gonna be okay?" he asked, reaching for her hand.

She nodded. "I just need to lie down, that's all."

When the light turned green, he drove the sleek sedan past a Burger King on his left. Looking ahead, he switched lanes while pushing his thoughts to the bright side of his life. His biggest joy was his freedom. He knew he had a rare chance to live the life he did by doing adult porn. How many ex-cons could boast of the life he had? Damn few! Trevon refused to risk his freedom again. Killing Yaffa last year was done in a rushed rage. But even now he held no regret, nor a touch of remorse. He killed for a woman he was deeply in love with.

Reaching Coconut Grove, he parked his Audi behind LaToria's brand new Aston Martin DBS Superleggera Volante. After walking her inside, he glanced out into the backyard to check on his bullmastiff, Rex. He lay on his side in the shade, asleep. Trevon kissed LaToria on the cheek and gave her plump ass a squeeze before he turned to head for the door.

"Trevon." LaToria stood in the living room with a stressed expression.

"Yeah, what's up?" He turned, standing by the door.

She sighed, unable to speak what was on her mind.

"Baby, you sure you're okay with me—"

"I'm fine," she said blurted. "Just bring me something to eat on your way back home."

"Pizza or chicken?" he asked.

She forced a smile. "Both," she replied. "I'm eating for two, remember." Trevon paused at the door with an inkling that she was lying through her teeth. Though she wore a high voltage smile, her eyes told him differently. Not wanting to stress her out, he kept his view to himself.

TWENTY MINUTES LATER, Trevon was seated in front of Janelle's desk, inhaling her light peach-scented body spray.

"I heard the news about Swagga," she said.

"Yeah, LaToria didn't take it too well."

"I'm not surprised about that."

Trevon removed his iPhone from his pocket to make sure the ringer was off. "Sorry 'bout that," he said, keeping his eyes above her breasts. The purple satin blouse clung tight against her perky twins. She was dressed professionally in a pantsuit that did little to cover her natural sex appeal. He managed to avoid any lustful looks at her.

"Well," she said, leaning back in her chair. "Are you ready to discuss your future here with Amatory?"

"It's why I'm here."

"So, what have you decided?"

He wanted to make the right choice. "I'll finish out my contract and do the rest of the films."

"I assume you and Kandi have discussed this at some length?"

"Yeah, but mainly I was the one stressing it. She said it won't bother her for me to continue to do porn without her."

Janelle nodded at the wall to Trevon's left. "Don't take this the wrong way, but Kandi knows how to draw the line between her emotions and business."

Trevon looked at the cover art posters of the DVDs that were produced by Amatory. "She told me that herself. But being honest, I told her I couldn't stand to watch her be with another man. So you know I'm happy about you allowing her to opt out of her contract."

"I already knew that, Trevon. I won't force you to do the films. I'm really happy for you and Kandi, but at the same time, I don't want to leave money on the table. By you doing the last nine films, I promise you that you'll be set financially."

"I don't doubt that," he said, thinking of the money still being made off the DVD he made with LaToria. With each DVD sold, he earned $1.80. Trevon's future looked properous if his next future film could sell like the first. Last week, Janelle had sent him and LaToria an e-mail to inform them of the success of their DVD ranking number one in sales. In less than four months, the DVD had reached a number of 575,000 copies sold! He was looking forward to his first royalty check.

"Have you read the latest reviews on your DVD?" she asked.

"Nah, been too busy with going to the gym and running errands for LaToria. Umm, did someone post something bad?"

"Nope. Far from it." She smiled. "Each day your female fan base is growing. Anyway, a fan posted a review saying how she loved the film and how much she envied Kandi. She gave the DVD five stars and asked if there would be more DVDs with you in it."

Trevon, in all truth, tried to stay grounded and humble. From ex-con to porn star was not an everyday switch. "Umm, I guess we gonna grant her request, huh?"

"Most surely!" Janelle replied.

Trevon adjusted his thoughts to focus on his actions as just business. He was sure of his love for LaToria. It was an issue he didn't doubt nor question. "When do we start filming?" he asked.

"Later next month." She reached for her iPad. "Here, I want you to look at something."

Trevon found himself briefly dwelling on whom he would be

making his next film with. His thoughts were broken when Janelle turned the screen of the iPad in his direction.

"This is Chelsea Kelliebrew. I signed her last month to a four-film deal right before the Christmas holiday, and I'd like her debut film to be with you."

"She looks young." He observed.

"She's only twenty-two, and she's ambitious. Being with her will cover your venture into interracial films."

"She a true blonde?"

"Yep. She's five-foot-four and a former swimsuit model. She looks so much like Kylie Jenner, huh?"

He nodded in agreement. "What will the theme of the film be?"

"It's still up in the air right now. But I did inform my screenwriters that I want it to be outdoors. The bedroom scenes are becoming the norm," she explained. "Also, I want you to do an anal scene with her. Are you okay with that?"

Trevon sat up and met Janelle's unsmiling expression. His conscience was tearing at him. Even if it was just *business*, he felt wrong to be casually making plans to have sex with another female. He looked at the image of Chelsea modeling a two-piece string bikini. There was no need to deny how sexy she was, even for a white girl. "I'll do it," he finally said, after thinking on it.

Janelle lifted her eyebrow. "I'm not getting the vibe that you're *sure* about doing this."

"Uh, have you told her about me yet?"

"A little. By now she has viewed your video with Kandi. Trust me. If you want to be a top seller, you have to do interracial films. Though it's not my favorite." She shrugged. "It's business and business is money."

"I don't doubt you one bit. It just feels like I'm doing LaToria wrong," he admitted. "I guess I need to stop mixing my work with my private life."

"Just do what's in your heart, Trevon. If you need some time to rethink—"

"Nah, I'm good." He sighed heavily. "I said I'll stick to the contract, and that's what I'm gonna do."

Janelle hoped his actions would match his words. "And I won't doubt that."

"So, when will I meet her?"

"Sometime next week. She's moving down from Orlando and should be settled in her new spot soon."

"Ai'ight. So, what's the deal with the other films?"

"I'd like to have you doing a different class of subject with each film. With Chelsea, you'll be doing interracial like I said, so the other films will differ."

"How?"

"Well, I'd like you to do a film with a plus-size female and one with an older woman. Also, I think a threesome is a good idea as well. I have a few more ideas, but the interracial film with Chelsea is a must do."

Trevon turned his attention back to the picture of Chelsea.

"She looks even better in person," Janelle commented. "And FYI, she has never been in front of a camera, so this time you'll be the teacher."

"Hell, I'm still learning the ropes myself." Trevon leaned back in the chair. "Oh! What does FYI mean?"

Janelle smirked. It slipped her mind that Trevon was still a newbie when it came to the current social media lingo. "It means, for your information."

"I'll have to remember that." He grinned.

Janelle turned the iPad off, then fingered a loose tress of raven black hair over her shoulder. "So how's life really treating you?"

Trevon shifted in the chair. "This drama with Swagga gettin' off free has me pissed! I know I did my dirt as well behind what went down in that warehouse. But still, Swagga tried to burn LaToria alive, and I just have to stand by and watch him go free!"

"Would you feel better if he went to prison?"

"I can't ever wish prison on anyone. Not after doing all that time I did."

"You can't let this problem get the best of you. Like you just pointed out, you yourself were lucky with not being charged with killing Swagga's bodyguard. Just move on, Trevon. Let it go. Focus on your future with LaToria and the baby."

"I swear I'm trying," he said.

"Try harder. Do it for yourself."

He nodded.

After a few exchanged words about the new film, the meeting came to an end. It was official. Trevon would continue his career in the adult film industry with Amatory Erotic Films.

"Is there anything else that's troubling you that you'd like to talk about?" she pressed.

Trevon wasn't sure if he should open up to Janelle. He had another issue troubling him, but he assumed she would view him differently if he spoke on it. Biting his words, he lied and said that everything was all good.

STROLLING to the back of AEF private parking lot, Trevon continued to dwell on the choice he made. It was only business; he reminded himself. Nearing his A8, he glanced at Janelle's Lamborghini Urus, wondering if he would one day own a high-priced whip as such.

Sitting behind the steering wheel of his sedan, he reached for his shades on the dashboard. Times such as now, he was filled with a peace of mind. It bothered him that he couldn't feel this way when he was with LaToria.

After making two stops to pick up LaToria's food, he headed home with the system reverberating in the trunk. The timeless classic by Tupac *"Shed So Many Tears"* came alive inside Trevon.

This ain't the life for me, I wanna change
But ain't no future right for me, I'm stuck in the game.

He kept the song on repeat until he pulled up in his driveway. To his surprise, LaToria's Aston Martin was gone. Slowing to a stop beside her black Escalade. He was caught off guard when his phone chimed. He took notice of the unknown number on the screen.

"Hello?" he answered.

"Hey handsome!"

Trevon leaned up in the seat. The voice sounded familiar, but he wasn't too sure. "Who is this?"

She laughed. "Turn around and you'll see."

Trevon twisted in the seat and was moved beyond words from the sight that greeted him.

2

WHY WE STRESSING!

January 20
Friday, 6:38 P.M. – Coconut Grove, Florida

"Jurnee!" Trevon said when he stepped out of his ride.

"Surprise, surprise!" she cooed, strolling toward him in a pair of designer jeggings.

"Why didn't you give me a heads up you were dropping by?" he said, easing his arms around her tiny waist. "LaToria told me nothing."

"That's because I didn't call her," she replied. "So what's going on? Where's Kandi?"

Trevon shrugged. "Out, I guess. You, um . . . with someone?" he asked, nodding at her tinted Bentley Bentayga SUV.

"No, honey. I'm alone. And who is Kandi with? I see her truck is here."

"She has a new ride."

"Really? What did she get?" she asked, propping a hand on her ample hip.

"An Aston Martin DBS."

"What! Is it red?"

"Yeah, how did you know?"

Jurnee smiled. "I guessed."

"You wanna come inside? I'll call LaToria to see where she's at. I'm sure she'll be shocked to know you're here."

Jurnee hadn't seen Trevon and LaToria since Christmas of last year. She followed him inside, helping him carry the food. *A red Aston Martin, huh?*

"How are things with ole dude you met?" he asked when they entered the kitchen.

"Didn't work out," she said, sitting at the table.

"Word! I thought you two were perfect."

"I'm good," she said, sounding sad. "I ended the relationship before things got out of hand."

"What went wrong?"

"He put his hands on me, and I don't play that shit."

"He hit you!"

"Yep. It was the first and last."

"That's fucked up. But you did right to leave him. So what are you doing now?"

Jurnee ran her fingers through her thick mane of curly black hair. "I need to relax. I think I'll get my job back at Amatory as Janelle's assistant. I know she's gonna flip when I tell her what happened."

"Why would she?" Trevon took a seat at the table across from Jurnee.

"Because she told me not to get involved with the bum. Oh well, that's a lesson I had to learn." She shrugged.

"Fuck that lesson! No man should be hitting you."

Jurnee stared at Trevon, thinking how lucky Kandi was to have a man like him at her side. A moment of awkwardness flashed through Jurnee when she looked around the kitchen. Memories popped in her mind back to the night she shared Trevon with Kandi. *Damn, I'm tripping. This is my bestie's man, and I'm up in here thinking about fucking his sexy ass.* "When you call Kandi, don't mention I'm here. I want to surprise her, okay?"

When Trevon pulled out his phone, she excused herself to the bathroom.

Trevon stared at Jurnee's bouncy ass as she strutted down the hall. Grinning, he dialed LaToria's number. On the fifth ring, she answered.

"Hey baby. Where you at? Your food is gettin' cold."

"I'm in front of the Omni Mall waiting for the bus."

"Quit playing."

"I'm not fucking playing!" she shouted. "Can't you hear the damn traffic in the background?"

Trevon was used to her mood swings. "Why are you waiting for a bus, LaToria? Where's the car?"

"I don't have it no more!"

"Was it stolen?!"

"Fuck that car, okay! Are you coming to pick me up or not?"

"Yeah, but why didn't you call me?"

"Now is not the time, okay? Are you coming or not?"

"Baby, you know I'm coming. But when I get there, you need to tell me what is going on! Are you okay?"

"I'm fine. Just . . . please hurry up and come get me." Her voice quavered, sounding as if she was on the verge of crying.

SILENCE CLOGGED the A8 with LaToria seated beside Trevon.

"What is going on, LaToria?" he asked, slowing for a red light. "You gonna tell me what happened to your car?"

She stayed silent.

"Oh, so now I'm talking to myself," he said without raising his voice. "I told you how I get when you go out without telling me nothing! And yet, you up and do it anyway like it's cool and then—"

"I'm not a fucking child, Trevon!"

His grip tightened on the steering wheel. Clenching his jaws, he fought hard to manage his temper. "Ain't gonna sit here and argue with you," he stated, while staring straight ahead.

"Good, then don't!"

"I got the food you asked for."

"I'm not hungry!"

"You ai'ight today? If this is about me sticking to my contract with Amatory, then yes—"

"Trevon, listen!" she shouted. "I told you I don't give a fuck about that shit! I don't care who you fuck or who sucks your dick, okay! I just don't care . . . I don't care what you do!"

Before Trevon could respond, a horn blew behind him. The light turned green. They made the rest of the trip home without saying a word. LaToria's emotions were so pent up that she paid no attention to Jurnee's Bentayga parked along the curb. Shoving the door open, she struggled out to her feet and rushed to the front door, leaving Trevon behind.

JURNEE KNEW there was tension between Kandi and Trevon the moment Kandi stormed inside the house.

"What the hell are you doing here?" LaToria shouted at Jurnee in the living room.

"I came to surprise some friends," Jurnee replied calmly. "But I didn't expect you of all people to welcome me like this."

LaToria rolled her eyes. "Whateva!" she huffed, stomping to her bedroom.

"And what's gotten up your ass?" Jurnee asked.

LaToria brushed Jurnee aside and slammed the bedroom door.

A few seconds later, Trevon entered the living room and sat down on the purple crescent-shaped leather sofa. "From the look on your face, I see that Hurricane LaToria just blew through here."

Jurnee nodded. "Were y'all two arguing?" she asked.

"I won't call it arguing," Trevon replied, picking up the remote for the 70-inch 3D flat screen TV.

"Well, she sure as hell ain't happy." Jurnee looked at Trevon and sat down beside him. "She wasn't happy to see me at all. Maybe I shoulda called," she said, looking worried.

"Nah, you're good. She just going through those pregnancy mood swings or something." He flipped idly through the channels.

Jurnee shrugged. "If you say so."

He lowered the remote. "Why do you say that?"

"I don't know. Maybe she has something on her mind."

"Yeah and talking to her now will only stress me out."

"I hope I'm not being too intrusive about your personal business. But how long has she been having those mood swings?"

He turned the TV off. Silence. "Shit seemed to change after we got back home from the holidays," he murmured. "I'm just dealing with it because I know our relationship won't be perfect."

"Want me to go back and talk to her?"

"It's on you if you want to," he replied.

"I'll go and see what's got my girl in a bitchy mood." She adjusted the form-fitting corset over her lush breasts. "Be right back." She stood, consciously aware of the stretchy jeggings that catered to her luscious figure. At the age of forty-one, she was proud to flaunt what she had to display.

Trevon smirked at the strong likeness Jurnee had toward Jennifer Lopez, and of course, he stole another glance at her thick, succulent ass. She was a Dominican goddess, a tasty piece of eye candy.

JURNEE GAVE a warning knock on LaToria's bedroom door as she breezed inside.

"I don't feel like being bothered!" LaToria said before Jurnee had a chance to close the door. She lay on the bed with her back facing Jurnee.

"What in the hell is going on with you, girl?" Jurnee stated.

LaToria rolled over. "Ain't nothing going on with me!"

"The hell it ain't!" Jurnee fired back. "I know damn well you're not doing what I think you're doing."

"I dunno what you're talking about," LaToria remarked.

"That Aston Martin!"

LaToria smacked her lips, shoving the pillow aside so she could sit up and confront Jurnee. "I don't have it no more! Happy now?"

"You should have never had it in the first damn place!" Jurnee lowered her voice. "I can't believe this mess. After all Trevon has done for you, you have the guts to—"

"Stop assuming shit when you don't know what the hell is going on!"

"Then tell me, so I won't have to assume!" Jurnee crossed her arms.

"It's none of your business," LaToria said, rubbing her temples.

"Now it's none of my business, huh? Why wasn't your ass saying that when this issue came up when we went to New York last year? If I can recall, which I easily can, mind you! You made it my business by coming to me, and I made it my personal business by doing what I did for yo' ass!"

"I don't wanna argue."

"Fuck what you *don't* wanna do! I wanna know why you're doing this dumb shit, girl? That man in there loves your ass to death!" Jurnee pointed in the direction of the living room. "S'pose he was doing what you're doing to him, huh? How would you feel then?"

LaToria wanted to scream. Instead, she began to cry. "It's not like that, Jurnee. I would never—intentionally hurt him."

"Oh, so it's all good to hurt him by mistake? What is wrong with you?"

LaToria's teary eyes sent a line of tears down her cheeks. "I'm trying to make things right." She sobbed. "You just don't know the fucked-up position I'm in right now."

Jurnee wasn't moved to feel sorry for LaToria at the moment. "Does Trevon know how you really got that car?"

"No."

"Girl, what are you getting yourself mixed up in?" Jurnee sat next to LaToria and eased her arm over her shoulder. "You're pregnant with Trevon's baby, and I don't want you to mess up what you two got going. You'll only regret it."

LaToria closed her eyes, leaning against her friend for the support she so desperately needed.

"It's gonna be okay," Jurnee said, gently.

LaToria wanted to believe in Jurnee, but deep down she knew differently and kept the truth of the matter to herself. She knew her past actions would not be understood by Jurnee nor Trevon. *If she could make things right, she would do so without a hint of hesitation.*

"Now, what's up with this sour mood you're in?" Jurnee asked after a brief spell of silence.

LaToria shrugged. "I don't know."

"You and Trevon were so happy last month. Do you need to share something with me?"

"No, I'm okay. Just got a lot on my mind and stuff." LaToria wiped her eyes with the back of her hand.

"So, you're telling me that nothing is going on with you and Mar—"

"No!" LaToria sat up, unable to look at Jurnee. "What happened up in New York is over, okay? Just, let me do what I got to do. I'll fix it all, and I did that today by gettin' rid of the car."

"I still don't understand why you even had it in the first place."

LaToria sighed. "It's done and over with, Jurnee, so please drop it," she pleaded.

Jurnee wasn't easily convinced, but she decided not to press any deeper.

"I'm sorry about snapping at you earlier," LaToria apologized.

Jurnee kiddingly rolled her hazel-brownish eyes. "Just don't let it happen again." She nudged LaToria. "You know it's all good, but who you really need to be making up with is that man of yours."

"I know," LaToria whined at hearing the truth.

"Well, getcha phat ass up and go do it." Jurnee laughed.

"'Ho, don't get it twisted, 'cause I'ma snap this body back ASAP after I have this baby," LaToria promised. "Okay, enough about my man. Where is yours? I—"

"We broke up." Jurnee's mood instantly turned sour.

"OMG! What the fuck happened?"

Now it was Jurnee's turn to build up a wall around her matters that dealt with her heart. "I'll tell you later. And before you start to pester me, I need to ask if I can spend the night?"

LaToria frowned. "So now you gonna hide stuff from me?"

"No. Ain't hiding nothing from your ass. I said I will tell you later, and that's just what I'm gonna do. So can I chill here or not?"

"Yeah, you can chill. And I don't know why you even felt you had to ask. But anyway, I'ma take your advice and go make up with my man."

"Good, 'cause that's all your sassy ass need is some good dick!" Jurnee laughed.

"And my man has plenty of it!" LaToria boasted, giving Jurnee a high-five.

Neither felt at ease to speak on the oral threesome they shared with Trevon. By an unspoken agreement, they figured it was simpler to pretend it never happened.

LATORIA'S THREE-BEDROOM house gave Jurnee the comfort of her own bathroom. Standing at the sink, she gazed at her reflection. Heavy cosmetics hid the discolored bruise around her right eye. She was at least thankful the swelling had lessened to a point where shades weren't needed. Feeling the signs of an oncoming headache, she squatted down to search the cabinet under the sink. To her surprise, she discovered an opened box of panty liners. She found it odd for the box to be in the guest bathroom. Moving it aside, a white folded piece of paper caught her eye sticking out the top of the box. The form drew her curiosity when she spotted LaToria's name on it. Eager to read the form, she removed it and reached over to lock the door. Unfolding the medical form, she gasped at what she read.

"Why?" she muttered, shaking her head. *LaToria wants an abortion?*

Jurnee stayed silent, her mind running too fast to grasp any thoughts. She read the medical form carefully, specifically checking the dates. Closing her eyes, she wondered why LaToria was planning to have an abortion later in the month. She replaced the form back like she found it, knowing LaToria wasn't being honest with her nor Trevon.

3

GOTTA PAY YOU BACK

January 20

Friday, 9:32 P.M. – Fort Lauderdale, Florida

"Where is Marcus?" Kendra demanded, using Swagga's real name.

Swagga's new bodyguard, thirty-three-year-old Rick, knew it was a wise choice to lie. "I'm not sure." He shrugged his beefy, tattooed shoulders.

"Bullshit!" she said, throwing her wine glass to the floor. "You're his damn bodyguard, so shouldn't your black ass know where the fuck he's at? I'm not going through this shit today. Now where is he?"

"Please calm down, Kendra. It's his party. He's around here someplace."

"Uh-huh, probably with that pink-haired bitch I saw all up in his pocket a minute ago!" She scanned the crowd, not giving a damn about the sideways looks she was getting. None of the guests were her friends. All the people within her view stood in the lanes of 'dick riders' or straight up groupies. All they cared for was Swagga's money. Kendra was fed up with Swagga's bullshit constantly being thrown in her face every day. Things started out sweet when Swagga appeared willing to keep it official within their relationship. It lasted all of three short weeks until she busted him with a thirsty ass groupie in the gym sucking his dick. Kendra forgave him, but she didn't forget. Fuck the money, the mansion, and fuck Marcus aka Swagga. Kendra refused to be dogged out by any man. She tried to give Swagga a chance on the strength of their daughter, but she could only deal with so much. Spinning on her toes, she rushed toward the stairs with Rick on her heels.

Stomping up the stairs, she was glad her daughter wasn't with her today. She left Rick at the bottom of the stairs and stormed inside the spacious bedroom she shared with Swagga. It took her five minutes to stuff two Gucci suitcases full of her clothes. Today should have been a happy day for her. However, she no longer had the fear of her man going to jail. She knew he was cheating on her with a bottom ass bitch that wasn't worth shit!

Rolling the suitcases down to the garage, she headed straight for a Mercedes-Benz AMG G63. She loaded the suitcase into the back of the SUV and slammed the door with all of her strength. She climbed inside the G63 and had her finger poised to press the *push to start* button when Rick tapped on the tinted window holding up his phone. Kendra started the engine before she reluctantly lowered the window.

"Swagga wants to holla atcha," he said, catching his breath.

Kendra snatched the phone. "What!"

"Shit, dats what I need to be askin' yo' ass! What the fuck is wrong wit' you?" Swagga yelled.

"Where are you?" she asked, raising her voice. "Better yet, who is with you?"

"Huh?"

"Muthafucker, you heard me. So stop trying to play me! But you know what? I'm tired of your bullshit, so have fun with that skank bitch you fooling with!"

"Yo, why you actin all foolish and shit! I just beat a fuckin' charge that coulda laid my ass down, and you buggin' 'bout dis dumb shit! I swear I'ma—"

"Goodbye, Marcus!" She handed Rick his phone, then slid the tinted window up. She had no more words to exchange with Swagga.

~

"DUMB ASS BITCH!" Swagga yelled after Rick told him about Kendra leaving. Leaning his head back, he closed his eyes on the sofa in the game room.

"You okay, sweetie?" a soft voice asked.

Swagga nodded. "Just finish what you was doin'," he said, running his fingers through the pink hair of the groupie he just met. She smiled and gently slid her soft lips down his shaft. Swagga couldn't recall her name, but he knew her measurements —34B-26-42! Remembering his past, he made her get butt ass naked before anything jumped off. Of course, he hid his true reason for asking her to strip because he was still ashamed of his slip-up with Chyna. Focusing on the pleasure he was getting, he assumed Kendra would bring her ass back once she calmed down. Swagga opened his eyes and stared at the groupie, doing her best to swallow him whole. Up and down, she slurped on his raw, stiff meat while cupping his balls.

"Eat it up, baby. Dis yo' dick fo' tahday." He reached down to squeeze one of her pointy nipples that jiggled with her movements. Without being asked, she ran her wet tongue up his shaft and then back down to his balls. Her head work was on point. Swagga moaned and lifted his ass off the cushion. Four minutes later, her head was still bouncing over his lap without pause.

Swagga asked her to slow down when he felt a nut building. He wanted to be on his feet when he came. "Yo, what's yo' name again?"

"Nashlly," she cooed, rubbing her lips against the tip of his erection.

"Okay, Nashlly. Now show me why I should let you be in my next video."

She did so by taking him deep inside her mouth while palming his ass.

~

LATER THAT NIGHT, after the party ended, Swagga and Rick had a trip to make. With Rick driving Swagga's Rolls-Royce Cullinan, they ended up at an empty public park in West Palm Beach.

"Is this guy official?" Swagga asked, working on his third Newport.

Rick nodded. "I've known him for a few months. So yeah, he's official."

"A few months! And you trust dude to put in this type of work?" Swagga asked, with doubt creeping in.

"Relax, okay? Shit, you've known me for less than three months, so what's the big difference? Let me handle it like I promised you."

"I hope this ain't no bullshit." Swagga settled deep into the plush leather seat, wincing from the smoke burning his eyes. Looking ahead, he only saw darkness. "I know dis fool ain't gonna be late! My time is money."

"He won't be late," Rick replied, waiting for a pair of headlights to appear. "We're early, remember?"

Swagga rubbed his nose. "Yo, you see that pink-haired bitch I bagged? I might feature her in my next video. Ass soft as hell!"

"Yeah, I saw her," Rick said. "And I think Kendra saw her too."

"I don't give a fuck! She just on some bullshit right now. By next week she'll be back on my dick," Swagga claimed, full of pride.

Rick slid the sunroof back, allowing the smoke to clear.

"My bad," Swagga said, lowering the window to thump the cigarette out. "I forgot you don't smoke."

Before Rick could respond, his eyes were drawn to the

rearview mirror. "Here's our man," he said, picking up a black .40 caliber handgun off his lap.

Swagga didn't question Rick's actions. If he felt some heat was needed, he would roll with it. A level of trust was still being built on Swagga's end, but so far Rick hadn't set off any ill vibes.

"Let me make sure everything is all good first." Rick was all business now.

"Do whatcha do," Swagga replied, hiding his nervousness.

Rick opened the door as a dark colored sedan pulled alongside them with the lights off.

"I'll be a minute," Rick informed before he climbed out of the Rolls-Royce SUV.

INSIDE THE DARK gray BMW 7-series was a middle-aged Bahamian by the name of Fritz.

"Long time no see," Rick greeted Fritz as he slid inside the BMW.

Fritz loosened his silk tie and replied. "And time a keep ah movin' wit' out us. So what is it that I can do fah you?"

"My boss needs to smooth out a few bumps in his path."

"Bumps, eh?" Fritz rubbed his chin. "How many?"

"Just one."

"He knows me price?" Fritz said, sitting a black cigar box on the dashboard.

"Money ain't an issue here."

"That be one of me favorite sayin'. So, how do ya boss want dis bump taken care of?"

"Make it look like an accident. Anything else will have the police looking our way."

Fritz nodded. "Dat can be done. And when does dis bump need my attention?"

Rick rubbed a palm over his cornrows. "Whenever the opportunity comes."

"That won't be a problem," Fritz replied. "Can you meet me tomorrow at the Fontainebleau? You should bring all the details you have on dis issue you wish for me to take care of."

"What time?"

"Noon."

"Okay, I'll call once I get there."

Fritz nodded. "See you tomorrow."

Rick exited the sedan and climbed back inside the Cullinan.

"What dude talkin' 'bout?" Swagga asked as soon as Rick was seated behind the wheel.

"Gotta get up with him at the Fontainebleau, tomorrow at noon."

"Y'all got all that shit in order that quick?"

"Fritz is all about his business and no bullshit." Rick turned the headlights on, and then he pulled away from the parking spot.

"Did you tell 'im how it needs to look like an accident?"

"Relax, yo. I got this. By June your issue is gonna be a memory."

Swagga ran his fingers through his locs and let out a deep sigh. It was hard to relax due to his issues, but Swagga was set firm on keeping his hands clean. Pulling out his phone, he dialed up an urban model who was eager to get up on his dick again.

Rick drove with his mind, dealing with his actions. He knew the risks that rode with hiring Fritz to commit murder. Those risks were overlooked by the twenty racks (*$20,000*) that Swagga would drop in his pocket. Easy money, in his view. Being Swagga's bodyguard had many perks that Rick worked hard to gain. He would do his job and get money. He stood 6-feet 5-inches, 315 pounds. He was imposing, even without the sight of his licensed weapon. Added to his immense size, he easily favored the late brawler, Kimbo Slice.

"How's the new track coming in the studio?" Rick asked when Swagga later ended his call. They were cruising down I-95 South, entering Dade County.

"'Nother banger, I hope," Swagga responded, with the seat reclined.

Rick slowed the Rolls-Royce when the radar started to beep. Lowering the speed to 85, he switched lanes to ease by a slow traveling van in the lane ahead. "You still need me to run that security check for your video next month?"

"Yeah go head an' do that."

When the two vehicles were side by side, the van seemed to match the SUV's speed. Turning his head, Swagga noticed the sliding door was cracked. He continued to study the van. The driver was hidden behind a poorly done tint job. Glancing back to the sliding door, he suddenly sat up. He narrowed his eyes at what looked like a hand gripping the edge of the sliding door. He sat petrified when the sliding door was shoved open, revealing a masked gunman pointing an AK-47 directly at him.

Swagga's panicked screams filled the interior as the hail of bullets ricocheted off the passenger side door and window.

Rick instinctively jerked the wheel to the right, crashing hard against the van. The impact threw the gunman on his ass, and before he regained his balance, Rick floored the pedal, weaving past a small sedan. Cars in their wake swerved and locked their brakes.

"You okay!" Rick shouted.

Swagga clutched his chest. "Why the fuck you do that shit?" he panted.

"Had to throw his aim off!" Rick glanced up at the rearview mirror, trying to spot the van. "This vehicle is armored but the tires ain't."

Swagga twisted around in the seat, feeling embarrassed. He forgot his ride was bulletproof. "You see 'em?"

Rick shook his head. "Nah! I think they weren't expecting this shit to be armored."

Swagga turned back around. "Take me home," he said.

Rick nodded. "I think you'll need more protection. Let me get my full team with me until we find out who is behind this."

Swagga's fear stood deep in the uncertainty of who was behind the attempted hit. Whomever it was, the motherfucker was bold and knew about his movements.

"Did you recognize anything about that van?" Rick asked as he sped along the interstate with the hazard lights flashing.

"Nah. Nothing but that, AK." Swagga turned in the seat again. "Damn, it's like they knew where to find me ..."

Rick glanced at Swagga. "I think we were followed somehow." He hated to admit it because it was his duty to be on point and observant at all times.

"We got company!" Swagga pointed to the rear.

Rick didn't need to look behind him. He could hear the sirens and see the flashing blue lights in the side mirror. Someone had called the police and Swagga's Rolls-Royce was easy to spot. Slowing down, Rick removed his .40 and laid it in plain view on the dashboard, along with his gun permit to carry a concealed weapon. "Call your lawyer and tell 'im you gonna need his assistance. When I pull over, let me do the talking." Rick stayed calm, despite the three Florida State Trooper Dodge Chargers filling the rearview mirrors.

Swagga fumbled his phone twice before his nerves settled. He had no reason to worry. Rick had a strict code of not driving dirty with drugs that were used daily by Swagga. Willing himself to match Rick's calm stance, Swagga hit the speed dial to contact his lawyer with hopes that Rick knew what he was doing.

AN HOUR LATER, the banged-up van pulled into a vacant building with the headlights turned off. The driver slowed to a squealing stop while his partner pulled down a rusted metal door. All was quiet in the seedy area of Overtown.

"What the fuck went wrong!" the driver shouted, his voice echoing off the bare cinder block walls. "Why the hell ain't nobody tell me about his truck being bulletproof. We coulda gotten our asses fucked all the way up!"

"Bruh, I'm just as surprised as you. I hit that bitch at point-blank range, and the bullets just bounced off."

"Fuck!" The driver shoved the door open.

"What do we do now?"

The driver sighed. "Get rid of that AK and this van. I'll call you later on. Gimme a few days to think about this shit."

4

SEXING YOU

January 20
Friday, 11:08 P.M. – Coconut Grove, Florida

"Uhhmmm . . . take this poo-poo, Smooch!" Jurnee heard Kandi's euphoric laced moan through the slightly open bedroom door. Biting her upper lip, she continued to massage her olive-toned breast while smearing the heavy wetness between her thighs. Focusing on the sounds, she matched the strokes against her clit with Kandi's constant pants. Hunching her hips up and down, she shoved her middle finger between her wet folds. Rocking against her digit, she pinched her nipple. With her eyes shut, she vividly fantasized about a union with Trevon. She envisioned herself riding the raw, extended span of his dick. Staying with that idea, she continued to please herself.

She slid another finger inside her tight slit and arched her back, driving her fingers deep. "Aaaahhh," she whined, longing for someone to touch her all over. Releasing her nipple, she used both hands on herself. Reaching that higher level, she became lost with her self-pleasurement. The sounds of Trevon and Kandi had ended minutes ago. With her eyes shut, she finished herself off by rubbing two fingers on her clit.

Just as her body reached its height, she felt someone moving across the bed.

"Shhhh. It's me," Kandi whispered in the dark. "Trevon is taking a shower, so we got to be quick and quiet."

Jurnee sat up. "Did he cum inside you?" she asked.

"Yeah, why?" Kandi replied, reaching between Jurnee's legs.

"Let me taste you."

"How about we taste each other?" Kandi suggested.

In the dark, they quietly licked and sucked each other. The act was unique for Jurnee. She slurped between Kandi's soft thighs, relishing the warm cum that Trevon left behind. She swirled her tongue between Kandi's pussy, making her moan and quiver.

Their climax came in a rush. Both hated to untwine their limbs, but it was done with Kandi rolling quietly off the bed. In the dark, they shared a brief kiss with their soft breasts mashed together.

"I need to talk to you in the morning," Kandi whispered.

Jurnee crushed her urge to confront Kandi about the abortion papers she discovered. Maybe Kandi was going to explain herself tomorrow?

"LaToria snuck out of Jurnee's bedroom with guilt riding on her shoulders. Entering her bedroom, she was relieved to hear the shower still running. Pushing the bathroom door open, she joined Trevon in the steamy shower. Just for the hell of it. She reached between his legs to rub his soapy penis.

"I thought you were in the bed," he said, pulling her closer.

"I'm hungry," she purred.

"For what?"

"Some more of this dick," she admitted, shamelessly making him hard with the touch of her hand.

He squeezed her ass and lowered his mouth to her breasts. LaToria moved her grip back and forth over his dick, making it stretch to its full measure. Parting her legs, she moved a step back, releasing him. "Fuck me from the back and hold my waist while you do me."

Trevon lightly slapped both of her ass cheeks when she turned around to bend over against the wall. "Make it clap fo' me."

"Okay, Smooch," she said, looking over her shoulder. With a sexy look, she made her ass bounce and clap for her man. Her lust sizzled to have him back inside her. Teasing her, he slid his dick between her ass cheeks while she continued to twerk.

"Now!" she moaned. "Slide it in me, Smooch. Gimme all that dick!"

He slapped his erection up against her pussy a few times before he pressed the tip against her opening. Looking down at the union, he held his breath until he was fully piercing her insides. His first thrust made her breasts sway. Being raw inside her was a sensation that he would never tire of.

"Dis how you want it?!" he asked, stroking her with a smooth pace that had her chanting his name.

LaToria loved the dick. She wasn't acting, her pleasure was real. Being with him made her feel desired beyond sex. Catching her by surprise, she jerked up on her toes when he pushed his thumb inside her ass.

"Yeah, Smooch!" she shouted. "Fuck my ass and poo-poo!

"Damn, that was the bomb," Kandi later purred, spooning in the bed, naked with Trevon.

"That pregnant pussy got me open."

"Boy, shut up." She smiled, snuggling closer against him. "And you know it's poo-poo, not pussy."

A brief silence fell between them. Trevon closed his eyes, inhaling the coconut lotion that coated her soft skin. He felt lucky to have her. Sure, she had her faults, just as he did, but he loved her. Even with LaToria's strong Nicki Minaj resemblance, he was able to respect her beyond the stance of mere looks. Most evident to him, she took him in with all his faults and scarred past. Their future? In truth, it scared him. Was he ready to be a father? A husband? With a hand on her belly, he reminded himself to take it day by day. The moment now was perfect, and that was the life he sought to have with LaToria.

WHILE TREVON and LaToria found rest, trouble was wide awake up in Washington, D.C. Tahkiyah Bradford sat inside a dark silver BMW M850i coupe parked outside The Park at Fourteenth Club with its engine running. Tonight, she had no plans to enter the club, even with the lure to mingle with a celebrity or two. Behind the tinted window, she scanned the parking lot. She wore a heavy padded dark green leather coat that hid her soft contours. What couldn't be hidden was her ageless beauty. At the age of fifty-four, she easily fooled many to believe that she was in her mid to late thirties. With her light skin tone and doe-like hazel eyes, her looks were fittingly classified as gorgeous. Shifting in the leather seat, she removed her designer glasses and rubbed the bridge of her nose. Her hair was pulled back into a bun, showing that she wasn't out to mingle. Sliding her glasses back on, she skimmed her fingers over the two items in her lap, a smartphone and a black 9-millimeter. A horn blew behind her. She ignored it, keeping her gaze focused at the entrance of the parking lot. She wanted some good news tonight. What she craved even more was peace and some sentiment of closure in her life. Just when her tolerable patience began to waiver, a Chevy Silverado 1500 pulled into the parking lot with dirty snow caked around the fenders. Tahkiyah placed her smartphone on the dashboard and thumbed the safety off the 9-millimeter. Minutes later, she had company.

"Cold out, ain't it?" a white male with a full salt and pepper beard said as he shut the door.

Tahkiyah sighed. "Do you have the information I requested? I didn't drive all the way out here to discuss the weather!"

"Yeah, I got it," he replied, unzipping his parka. "Here, take a look at these." He handed her a sealed manila envelope.

"Thank you," she murmured.

"Mind if I light one up?" the man asked, reaching inside the parka for his cigarettes.

"Yes, I do mind," she replied stiffly, without looking at him.

Sighing, he waited until she broke the seal on the envelope. "The pictures that I mentioned in my e-mail are enclosed."

"I would hope so since I paid you sixty percent up front." She shifted through the papers until she reached a stack of pictures.

"That's her house," he explained.

"And you're sure it's her? I can't afford any mistakes with this."

"Without a doubt. I ran a full background check, and the birth certificate and social security number you gave me were a match."

Tahkiyah stayed silent until she picked up a second picture. To get a better look, she reached up to turn the interior light on. "Is this her?" she asked with her heart racing.

"Yeah. That's as close as I could get."

Tahkiyah couldn't remove her eyes from the photo. "What's her name?" she asked quickly.

The man cleared his throat. "LaToria Nicole Frost."

"LaToria," Tahkiyah repeated to herself.

"Yeah. I can find out more about her if needed. Starting with her job and stuff like that. She also—"

"You've done well enough," she said. "Our terms of business ends here."

"Are you sure? I can easily—"

"I said were done!"

"Fine with me." The private investigator zipped up his parka and made a rude exit without saying goodbye.

Alone once again, Tahkiyah was faced with a choice. It took her several minutes to make up her mind. Doing so, she reached for her smartphone. Doubting her boyfriend, Anthony was awake, she elected to send him a text message.

I'm okay. Will call u soon. Please manage things in the office until I return. Promise 2 explain. XOXO

Making it hard to change her mind, she pulled out of the

parking lot and headed south. She wasn't packed for the trip to South Florida, but time nor money stood a matter with her. She would buy clothes and whatever else she needed when she reached her destination. She was unable to let the past rest. She would face LaToria and worry about the results of it later.

Haters tried to murder me 2nite!

Swagga tweeted when he finally made it home at two in the morning. He was still jumpy from the shooting, so to ease off the edge, he filled his lungs with some killer weed.

"I feel like Scarface up in dis bitch!" Swagga shouted from a brown and black gator sectional sofa in the huge living room. He took a long pull on the joint while his manager Harry Storm shook his head, frowning.

As promised, Rick had beefed up Swagga's security with an addition of four men.

"I need me a new ride." Swagga's voice dragged.

"Shouldn't you be more concerned about who tried to—"

"Can you handle it or not?" Swagga yelled at Harry. "Dat's the fuckin' police job, not mine!"

Harry removed his glasses. He hated how Swagga tried to play the gangsta role. "I'm your music manager, not your personal assistant, Swagga."

Swagga sat up, staring at Harry. "Muthafucka, you work fo' me! It's my name dat push yo' checks, so you better switch up that—"

"Swagga, chill," Rick said from across the room. "He has a point. This is some serious shit we dealing with."

"Man, it is what it is." Swagga leaned up and grabbed a bottle of Crown Royal Black off the floor.

Harry slid his glasses back on. "You need to get back in the recording booth," he said, absently looking at Swagga filling his glass for the third time.

"I know," Swagga slurred. "Can't you see I'm stressed? You a good ole white boy, so I doubt nobody eva popped no slugs atcha."

"And I hope to keep it that way," Harry replied.

Swagga looked up from filling his glass. "See what I mean, Rick? Harry, don't back down, yo! He gonna have the same drive to get me back on top of the rap game!"

"What are your plans?" Harry asked, just as Swagga lifted the glass to his lips.

"I'ma be ready Monday." Swagga lowered the glass. "Lemme clear my mind of all this shit."

Harry stood. "Good."

"Why don't cha spend the night?" Swagga offered.

Harry shook his head. "Wife is waiting up for me."

Swagga shrugged and raised the glass to his lips.

"I'll have one of the guards see you to your car, Mr. Storm," Rick said, as Harry picked up his leather briefcase.

Swagga continued to get high and drunk in the comfort and safety of his mansion. Smiling, he thought back to last year, and how he hated so much on Trevon and Kandi. Thinking of her made his dick hard.

"Google. Turn the living room TV on." he said, "And play video six."

Three seconds later, Kandi's naked, oiled up, 48-inch ass filled the 100-inch screen. She was outside by a pool with two black men. Swagga owned all of Kandi's adult films, all but her last, that included Trevon.

"Bitches ain't shit," he slurred, watching the men rubbing Kandi's ass while she stroked them below their waists. Swagga held no remorse about trying to kill Kandi to keep his deeds with Chyna a secret. Watching the porn easily reminded him of his times with Kandi in bed. Not wanting to spend the night alone, he picked up his phone to call up one of his groupies.

5

—————

THIS CAN'T BE REAL

January 21

Saturday, 10:14 A.M. – Coconut Grove, Florida

"Since when do you get out of bed before noon on the weekend?" Kandi startled Jurnee as she attempted to quietly close the front door.

"Hey girl." Jurnee smiled nervously at Kandi on the sofa. "I had to run to the ATM right quick," she said, slipping the yellow leather strap of her Coach bag off her shoulder. "I didn't wake you up, did I?"

"Nah," Kandi replied, sitting up and yawning. "I just got up about a few minutes ago. I came in here to watch the news, but I fell asleep."

Jurnee grinned as she sat down on the sofa. "Trevon put that ass to bed last night, didn't he?"

"Naturally," Kandi answered. "And you helped me out too."

"I take it that you didn't mention what we did to Trevon?"

Kandi nodded.

"It's not good to be keeping secrets from your man," Jurnee warned.

"It ain't a big deal. Besides, he knew I was bisexual before we hooked up, so I won't stress it, okay?"

"That ain't the point I'm trying to make, girl."

Kandi rolled her eyes. "What's up with you and your man?"

"We broke up," Jurnee stated, crossing her arms.

"Over what?"

She sighed and cleared her throat. "He hit me and yelled in my face, and you know I don't play that shit. So, I left his ass!"

"Are you okay?"

Jurnee shrugged. "I just need some time to get my life in order about what I want to do."

"You talk to Janelle yet?"

"Nah. But I plan to on Monday."

"Well, you know you're welcomed here."

Jurnee looked around the living room. "Is Trevon up?"

"Not yet."

"So, what did you have to talk to me about?"

Kandi tugged at the edge of the *Black Lives Matter* tank top she wore with no panties. "Have you ever done something that you regret doing?"

"Uh . . . yeah?"

"What was it?"

"Well, I guess my biggest regret is not allowing myself to fully open up to a man. It's not a day that goes by that I don't think about what it would be like to be in your shoes."

"My shoes?"

"Yeah. I think about having a baby."

"Really! Shit. You ain't never tell me that."

"It's true," Jurnee confessed. "I know life isn't perfect, but I want the best for you and Trevon and the baby."

"Life ain't never perfect," Kandi muttered with a pout.

Jurnee could see that something was troubling her friend. "What do you feel is wrong? You have Trevon, right? And the baby—"

"Things just ain't perfect, okay!" Kandi said before she got up to pace the floor.

"What am I missing, Kandi?" Jurnee stood. "Ever since I've been here, you've been acting funny. Why aren't you happy?"

"It's real fucked up right now."

"What's fucked up?"

Kandi didn't answer.

Jurnee glanced down the hall before she spoke. "Is Trevon cheating on you or something?" she whispered.

"No," Kandi groaned, wiping her tears.

Jurnee walked up to Kandi and laid her hands on her shoulders. "You need to tell me what's going on with you."

Kandi lowered her chin. "I can't." She sobbed.

"Yes, the hell you can!" Jurnee pressed, her voice filled with exasperation. She struggled not to mention the abortion paper she found last night. Her hopes stood high on Kandi being open with her about her problem.

Kandi turned from Jurnee to sit back on the sofa. "It's about what happened up in New York."

"I thought you said you took care of—"

"Dammit, I lied, okay!"

"I'm starting to notice that."

"You're not being helpful!"

"How can I when you are keeping shit from me?"

Kandi ran her fingers through her hair, sighing. "It's about the baby."

"What's wrong with the baby, Kandi?" Jurnee replied mildly.

"When we were up in New York, I—" Kandi paused when her phone rang. Hearing the special ring tone, she answered quickly. "Martellus! I told you not to call this number!"

Jurnee frowned when she heard Martellus' name. She made no effort to conceal the disappointment on her face as Kandi got up to take the call into the kitchen.

"Fuck you, okay!" Kandi said, seething. "Didn't I make things clear to you yesterday?" She sat alone in the kitchen.

"You know you're wrong, Kandi! How the hell did you expect me to just let this shit go? My views are just as important as yours!" Martellus said.

"No, they're not! I told you I'll take care of this. So now you won't have to worry about breaking your wife's special little heart. And plus, you—"

"I'm getting a divorce, Kandi. I was trying to tell you yesterday before you ran out on me," he said desperately.

"Bullshit!"

"It's true, baby. The papers have been filed, and I've told you you're the woman I need and want in my life."

"Don't be telling me a lie," Kandi whined, gripping the phone.

"I'm serious. I love you, and I'm willing to prove myself to you beyond mere words, baby. But to make this work, you have to give me—give us a chance. Do you love me?"

Kandi stared at the kitchen island with her lips quivering. "Why are you doing this to me?"

"All I know how to do is love you. Now, if I'm wrong for that. Then it's something I can't explain."

"I'm with somebody." She sobbed.

"You don't love him. We have a strong past, and if given the chance, we can have a stronger future. He can't make you happy like I can. Why pretend? I'm leaving my wife for you because I've grown to care for you, and I love you, baby."

"But—"

"Ain't no buts. I've done all that you've asked of me, and I did it out of love, not lust. Think about what we did when you came to New York. It wasn't lust and you know it. I . . . don't want to have an affair with you anymore. I want you firmly in my life, no bullshit."

". . . I don't know." She cried.

"Baby, listen to me. My flight leaves tonight at nine. I need to see you before I go. Can you do that for me?"

"Yes," she said, wiping her eyes.

"Promise?"

"I promise."

"I love you, Kandi."

Kandi closed her eyes and spoke the words he wanted to hear. "I love you the same."

∾

It wasn't until noon when Trevon finally rolled out of bed. Hearing the TV in the living room, he assumed he would find LaToria. To his surprise, Jurnee was sat alone on the sofa watching the news.

"Hey, what's up?" he asked, having forgotten that she was visiting.

"Good afternoon, sleepy head." She smiled at the sight of him wearing nothing but a pair of black briefs.

"Damn, it's that late?" He yawned.

"That it is," Jurnee answered, fingering a lustrous curl of hair that hung near her left breast.

"Um, where LaToria?"

"Left for a nail appointment about an hour ago." Her eyes moved over his muscular torso and descended below his waist. The close-fitted briefs did little to hide his dick, even when it was soft.

"She say when she comin' back?"

Jurnee shook her head. "Why don't you call her?" she suggested, since she felt Kandi had lied to her.

"Nah. Ain't tryin' to argue with her today."

"Just trying to be helpful."

"Thanks," he said, scratching his beard. "Um, lemme put some clothes on."

"You going somewhere?"

"Wasn't planning to," he answered. "Just gonna feed my dog, then make breakfast."

"Let me cook for you." She stood, pleased to see his eyes

moving over her body. "Something wrong?"

He returned her smile. "Umm, don't get upset, but I was just thinking how—like—you, um, sorta favor Jennifer Lopez."

Jurnee smiled, doing all that she could to keep her eyes above his waist. Sure, she had seen him naked and sucked his dick, but that was *before* any feelings were noted between him and Kandi.

Later, she stood in the kitchen, frying bacon and eggs while Trevon took a shower. She bit her words again on what she had discovered in the bathroom about the upcoming abortion. Things weren't right. She wasn't fooled by Kandi's lie. Deep down, she knew her friend had rushed out to visit Martellus. Anger started to consume her. *Why do women dog out good men?* She could see the love that Trevon held for Kandi, but behind his back he was being played. This placed Jurnee at the crossroads. Tell Trevon the truth, or stay quiet and respect the bond and friendship she had with Kandi?

KANDI TRIED to convince herself that she was doing the right thing. Sneaking out to see Martellus had her heart twisted. He had spoken the truth earlier about the past they had together. Kandi had met Martellus Hart when she was only nineteen and dancing at the strip club up in Atlanta. Back then she wasn't up to speed on the game that men played to get inside her. Meeting Martellus was a new adventure for Kandi. For starters, she was drawn to him by the way he carried himself in a professional manner. He was twenty years older and married, but Kandi ignored both and dove headfirst into an affair that would span over the next five years.

Kandi showed no guilt when she entered Martellus' suite on South Beach. Looking into his brown eyes, she saw the need that drove him to unbutton her blouse.

"I'm glad you came," he said, brushing his lips against her neck. "Let me make love to you. I'm at the point where I can't share you anymore."

Kandi raised her hands up to his naked waist. He was warm.

"Touch me, baby. Look at what you're doing to me."

She slid her hands down to grip his solid erection. With her eyes shut, she stroked him slowly. It all felt so right to her.

"Show me how much you love me," he said, removing the red bra she wore. "I need to feel those soft, warm lips. Please, baby."

Kandi pushed him backward until he fell back on the bed. Going down to her knees, she moaned out his name and then slid her tongue up the underside of his swollen flesh. Unable to stop herself, she wrapped her glossy lips around his dick, bobbing up and down at a slow pace.

"Is it good?" Jurnee asked, standing at the stove. She already knew the answer, since Trevon was asking for seconds.

"Hell yeah! How did you know I like my grits with cheese?"

She shrugged. "Lucky guess."

"Hey. Did LaToria tell you about the film we got on Swagga?"

"Um, no," she answered, filling a glass with some milk. "Only thing she said about him is that she was upset about him beating the case."

"Well, you won't believe it until you see it. But our boy Swagga is gay!"

"Stop playing!"

"Nah, for real. It's the reason he went after LaToria. For some reason he thought she had the film of him with a transgender by the name of Chyna."

"And you got the film?"

"Yep. It's on my phone."

Jurnee looked down at her food.

"Yeah, you might wanna eat first," Trevon suggested.

"Does Swagga know you got it?"

"Nope."

"How long have you had it?"

"Since Christmas."

"What do you plan to do with it? I assume Swagga doesn't want it to be made public."

"Not sure right now. LaToria doesn't think it will do any harm to him. She feels that the public view on being gay isn't the same as it used to be."

"She has a point. Look at the gay marriage laws being passed in some states. And I myself can't dog Swagga, because I'm bisexual myself."

"Yeah, but you don't do it in secret and put others at risk. Swagga on some down low shit."

Jurnee shrugged. "How are things at Amatory?" she asked, moving to a new topic.

"Good. I went to see Janelle yesterday, and I'm up for nine more films. She has my next film being an interracial one with a girl by the name of—"

"Chelsea Kelliebrew." Jurnee jumped in.

"You know her?"

"Not really. But I did her interview at the office last year. And if Janelle didn't mention it, doing an interracial film is a good move for your career."

"She said the same," he replied, failing to keep his eyes off her soft line of cleavage.

After they finished breakfast around 2:10 p.m., they went outside by the pool.

"Have you and Kandi come up with a name for the baby?"

"Nah." He smiled. "She wants the gender to be a surprise."

"What are you hoping for?" Jurnee asked, sitting on a deck chair across from Trevon.

"A girl." He beamed. "Look, don't tell LaToria, but I'ma ask her to marry me after the baby is born."

"Seriously!"

Trevon nodded. "I just wanna do right by her and do-"

His words came to a halt when his iPhone chimed. He grabbed

his phone off the end of the deck chair and flashed a smile when he saw LaToria's caller ID on the touchscreen.

"Hey baby, what's up?"

"Nothing," she replied tersely.

He cleared his throat. "Um, I missed you this morning. You should've woken me up with a goodbye hug or kiss."

". . . I'm sorry, Trevon."

"It's all good, baby. You know how I don't like to wake up without you in my arms. And since that didn't happen, I'ma put it on you when you get back—"

"Is Jurnee still there?"

"Yeah."

"I need to talk to her right quick," she said, impatiently. "And take me off the speaker."

Trevon fought within himself not to check LaToria. Biting his words, he handed the phone to Jurnee. He stayed close by to listen in on the one-sided conversation. It turned out to be useless. Jurnee was speechless from the words that filled her ear. When Jurnee held the phone out, he snatched it back.

"LaToria, what's going on with you?"

"Trevon, I'm sorry," LaToria cried.

"Sorry about what, baby? Why are you crying?"

"Don't hate me."

Trevon turned from Jurnee. "What is going on with you, baby? You are starting to scare me, okay. Just . . . come home and we'll talk things out together."

"Trevon, I'm not coming back home. What we had between us is no more. I'm sorry, and I never meant to hurt—I can't be with you no more."

6

AIN'T THIS A BITCH?

January 21
Saturday, 2:21 P.M. – South Beach, Florida

"Where the fuck this fool at?" Swagga muttered to himself as he glanced at his diamond encrusted Rolex for the fifth time in thirty minutes. He sat up in the black leather seat inside Rick's Chevy Suburban to scan the Fontainebleau Hotel across the busy street. Overlooking the bikini-clad women parading up and down the sidewalk, he searched for Rick.

Becoming annoyed, he yanked a brown Gucci towel off his head. "Fuck!" he shouted.

At least the tinted windows were cracked, and it was needed due to the heat. Swagga ignored the beads of sweat on his forehead. He couldn't step out of the SUV without taking the risk of being recognized. Sighing, he wondered what in the hell was taking Rick so long. He picked up a loaded 9-millimeter Rick left behind. His sweaty hand squeezed the black polymer grip.

"I got nineteen in the clip an' one in the chamber. I'm bustin' on you fool like my name is anger. Hatin' on me. Fool, it's easy—" Swagga paused in his freestyle when he caught sight of the Black couple exiting the hotel. Wide-eyed, he peered through the window thinking his mind was fucking with him. "Now ain't this some real live bullshit!" Swagga shook his head at the clear view of Kandi in the arms of Martellus. "That greasy, baldheaded, snake ass muthafucka!" Swagga gripped the gun tighter at the sight of Martellus all hugged up with Kandi. His finger itched at the idea of dumping the clip against Martellus' smug face. As for Kandi, he would save one for her pretty red ass. His gaze stayed on them up until the valet rolled up in a red DBS Superleggera Volante Knowing that Trevon was being played eased a crooked grin on Swagga's face. When the DBS drove off, Swagga turned his attention toward the packed beach. Flat asses were the thing of the past. Real or fake, Swagga was open off a swollen ass. From where he sat he saw two white women sunbathing side by side on their stomachs. Both were topless, wearing a thin bikini G-string.

"Damn, them asses phat!" he murmured, knowing his chances were high that he could fuck them both. Building a taste for the *white* kind, he figured he would hook up with another groupie that happened to be a cheerleader for the Miami Heat.

Turning back to the Fontainebleau, he was relieved to see Rick jogging across the street.

"Damn, bruh! What the fuck took you so long?" Swagga asked when Rick was inside. "Hot as hell up in here!"

"Shit like this can't be rushed," Rick replied, removing his Smith & Wesson .40 from his waist. "Fritz is not a man to rush."

"So er'thang good or what?"

"All we gotta do is go about our biz." Rick placed the .40 inside the custom-built door panel. "Let Fritz do what he do. Trust me on this."

Swagga waited to speak while Rick removed his backup piece from a holster strapped under his left pants leg. "What kinda heat is that?"

Rick held the subcompact black polymer frame pistol near the steering wheel. "It's a Sig Sauer with a 2.9-inch barrel."

"Shit, small as hell," Swagga retorted.

Rick shrugged. "It holds six rounds, and it's a major upgrade over the thirty-eight." Rick nodded at the larger 9-millimeter he left with Swagga. "You done with that?"

Swagga's interest in guns ranked at the bottom of his list. Handing the loaded gun back to Rick eased a heavy weight off Swagga's mind.

"Ai'ight, where we headed?" Rick asked, pulling from the curb. "If it's not back to the crib, I'ma need to call the whole team, and plus we need to switch—"

"Just take me back home 'cuz I ain't tryin' to go through all that shit."

"You heard from Kendra?"

"Nah. And I ain't gonna call 'er ass!"

"You should if you want my opinion."

"Yo, I've been thinkin'." Swagga brushed Rick's last words off. "Look, while you was up with ole boy. Three rides came by thumpin' and none of 'em were bangin' my shit. DaBaby, Quavo, and Rick Ross are eatin'! Here I am on some bullshit when my ass need to be in the fuckin' studio!"

"So get on your grind. Let me handle your safety. Yeah, I don't always agree with things you do, but I got your back, and that's on my hood."

Swagga slid the towel back over his head. "You ain't seen shit yet! I know I can put this rap game on smash.

"What up with you going on tour this summer?" Rick asked, constantly checking the rearview mirror for anything suspicious.

"Harry 'pose to be workin' on it," Swagga replied, trailing his thumb along the fresh crease of his acid-washed Red Monkey jeans. "Yo, can I trust them other guys you got working wit' you?"

"Relax, bruh. All of them are proven."

Swagga *tried* to relax inside the SUV while Rick took the long road home by avoiding I-95 North. They rode in obscurity inside Rick's Suburban, which was needed for today.

"I still need a new whip to replace my Cullinan," Swagga reminded Rick when they reached the city limits for Fort Lauderdale.

"Do you still got your eyes on a Ferrari 488 Pista?" Rick asked, driving through a green light.

"Nah., I think the McLaren look betta—matter of fact. Guess who I saw at the Fontainebleau?"

"Was it Megan Thee Stallion?"

"Fuck no! She ain't neva' hit me back, but anyway I saw Martellus."

"Word?" Rick nodded at hearing the name. Upon taking the job as Swagga's chief bodyguard, Rick requested a list of names of people that Swagga had beef with or any type of issue. Those names were on Rick's alert list, and none would ever be within arm's reach of Swagga, nor would they get on RSVP to any function hosted by Swagga. Rick was aware of all beef that Swagga had, with whom and why.

"What is he doing down here?" Rick asked.

"Creepin' wit' Kandi, of all people."

Rick glanced at Swagga. "Your Kandi?"

"Bitch don't belong to me, but yeah, her. I guess she steppin' out on Trevon."

"Want me to see what he's up to?"

Swagga cracked his knuckles. "That might be a good move. I know Martellus will do some grimy ass shit, so I ain't gonna expect nothin' less from him. What I wanna know is how long he been fuckin' Kandi?"

"I'll look into it and make some calls."

"You do that," Swagga said. "'Cause if our boy Fritz come through. I might add Martellus to the menu too."

MOVING FORWARD

January 21
Saturday, 5:16 P.M. – Coconut Grove, Florida

Back in Coconut Grove, the dead silence frightened Jurnee for Trevon's safety. For the last several minutes, she stood anxiously at the locked bedroom door.

"Please make a sound or something," she begged, her eyes wet from crying. "I know you're hurting over this mess Kandi has done, and I swear to you I didn't know anything about this." She knocked. "Please open the door and talk to me, or just talk to me through the door so I'll know you're okay. Trevon, please . . . I'm really getting scared out here, so don't make me look crazy by calling the police to come kick this door down!" She crossed her arms. "I won't leave until you open this door or say something. C'mon now, Trevon. Please open the door." She banged on the door as hard as she could. "I'm calling the police!" she shouted with tears welling. Just as she pulled up the 911 icon on her phone, she heard the lock click. Jurnee froze with her heart jumping. Calming herself, she reached for the doorknob and slowly opened the door. She stepped inside the bedroom and found Trevon sitting at the foot of the bed, with his head down.

"Why do you care?" he asked, looking up at her with hurt showing on his face.

Jurnee closed the door. "I'm sorry this has happened to—"

"What did she say to you?"

"She told me not to try to talk her out of going back to . . . Martellus."

"Who the fuck is he!"

"Kandi met him when she was dancing up in Atlanta, and they started an affair back then. And—"

"He's married?"

"Was," Jurnee answered.

"So, she's been fuckin' this guy behind my back since day one!"

Jurnee couldn't reply.

"How the fuck she just up and run off!" he shouted. "Ain't done nothing to be treated like this and yet—" He paused, turning his head away.

"I don't like this, Trevon. You gotta believe me, okay?" Jurnee sympathized.

"Where are they going?"

"I really don't know. He has a home up in New York and one in Denver."

Trevon shamelessly wiped his eyes. "Oh, he got money, huh?"

She nodded. "Plenty. He owns a record label, and last year he tried to buy an NBA team."

"So, she left me for money," he stated, shaking his head.

"Trust me, I'm not standing up for her, but I think it's more than that."

Trevon looked around the bedroom. Signs of LaToria were everywhere. A pair of her panties were folded up beside a pile of clean towels. On the dresser, her perfume and cosmetics reminded him of how she would apply lip gloss in the nude. "This can't be real," he muttered.

"Don't let this break you." Jurnee moved across the room and placed a hand on his muscular shoulder.

"Ain't—" His words couldn't express the pain over losing LaToria.

Jurnee sat down and waited a few seconds before she spoke. "Why was she going to have an abortion?"

"What!" He shot to his feet. "Who told you some bullshit like that?"

She shook her head. "No one. But I found this in the bathroom." She reached inside her jean pocket and pulled out the medical form.

"What's this?" He asked, unfolding the paper.

"She was—or is—still planning to have an abortion later this month."

His entire world was crushed. Losing LaToria was one thing, but for her to kill their child to lay under another man was out of order. "How the fuck can she do this to me!" He shook the form in Jurnee's face.

"I'm on your side—"

"Fuck being on my side!" he shouted. "She gonna kill my first-born and push me out of the picture like my voice don't count! This . . . this some bullshit! How can she even look at herself in the mirror! *How*!"

She winced when he shouted.

Trevon, even in his rage, saw the sudden fear in Jurnee. She had tears in her eyes, but he knew the deeper fear of being abused had caused her to jump. Dropping his hands, he went down on one knee. "Don't be afraid of me, okay? I . . . I shouldn't be yelling at you, I'm sorry."

She nodded. "Kandi is wrong." She sobbed, reaching for his hand.

He didn't know the words to speak. Doing what he felt was right. He took her into his arms. "I can't let her kill my child," he said, meaning every word. "I can go on without her, but I want my seed."

She agreed with him. Making a quick choice, she spoke what was dwelling in her mind. "I'll help you," she said.

"You don't have to—"

"No." She lifted her head off his shoulder to look into his eyes.

He placed his hands on the bed next to her hips. Her arms remained around his neck, their faces inches apart. "I don't even know what I deserve."

"You deserve better," she said. "I know LaToria is my best friend and all, but right is right and wrong is wrong. It's like . . . I don't know who she is."

He lowered his head. "I don't know what to do."

"We'll figure it out," she assured him, easing her arms from around his neck.

"I gotta find a place to stay, and if—"

"This isn't Kandi's house, remember. It's Janelle's name on the title, and I'm sure she'll let you stay here once we explain what happened."

He stood and crossed the room. Stopping at the dresser, he saw a broken man in the mirror. "I was a fool to even think she really loved me." He picked up a picture that he took with LaToria last year.

"Don't think like that. She's the one with the issues, not you," Jurnee told him.

"Where do I start?"

"You start by moving on with your life. You can't let this eat at you, Trevon. I know it hurts because I know how you feel about Kandi."

He shrugged, placing the picture face down on the dresser.

"You still have your career—"

"I can't—"

"Yes, you can!" She came to her feet. "Don't let this break you!"

He turned to face her. "Why do you even care?" he asked again.

"Why shouldn't I care?"

"Don't answer a question by asking one."

"You want me to be honest?"

He shook his head. "No. I *need* you to be honest."

She crossed her arms, lowering her eyes to the floor. "I don't know why I care, but I do, okay?"

"LaToria said she cared about me too, so how—"

"I'm not her!" She looked up.

Trevon shifted his feet. "I'm sorry 'bout that."

"Are you gonna be okay?"

"I guess. It just seems like none of this shit is real." He shook his head. "One minute I'm about to get an engagement ring and the next . . . I just need to get outta this fuckin' house before I spaz out."

"Where are you going?"

He shrugged. "I don't know."

Standing in place, she wondered how he would feel if she spoke the truth on why she cared about him. Assuming the worst, she stayed quiet as he made his exit.

Trevon was trudging down the hall when Jurnee called out his name. Coming to a stop, he turned. She eased up to him, her eyes still wet from crying.

"Do you want me to be here when you get back?" she asked softly.

Trevon sighed. "I don't care, Jurnee. I . . . I just don't care."

"That's the last thing you should do is not care," Jurnee said.

"So, what do you suggest?"

"Let me go with you. How about we get out of this house and grab a bite to eat?"

He thought about her suggestion. "Why not?" he said as he fought to hide his pain over LaToria. "Let's go before I lose my fuckin' mind."

"SHE'S NOT ANSWERING any of my calls," Trevon told Jurnee as they later sat inside his A8 outside of the Sushi Samba Restaurant.

Jurnee noticed the pain in his voice. "She can't hide," she said, rubbing his shoulder. "Like I told you in the restaurant, Martellus has a record company, so we'll just reach him—"

"And say what?" Trevon blurted. "You think I'ma ask for LaToria back?"

"But I thought you wanted—"

"It don't matter no more. I mean, really. How can I stop her from having the abortion? Hell, I can't even leave the state without going through a ton of bullshit with my probation officer! If she don't want to be with me no more than fuck it. And fuck her!"

"Do you really mean that, Trevon?"

"Ain't got no choice," he said.

"You always have a choice," she pointed out.

"Do I really?"

She reached for his chin, turning it toward her. "Look at me, papi. You can waste your time running after Kandi or move on with your life and become the superstar in this business. Kandi made her choice, now you make yours."

He nodded. "I guess this will be a life lesson learned, huh?"

"Damn right! Get money over pussy. Stick with Amatory, and you'll be rich and famous, papi. If Kandi was meant for you, or you for her, then this shit wouldn't be happening."

"But what about my seed?" he asked wistfully.

"I don't have all the answers, papi."

They sat in silence, trapped in their thoughts. Trevon dwelled on the disappointment his mom and sister would feel over the news about the breakup.

As for Jurnee, her thoughts jumped back to weighing the option of telling Trevon the truth about why she really cared about him.

"It's getting late," she said, looking at her phone. "Don't you have a certain time to be in?"

"Yeah, by ten if I ain't working."

"I wouldn't mind keeping you company. We could order a movie and just chill if you want to," she suggested.

"To be honest," he said, seeing it was ten minutes past 8 PM.

"I'd rather stop at the liquor store, get something to drink, and just get fucked up because being sober is the last thing on my mind."

Jurnee smiled. "Sounds like a plan to me."

Seconds later, the Audi exited the parking lot with the latest song by Lucci pounding in the trunk. As Trevon drove with Jurnee sitting beautifully at his side, he willed himself to become hard-hearted toward that false item called love.

8
____

BLAME IT ON THE HENNY

January 21
Saturday, 10:20 P.M. – Miami, Florida

Killing someone was not a difficult task when it was fully thought out and planned. Fritz was alone at an undisclosed location in the Northwestern area of Miami. In the one-bedroom apartment, the wall in the tiny bedroom was covered with pictures of his new target. Fritz was shirtless, smoking a thick, genuine hand rolled Cuban cigar. Smoke wafted up near the stained popcorn ceiling, marred by three bullet holes. Sitting up on the queen-size bed, Fritz took a close study of the man in the pictures. Rick had supplied the pictures and all the vital information that Fritz had requested. In the coming days, he would begin tracking his new target to get a deeper knowledge of his daily movements. Being close and unseen was an easy task for Fritz to accomplish. Committing an act of murder seemed the norm for him. There were men and a few women who took their last breath with Fritz's grinning face in their vision. The others died by what was deemed as an accident. From the ungoverned streets of Zimbabwe to the flashing lights of Hollywood, California, Fritz had proven his talent. A professional killer is how he viewed himself. At times he couldn't determine what drove his urge to kill. The money, or the rush of stalking his target and seeing fear pooling in their eyes when they realize their life on earth was about to expire.

Yeah, killing was easy in Fritz's mind. The muted TV was tuned on a bland sitcom that Fritz gave no attention. The cheap, outdated TV was being used for lighting in the stuffy bedroom with a brown carpet torn in various spots. This dwelling was only temporary for him. It would suit his needs until the job was done.

Inhaling the cigar, he picked up his phone. After dialing a local number, he placed the cigar in a chipped glass ashtray. His call was answered after the third ring. Knowing his number was known on the other end, he made no attempt to introduce himself. He also knew the person on the other end was strictly business as himself.

"I need a new vehicle by tomorrow night," Fritz explained. "And I don't need anything flashy." He spoke flawlessly spoke without an accent.

"Not a problem. You'll find what you need parked at our normal spot tomorrow. The keys will be taped inside the front left fender."

Frite ended the call and laid his phone beside the ashtray. He stared at the cigar and was about to reach for it when a knocking at the front door drew him to his feet. He grabbed a Glock 34 9mm off the bed and headed into the musty, dimly lit living room.

"I gotcha chicken, so hurry da hell up and lemme in!"

Fritz relaxed his grip on the pistol upon hearing Jenny's irritating voice. "Show some patience!" he shouted, thumbing the safety on the Glock and tucking it behind his back.

Unlocking the two doors, he stepped aside as Jenny flounced into the apartment in a glinty pair of black leather five-inch spiked booties. A heavy, cheap pineapple perfume and the aroma of fried chicken filled his nose, causing his stomach to growl. "Anybody follow you?" he asked, scanning the streets outside.

"Nooo . . ." she complained, rolling her eyes. "Ain't nobody important, and I don't have no pimp runnin' after my ass. Now let's eat. And maybe we can have some fun after we finish." She whirled her wide ass, unaware that her blonde wig was slightly crooked on her head.

Fritz locked the doors and joined Jenny on the tattered green cloth sofa. Like every man, Fritz had likings that he filled his downtime with. In Fritz's case, his mind was at ease when he could entertain himself with a willing prostitute and chicken.

"This was an excellent idea," Jurnee said, curled up on the sofa with her heels off. She kept her eyes on Trevon while sipping her third glass of Ciroc and Sprite.

"Life's a bitch, ain't it?" he said, lounging beside her with a bottle of Patron between his legs.

"Life is what you make it," she replied, raising her glass in the air. "Words from my girl, Mary J. Blige."

He lifted the bottle to his lips to finish it.

"Easy, papi," she warned as he gulped the bottle of Patron until it was empty.

He savored the tequila and the mellow feeling it induced over his mind and body. "Wh-what's that song you got on?" he asked.

"It's called 'Nothing Can Come Between Us' by Sade," she said, softly.

"I like it," he said with his eyes low.

"Really?"

"Yeah, but—" He paused, sliding a hand down his face.

"But what?"

"Nah, I was 'bout to say sumthin' stupid." He grinned.

She giggled. "Are you drunk?"

"Not yet, but I'm damn shole' tryin'." He sat up, placing the empty bottle on the floor. "What that Ciroc taste like?"

"Like me," she flirted, knowing she was slightly tipsy.

"You're crazy." He smiled, reaching for a second bottle of Ciroc on the table.

"Hey. I got a question," she said, handing him her empty glass. "Say, if you were like . . . alone on an island with one famous woman . . . um, who would she be?"

"Um . . . just one?"

"Yes." She giggled, tucking her feet up under her.

With a wide grin he said, "Um, I'll have to pick the MSWA, Jennifer Lopez."

She exploded into a fit of laughter.

"Why is that so funny?" he asked, enjoying the sight and sound of her mood.

She couldn't speak until her giggling ceased. "You're just saying that because you said I favor her." She nudged him on his knee.

"So." He shrugged, twisting the cap off the Ciroc.

"And what does MSWA mean?"

"Most sexiest woman alive," he said, filling her glass.

"You love yourself some Jennifer Lopez, huh?" she teased. "Well, if I was alone on an island. I swear I'd love to be with Gucci Mane, and it's not because you look like him," she lied.

"Yeah, whateva." He handed Jurnee her glass.

"Thank you." She waited until he filled his glass before she spoke again. "Let's, um, make a toast."

"For what?"

"To the future."

He lifted his glass. "Why not? 'Cause the past ain't shit."

"Moving forward," she said when their glasses clinked.

They kept the mood casual while consuming glass after glass of alcohol. "What time is it?" She asked, rubbing her forehead.

He studied his phone for a moment. "Uh, ten minutes past ten."

"I can't drink another drop." Jurnee stretched her legs out in Trevon's direction. "Rub my feet." She wiggled her neon blue pedicured toes.

"What I look like?" he asked as she laid her feet on his lap.

"My personal masseur," she slurred.

"Ain't nothing free."

"And what is your fee?"

"I'll let you know when I'm done."

She pulled her feet back, grinning. "Well, if I have to pay then I might as well get my money's worth and, um, enjoy myself." She giggled.

He remained seated as she slowly eased to her feet. His eyes roamed over her luscious ass and small waist. "Hey. What are your measurements?"

"Hold that thought," she said, steadying herself on the arm of the sofa. "Relax and give me a few minutes."

"Ain't movin' from this spot."

"Who said I wanted my feet rubbed in here? Since I have to pay, I get to set the, um—guidelines and stuff like that," she said with a sexy smirk.

He nodded. "Fine by me," he said, undressing her with his eyes.

She tottered with her first step but caught herself giggling. "I'm okay." She motioned him to remain where he sat.

When he was alone on the sofa, he kicked his shoes off, leaned his head back, and closed his eyes. His pain over LaToria diminished by spending time with Jurnee. There would be no more tears. Even in his current intoxicated state, he realized that Jurnee had spoken the truth about moving on through his loss of LaToria. Stress kept his eyes shut. Sleep crept up on him several minutes later.

Within fifteen minutes, he snapped awake when his iPhone rung. Sitting up, rubbing his face, he retrieved the phone off the table between the empty bottles. "Yeah?" he answered, without taking the time to see who was calling him.

"May I speak with Señor Trevon?" Jurnee giggled.

"Speakin'," he replied.

"I'm ready for my massage, and I hope you won't keep me waiting."

"I guess I should come and handle that, huh?"

"That would be a good idea. I'm in my bedroom waiting for you."

JURNEE LAY on her stomach when Trevon entered the bedroom. She had taken the time to set the mood by lighting seven vanilla scented Bright Black candles around the room. After a quick shower, she coated her skin with some luminous gold dust body lotion.

"Smells good in here," he said, closing the door.

She didn't speak until she felt him sit on the bed. "You like what you see?" she asked as *"Sweet Lady"* by Tyrese played softly from her phone.

He nodded at the sight filling his eyes. She was clad in a black honeycomb lace and fishnet negligee that exposed the bottom part of her bare ass. Looking at her back, he didn't see a bra strap.

"Can you start on my shoulders?" she asked, turning her head on the pillow in his direction.

"I think I can do that," he said, moving up on the bed.

Jurnee knew she positioned herself on front street by wearing the short negligee without any panties. She told herself she wouldn't shelter any regrets tonight. No matter how far things went.

"Mmm, that feels soooo good," she moaned when his hands began to knead the area around her neck and shoulders.

"Been a crazy day, ain't it?"

"Life ain't never perfect," she said with her eyes shut.

"Shit. We both back to being single."

"I won't miss him," she said, being honest. "Nor the sex, because I was making him wait."

"For real?"

"Yeah. I guess he assumed I was easy since I'm a former porn star."

He pressed his thumb along her shoulders, moving them in circles. "Um, when is the last time you had sex with a man?"

"That would be exactly eight months ago."

"And women still do it for you?"

She shrugged. "Why do you ask?" She opened her eyes.

"Just wonderin'," he said, grinning at her.

A few moments of silence moved between them.

"You ever think about that night I schooled you on the art of oral sex?" she asked.

"Puttin' me on the stage, huh? But yeah, it crossed my mind from time to time."

She smiled. "Mine too, and I can still taste your cum sliding down my throat. I really, really, enjoyed sucking your dick that night. Did it feel better when I sucked it slow or fast?"

Caught off guard by her bluntness caused him to stutter. "I-I, um—guess I'll say both."

She blushed. "I wanna tell you something." She turned over to her side. "That night I was with you. I wanted to feel your dick inside me, but your contract wouldn't allow it."

"Shit, I felt the same way," he said, sliding a hand up her thigh.

She sat up. "Can you take your clothes off? I want to see all of you."

"We don't have to do—"

"Shhh." She laid a finger on his lips. "It's just the two of us tonight, and I know you want to have sex with me, Trevon." Smiling, her lips brushed against his ear. "We can do it all night long. I wanted you the very first day you walked inside my office at Amatory." She stuck her tongue out and licked the back of his ear. Acting brazen, she lowered a hand between his legs and gripped his solid erection. Keeping the mood going, she pushed him to his back, sliding her fingers under his clothes. In the scented, candlelit room, their lips met in a long, slow, tongue-clashing kiss.

He enjoyed the softness of her breasts within seconds of their contact. By her heavy breathing, he knew the line of friends was about to be crossed. With their hands moving quickly, he was undressed, piece by piece. They met in the middle of the bed.

"I want you so bad!" she moaned, reaching for his dick. She was tired of fingering herself, or using the vibrator, or a detachable shower head to bring her pleasure. Her body wasn't just asking for any man. It was screamed for Trevon. Countless nights she had fantasizing about feeling all of him inside her. Unknown to anyone, just the sound of his voice would make her hot and want to throw the pussy on him that he would never forget. Slipping the negligee off, she was delighted to see the spark in his eyes. She licked her glossy lips and took his dick back into her hands. She caressed him while pressing her nipples against his arm.

Trevon gasped when Jurnee lowered her beautiful face between his legs, taking his balls into her mouth. He closed his eyes, enjoying how she slurped and popped them in and out of her wet mouth. Her soft hands massaged the length of his dick, making his back stiffen. She took her time pleasing him with her mouth. Seeing a drop of precum at his tip, she worked her way up his shaft with her tongue. She licked him clean, moaning with the sweet taste of his precum in her mouth. She licked all over it like a lollipop. Coming up on her knees, she lowered her soft lips down the length of his stiff, hard dick. With her breast against his thigh, she bobbed up and down, slurping.

He combed his fingers through her hair, then he held it up and out of her face so he could see. With his free hand he palmed, squeezed, and spanked her soft, golden ass.

She continued to suck on him, waiting for him to pop his delicious whipped cream inside her mouth. Up and down, she deep throated his flesh while caressing his balls. For several minutes she had him feeling like a king.

Allowing her to lead, he showed no hints of wanting to stop her when she mounted him.

"I need this dick," she moaned. Licking his neck, she raised her ass up a few inches, then reached down to hold his dick straight up. With nothing between them, she slid down on his throbbing meat, losing her breath. Her pussy was wet and tight. Slowly, she moved herself up and down. "Fuck, this feels good!" she moaned heavily. Balling up the sheets in her hands, she moved faster, her soft ass clapping against his flesh. Each time she went up, she squeezed her pussy muscles to grip his long dick.

Trevon was in a trance, watching her breasts jiggle and the erotic way she rode his bare dick. He encouraged her to keep going by telling her how good the pussy was. No thoughts of LaToria filled his mind as he later pounded Jurnee from the back while pulling her hair. They had a wild marathon of fucking that lasted closed to an hour. Jurnee had climaxed twice in that time and was gasping and out of breath when Trevon finally came deep inside her.

CAN I HIT IN THE MORNING?

January 22
Sunday, 12:30 P.M. - Miami, Florida

"I need your help," Tahkiyah said over the phone while closing the door behind a female hotel attendant.

"I thought our terms ended—"

"I'm not in the mood, Mr. Staton," she said, interrupting the private investigator. "Do you wish to be paid, or not?"

"What's your problem?"

Tahkiyah sat on the edge of the bed. "Why didn't you tell me that LaToria lives in a gated community?" she complained.

"I didn't feel it was of any relevance."

"Well, it is. How did you manage to get those pictures?"

"I got my sources. Uh, by any chance are you down in Miami?"

"Yes. I'm at the Mondrian Hotel. Now, can you help me or not? I need to get on the visitors' list somehow without LaToria knowing it."

"All right. I'll make a few calls, and I'll call you back around five or six."

"I'll be waiting," she said dryly.

Ending the call, she sat in silence for a few moments. She had to go through the plan she had set before herself. Her options were limited. Ignoring the truth was an issue she could no longer live with. Still somewhat exhausted from the road trip, she elected to take a long relaxing soak in the tub. Stripping free of her name brand, tailor-made clothes, she stood naked in the middle of the bathroom. Closing her eyes, she licked two of her fingers and lowered them between her legs. Her folds were warm and slightly moist. Anthony liked it when she touched herself in front of him. Doing it alone didn't bring her the same satisfaction as it did when she was being watched. She pushed two fingers between her delicate folds and then imagined she wasn't alone. "This isn't working," she murmured before she stopped touching herself. Her breasts were full, well rounded and youthful looking. She found delight in the way she still had a sex appeal that could turn Anthony on with little effort. She also craved it when he would caress or suck her nipples when he was inside her.

Relaxing in the hot, scented water, she closed her eyes after placing her glasses to the side. She hoped Staton would be able to get her through the gate at Quovadis Estates. The trip to Miami was for a reason, a reason that Tahkiyah was steadfast on seeing through.

AT THE SAME TIME, Trevon and Jurnee were just waking up in bed together. Across the room the sun threw its beam through a slit in the curtain.

"My head killin' me," Trevon complained, rolling to his back.

"That's your fault, Mr. Drink From The Bottle," Jurnee kidded. "You, um, want something to eat?"

"What's on the menu?" he asked, with his voice raspy.

"Name it," she said, feeling the warmth of his body next to hers.

"Uh. How 'bout some bacon, eggs, toast, and grits."

"That's simple." She turned to his side, hoping he wouldn't push her away.

"About last night," he said.

"What about it?" She moved closer, placing her hand on his stomach under the sheets. "You have some regrets about what we did?"

"Nah. But I don't want you to feel that I took advantage of you."

"Please." She rolled her eyes. "I was in my sober mind when I *gave* you this pussy, and I'm in my sober mind now. What we did last night was natural, and I enjoyed all of it."

He slid his hand down her back until he reached her bare ass. "Okay, it's all good then."

She looked into his eyes, slowly inching her fingers down. When she discovered that he was fully erect, she smiled. "You're gonna spoil me with this." She took him inside her hand and leaned up to cup her swollen nipple to his mouth. Closing her eyes, she tossed her head back while his tongue circled her nipple. Under the sheets, she squeezed his dick.

"I need to be inside you!" he groaned between her soft breasts. She released his erection and rolled over, parting her legs. He shoved the sheets back so he could view her body. She gazed up at him, rubbing her clit. He took her legs and placed them up on his shoulders and slid in deep and slow.

"Damn, you got some good pussy!" he moaned, taking full length thrusts inside of her.

"Shit . . . papi. Fuck me! Go faster . . . ahhh . . . I love your big dick!" she panted underneath him. "Do it! Fuck this pussy! Aaahhh, right there!"

In and out, he fed her soaked pussy with his manhood. The bed started to squeak from their weight and movements.

"You like it like this?" he asked, grinding between her legs.

"Yesss! Ahhh. This dick is so fuckin' good!" she screamed, digging her nails into the back of his arms. Closing her eyes, she entered a state of pure euphoria. He pounded hard and steady at a pace that had her fighting to catch her breath. He filled her thoroughly, causing her legs to tremble with each stroke. The wetness between her thighs became heavy, allowing him to easily slide in and out. Churning her hips, she murmured his name continuously, matching the tempo of his thrusts.

"You love this pussy!" She breathed as their bodies smacked together. He changed the angle of his thrusts by leaning up and pressing her legs back near her ears. Groaning, he maintained his fervid pace.

"Turn over," he said minutes later.

She rolled to her knees but kept her head on the pillow.

"Mmm. This ass looks so damn good!" he said, caressing her ass.

"Gimme that big dick," she purred, twerking her hips and ass. Reaching back between her legs, she wrapped her hand around his dick. She felt his hands moving all over her ass, making her shudder. Teasing him, she placed his tip against her syrupy pussy lips, and then moved it up and down its length. They moaned.

"Make me cum. Please fuck me good and hard." She released her grip and pushed backward while biting her bottom lip.

Ecstasy stung her from her nipples to the center where Trevon penetrated her. She wiggled her ass as he continued to thrust. "Fuck! Baby, you feel so good in me! Yes . . . gonna cum all over your big dick!"

"Shit!" He smacked her jiggling ass. "Pop that pussy fo' me!"

He had a firm grip on her hips, pounding in and out of her. He couldn't stop, even if he wanted to. No regrets.

"Aww fuck, aww fuck! Aww . . . shit, it's so good!" She shuddered.

"You love dis dick?" he shouted, running his length inside her.

"Fuck yes!" she moaned. "Owww . . . yes! I feel it in my stomach!"

"Mmm. You got my dick so wet!" he moaned, staring at her ass.

Jurnee squeezed the pillow, drowning in pleasure as Trevon stirred her insides. Staying face down–ass up, she took the dick happily, climaxing minutes later. She was speechless when he pulled out of her. No words were needed to meet his needs. Turning over, she slid off the bed, pulling him with her. She went down to her knees, wrapping both hands around his love tool. She jacked him off slowly, with a twist on her upward trip. When a drop of precum formed before her lips, she flattened her tongue against it and then wrapped her wet lips around it. Her eyes stayed open while she sucked his ebony penis.

He slid his hands through her hair as her lips glided back and forth across his rod. "Shit. Suck it, baby," he groaned. "Mmmm. Work it good fo' me, baby."

Jurnee went to work, slurping and sucking on his dick until spit started coming from the corners of her lips. She loved how his large manhood stretched her jaws. "Mmm, you taste so good," she said, giving his balls a gentle squeeze. Showing it was true, she took him back inside her mouth, loving the taste of his precum. She sucked it hard while jacking him off. His tip popped in and out of her mouth with a loud, wet snap. His head rolled when she gripped his ass and forced him to the back of her throat. She could feel his balls on her chin when she engulfed all of him.

He closed his eyes, holding her head with both hands. She hummed and moaned, giving him the best head in his life. She looked up at him when she felt his veins throbbing and growing thicker along the length that slid in and out of her mouth.

"Jurnee!" he moaned. His climax exploded in a sudden release, bursting inside her mouth.

She took it all, licking his dick clean after she slurped down every drop of his cream. Purring, she lifted his soft dick and suckled gently on his balls. When their eyes met, she twisted her tongue around his tip, smiling. "You ready for breakfast now?"

He nodded as he helped her to her feet. Her body was too appealing to ignore. His hands slid down her back, coming to a stop to palm both of her succulent butt cheeks.

He squeezed her ass, grinning. "You made me feel real good."

"So . . ." she said, tilting her head. "I too can say the same in return because I really enjoyed having you all up in me."

"Too bad we couldn't film it," he said, rubbing her thigh.

"Them days are ova for me. The only porn star under this roof is you, and I'm one lucky bitch to have this dick on tap." She smiled.

He was grateful for her company. She forced LaToria from his mind and showed him that he still had a life to live.

Kissing her on her forehead, he left her alone so they could take separate showers. They met in the kitchen, and Jurnee had indeed made his requested breakfast to replenish their bodies. At the table, it warmed her to see how he couldn't take his eyes off her. She had her long hair piled up on her head, with two stringy curls hanging down both sides of her face. Staying sexy was always an effortless task for Jurnee; who wore a pair of tight shorts and a V-neck tank top without a bra?

"So, you think I rushed things with LaToria?" he asked, feeling natural to be at the table wearing nothing but his briefs.

"Sure. See, I think you needed to enjoy your freedom. Hell, I still do. To me, I just felt like you were moving too fast."

"What about now?" he asked as she got up from the table with the empty plate.

"It's your second shot," she replied over her shoulder. "Life is too short to stress, so fuck the bullshit and focus on today and tomorrow."

He followed her to the sink with his eyes. He was thinking about how things would change between them after sex. So far, she wasn't acting clingy, nor speaking of any emotions that he assumed she felt. On his part, it was all about sex. Being inside her was a delight that he wanted to enjoy over and over. Looking at her from behind pushed his mind back toward sex. Sliding back from the table, he crossed the floor and moved up behind her, placing his hands on her succulent hips. Closing his eyes, he kissed her lightly on the back of her neck.

"You smell so good," he said.

"Thank you." She smiled, with her nipples stiffening under the top.

"You got anything planned for today?"

She shook her head, pushing her ass back against him. "I wanna tell you something."

"What's up?" he said, sliding his hands down the front of her shorts.

"I-" she moaned, "wanted to be your first when you got out of prison. I wanted you so badly when I first saw you," she finally admitted.

"You got me now."

She leaned her head back, moaning softly as his fingers moved over her clitoris. "Right there. Aaaahhh. Touch me, Papi."

"Take your top off for me. Can you do that?"

"You know I will. I'll do anything for you."

He skated his fingers up and down her furrow, coating his fingertips with her wetness. When she removed the top, her heavy 36 DD's popped free. Sucking on the side of her neck, he continued to rub between her wet folds.

She bit her upper lip as her body responded to his touch. She felt the hardness of his nature pressing against her ass. Knowing that he wanted her again had her floating. "Ahhh shit, that feels so good." She grabbed her breasts, mashing them together and pinching her nipples.

"I can make it feel better," he said, kissing behind her ear.

"Better than this?" she breathed. "You'll have to show me."

He removed his fingers from between her legs. "Turn your sexy ass around."

She obeyed, pleased with the attention he showered her with. Her breasts jiggled when she turned to face him. With her back against the sink, she was unable to move. Their eyes met.

"Now what?" she asked, rubbing his erection through his briefs.

Unexpectantly, he lowered his lips to hers. She squeezed his dick while kissing a man she wanted at first sight. He tongued her slowly, roaming his hands through her hair and rubbing the sides of her breasts.

"I wanna fuck you again," he moaned."

She nodded. "This pussy is all yours."

Trevon lowered his lips to her nipples, kissing both. "Get naked and wait for me on the sofa."

"Okay," she said softly. "But please don't make me wait too long."

She pranced out of the kitchen, swaying her hips and ass suggestively. Whatever he had in store for her, she was down with it. Reaching the living room, she quickly peeled the shorts off her ass and got comfortable on the sofa. Just as she was relaxed, he came out of the kitchen butt ass naked, with his imposing dick leading the way.

"Let me suck that dick," she said, reaching between his legs.

"Not yet." He grabbed her hand. "I'm runnin' shit today. Now lay back and bust that kitty open 'cause I'm still hungry." He smiled, licking his lips.

He sat down on the sofa, staring between her thick, olive-toned thighs. Once she was ready, he lowered her right foot to the floor and placed her left over the back of the sofa. Her pussy lips were puffy and bald. Her scent expelled a hint of cinnamon.

"Mmmm . . . you gonna lick my pussy." She squirmed and moaned. "Ahhh. Trevon, it's your pussy now!"

He inhaled the scent of her and licked her a few times before he inserted his tongue inside her.

"Ooohh, oohh, oohh, Trevon, papi!" She palmed his head with one hand while she tugged on her nipple with the other. "Mmmm. Keep licking it. Yess, yesss, ummmm!" she gasped as his lethal tongue lashed up and down the length of her sapping wet pussy.

He sucked on her moist vulva, relishing the taste and scent of them. He slurped at the flavorful discharge that left his lips and beard glistening.

"Shit, baby, don't, ummm . . . stop," she said, out of breath.

He slid two fingers inside her wet hole and swiped his tongue across her clitoris. He felt her muscles contracting around his fingers.

In a sexual daze, she touched his fine chiseled body as he moved on top of her, hooking her legs over his strong arms. Holding her breath, she reached down for his long dick and guided it back inside her.

10

SLOPPY SECONDS!

January 22

Sunday, 8:18 P.M. - Coconut Grove, Florida

"You alive in there?" Trevon shouted through the bathroom door.

"What's up? It's open," Jurnee replied.

Trevon entered the bathroom and grinned at Jurnee, relaxing in a peach scented bubble bath. "Just wanted to let you know I'ma head out to the store right quick. You need anything?"

"Nah, I'm fine." She smiled up at him. "Your probation officer gone?"

He nodded. "Yeah, he left about five minutes ago."

"Do you still wanna go out tonight?"

"Yeah, I got the okay from my probation officer because I said its business related."

"Good. I have just the spot we can go to."

"Where?" he asked. "Lemme guess. Club Liv at the Fontainebleau?"

She grinned. "It'll be a surprise."

"Ai'ight. I'll be back, and I let Rex in. And yes, he's housebroken."

She waited until she heard the front door close before she reached for her iPhone. Clearing her mind, she hoped she was doing the right thing by trying to reach Kandi. After the fourth unanswered ring, she was just about to hang up when Martellus answered.

"Hey, Jurnee."

She frowned. "I need to talk to Kandi if you don't mind."

"I hope you're not mad at me for being in love with Kandi?"

"If I wanted to talk to your ass, I would have called you!" she said sternly.

"We don't have to be bitter. You should want what's best for Kandi, and it's a no-brainer that it's me. I Googled that ex-convict, Trevon, and I was alarmed by what he—"

"Who the fuck are you to judge somebody! I bet your wife isn't happy about you fucking around on her, now is she? Listen, is Kandi around or not? 'Cause listening to your dumb ass is giving me a headache!"

"Hold on," he replied.

Jurnee only had to wait a few seconds before Kandi got on the line.

"Hey girl," Kandi said in a neutral tone.

"Are you on drugs or something? What in the hell is wrong with you!"

Kandi sighed heavily. "I'm grown, okay? And I don't need to explain nothing to you."

"It ain't about me!" Jurnee shouted. "It's about Trevon! The man you ran off on! The man whose baby you're carrying, and you blocked his number so he can't call. That's who you need to explain this bullshit you're doing to! I thought I knew you as a friend, but I guess I was wrong. Tell me. Is your prince Martellus paying for your abortion? He got your head so twisted that you're gonna kill the baby. Bitch, that's low!"

"Who—you don't know what—"

"Stop lying, Kandi! I found the damn abortion form under the sink. Now try to tell me I didn't!" Jurnee waited for Kandi to defend herself. When she stayed quiet, it only increased her outrage. "So, it's true, huh? How can you do this to Trevon? Running off . . . and I–I don't understand nothing you're doing! You think Martellus is gonna be faithful to you?" she scoffed.

"You don't know him like I do!"

"And I'm glad I don't!"

"Is Trevon around?"

"Why do you care? You got his number blocked, and I assume you'll block mine after this call."

"Just—tell him I'm sorry and I—"

"He already knows you're sorry, and I ain't telling him nothing. You wanna talk to him, call him your damn self!"

"Oh. So you've been keeping him company?"

"And if I have? What fucking business is it to your ass?"

"Did you fuck him in my bed? Ain't been gone two days and your grimy ass is probably still in my house fucking my—what if this was all a test, huh? Both of y'all failed! You ain't shit, and it only proves my point to be with Martellus!"

"Nah, bitch, you ain't gonna make us out to be bad people! You started this bullshit, and now you see your ass ain't gonna be missed. And FYI, hell yeah, we fucked, and no he didn't utter your name when he was all up in me!"

"Fuck you, bitch!"

"Whatever! Trevon *will* get over your ass, and I'ma make sure of that, personally!"

"Y'all can have each other! I don't give a fuck!"

"Good, bitch! I'ma enjoy bagging all your shit to toss in the trash 'cause we don't need no memories of your sleazy ass here! Trevon don't need you, and he'll be better off without you in his life—"

"And listen to you! We in the same boat, bitch. Only you had twice as many dicks up your funky ass than me! Fuck you! And next time, get your facts straight before you toss it up in my face! Oh, have fun throwing my shit out, 'cause, bitch, I'm good and always will be! And always remember this! You can never be me, so settle for being second and having my leftovers!"

KANDI SIMMERED as she threw her phone on the oversized bed.

"Are you okay, baby?" Martellus asked, rubbing her arm. "Aren't you tired from the trip?"

"No! I'm fine. I just need to put this shit behind me." She frowned.

"Is it true what you said about Jurnee sleeping with Trevon?"

"It doesn't matter, okay!" she said, turning away from him.

"I just want you to be happy here."

"I am," she said, gazing out the bedroom window at the snow-capped mountains in the distance. Her life had changed instantly when she boarded his private jet to fly away to Denver with him. He assured her that she wouldn't lack for anything, and that she would be the only woman in his life.

"Do you need me to do anything before I go?" he asked.

She sighed, turning from the window. "I haven't been here for a full day, and you're already leaving me alone?"

"Relax, baby. I have a business meeting to attend, and you're more than welcomed to come and sit and wait until it's over." He reached for her hands. "Or you can stay here and explore your new home and kick back off your feet. I'll be back before nine."

"I'll stay here."

"Are you positive, baby?"

"Uh-huh," she replied, looking at the bed across the room. She couldn't help but wonder if Martellus had slept with his wife on that very bed. *Of course he had,* she told herself. "I'm not sleeping in the same bed you shared with your wife."

He shrugged. "Okay, I can understand that. Uh, you can go online and pick out any new bed that you want."

"I need some clothes, too," she said tersely.

"Use my credit card and get all that you need," he said, lifting her chin. "I'm going to take care of you, baby. All of your needs. I promise you." He kissed her, sliding his hands up and down her arms.

"I hope so," she said, nuzzling her lips against his neck.

"When I get back. Do you think we can find another place to do it since you'll be getting rid of the bed?" he asked, grinning.

"I'll see what I can do. That big sofa downstairs looks like a good spot."

"Mmmm," he moaned, pulling her against his crotch. "That sounds perfect. And we can do it in front of the fireplace."

"Don't let your business come before me, because I'm gonna need some hot loving on this cold winter night."

He roamed his hands over her voluptuous body, wishing he could take her right now on the bed.

Later, after he left for work, she headed down to the first floor. Martellus' home was a lavish custom-built ranch with five bedrooms and four full bathrooms. Luxurious as it was, it wasn't something new to her. Trailing her fingers along the polished rail of the oak staircase, she paused halfway to admire the elegantly furnished family room with exposed wood timbers along the vaulted ceiling.

"Do you like the view?"

Kandi already knew she wasn't alone. "It'll take some getting used to," she replied, looking out the French doors that showed the expansive wooded backyard and snow-covered ground. "You must be Mrs. Biathrow. Martellus told me about you on our flight."

"Yes, I am. And is there anything you require, Ms. Frost?"

Kandi figured Mrs. Biathrow would be the one item that she would learn to live with. She had mixed emotions when Martellus first told her about his housekeeper. Kandi wasn't about to share her new home with no other bitch. She was somewhat calmed when Martellus further explained that Mrs. Biathrow's husband was his full-time chauffeur whenever he was in Denver. He went as far as giving Kandi the right to fire the housekeeper if she wasn't comfortable with her, but first she had to agree to at least meeting

Mrs. Biathrow. Kandi assumed the housekeeper would be an attractive woman that Martellus favored.

"You can call me LaToria," Kandi said, making a true effort to be friendly. The lady before her was dull looking, with pale white skin that showed no hint of being under the sun. She was bigboned with large breasts, wide hips, and a heavy ass. Kandi knew Mrs. Biathrow wasn't the owner of any two-piece swimsuits or thongs. Her dark hair was pulled back in a bland ponytail, matching her less than average looks.

In the large gourmet kitchen, Kandi elected to sit at the table with Mrs. Biathrow over a cup of hot cocoa. With a baby on the way, Kandi didn't see any wrong to have someone cater to her every need. She imagined herself turning this house into a home.

BACK IN MIAMI, Florida, Jurnee made every effort to enjoy herself with Trevon. Her pressing anxiety revolved around the last harsh statement that Kandi told her. For now, she didn't mention the call to Trevon. She wasn't sure how he would react.

Tonight, she used her A-List status to get inside the new trendy club, Taste Me, on Lincoln Road. Jurnee effortlessly garnered all types of looks by showcasing her mouthwatering figure in a Chanel bodycon dress with fishnet sides. Trevon wore Gucci from head to toe in a tight-fitting shirt and a pair of jeans. Up in VIP, they ordered a bottle of Grey Goose on the rocks.

"How'd you get us by that line?" Trevon asked Jurnee when they were seated at their private booth.

"I know the owner," she said, crossing her legs.

"Y'all go way back or something?"

"Yeah. I've known Novia for about five years now."

"Maybe one day I'll be known like you."

"You gotta put in work. Look at Mr. Marcus and how many films he made. He has his own company, and he's doing good."

"You ever did a film with him?"

She frowned. "Don't tell me you haven't seen all of my films yet. And I thought you were a true fan." She pouted. "But yeah, I did a film with him when I first started out."

"You think I could reach his level?"

"Absolutely! I think you need to do a threesome with The Body XXX and Tori Taylor, because them two are really doing it right now."

"Wishful thinking, huh?" He grinned, reflecting on the days he had masturbated off X-rated pictures while he was in prison.

"It can happen. I got their numbers on speed dial. Just run the idea by Janelle and see what she thinks," she suggested.

"I'll do that," he said as three attractive women breezed by the booth. The shortest of the trio stared at him.

"Do you know her?" Jurnee asked, after the women left VIP.

"Nah. Never seen her before," he said honestly. "Maybe she's a fan."

She shrugged. "Oh yeah. I meant to ask you while you were driving. Um, why were you looking in the rearview mirrors so much?"

"You noticed?"

"Uh, yeah."

He scratched his eyebrow. "I thought I was being followed for a minute. At first, I thought it was my probation officer, but he drives a Tahoe. I guess I was just trippin'."

"Who do you think it was? And how long were we followed?"

Trevon handed Jurnee her glass. "Nah, it ain't nothing. I'm just buggin' out. Let's enjoy the moment."

"This will be my only glass for tonight," she told him. "The rest of the bottle is all yours."

"What? You trying to get me drunk again, so you can take advantage of me when we get home?" he joked.

She smirked. "Papi, you know I don't need to do that."

"What's on your mind?"

"Um, you ever had a threesome?"

He shook his head. "I, uh, can't count what I did with you and—"

"Don't even mention her name," she interrupted. "So, would you like to do a threesome?"

"Janelle has one set up in a future film for me."

"I'm talking about your private life. Being with two women is an art. What you did with me, and you know who, was just oral sex. When you have to split that dick between two women, you better know what you're doing."

"And let me guess. You wanna show me how it's done?"

Smiling, she nodded. "I could hook it up."

"When?"

"Soon," she said, looking around the club. "You just sit back and let me handle it."

He rubbed her thigh under the table and whispered in her ear, "I never forgot your golden rule, so I'll remind you of it. Just go for what you know."

"That's so true," she replied. "And I need you to keep that in mind as you move on with your life. Do what makes you happy. Enjoy your freedom most of all. And don't deal with matters of your heart too much." She pointed at his chest. "Many men would break their legs to be in your position, so don't blow it because someone else made a stupid mistake."

"You really care about me, huh?"

"Sure, I do. I'm just a real ass woman."

"And a gorgeous one, too."

She blushed. "Let's do something wild tonight." She fingered her long, silky ringlets over her left shoulder.

"What do you have in mind?"

"Let's get a room tonight. I want to make your fantasy come true. Let me share you with another woman. It will make me sooo hot to see you fucking somebody else with that masterpiece dick you got."

"With no regrets?"

"None." She licked his ear and slid her hand down to his lap.

"Mmm, I knew it would be hard," she cooed, rubbing his dick print.

"Damn, what would I do without you?"

She squeezed his erection. "Dream about me."

"You ready to go?"

"Why? We just got here, Papi."

"The club will be here tomorrow. All I got on my—" He paused, looking toward the exit.

"What is it?" she asked, alarmed.

"Don't look, but Swagga's former producer, D-Hot, just came in through the back door."

11

———

A TABLE FOR THREESOME?

January 22

Sunday, 10:49 P.M. - Miami Beach, Florida

"**A**re you sure you wanna do this tonight?" Rick asked Swagga from the front passenger seat of a Bentley Flying Spur.

"Yeah, bruh. I gotta get back on my grind! Fuck all these bitches and all this bullshit. I 'on't give a fuck what time it is. I need to be in the studio," Swagga said from the rear of the car.

Rick turned back and made a call to ensure the security would be in place for Swagga's spur-of-the-moment visit to the recording booth. The Moroccan blue sedan was closely followed by two of Rick's men in a lifted Tuscany Harley-Davidson F-250. Rick's task was to keep Swagga alive, and failure was not an alternative. Rick moved his team in an efficient fashion when they reached the studio. It was all business tonight, not a groupie in sight. With the lights dim, Swagga went into a zone once the heavy bass filled his headphones. He bobbed his head, bouncing on his toes.

"Jeah! Uh-huh . . . Swagga in da buildin'! Jeah!" He went on hyping himself up for a freestyle flow. Nearing the microphone, he showed why he wasn't to be overlooked in the rap game.

Pops said I'll fail if I fail to plan fast lane paper chase Bentley Spur sedan shooters in the Harley D, F-250 wit drums beat the case face straight product out of the slums stunna, I'm the reason why bitches wonder about me on the low, I be takin' them under beat it down run it up, versus hot as the summer treat the packs like batons how I pass to the runners.

Rick's focus on Swagga ceased when his cell phone rung. Pulling it from his hip, he moved quickly to the corner when the coded number for Fritz appeared on the screen.

"Is there a problem?" Rick asked.

"None at all, mon," Fritz replied, using his accent. "Jus' lettin' ya know dat me caught up wit' ya issue. Me been him shadow an' him don' even know it. Tings not lookin' too heavy like ya explain. Me guessin' he not 'spectin' no trouble."

"He still in town?"

"Yeah. Clubbin' wit' a fine lady."

"Okay. Just do what you do, but don't forget how I want it done."

"I neva fahget da rules."

"Good. So is there anything else you need to tell me?"

"Naw."

"Okay. I'll relay the message to my boss."

"You do dat. Till next time."

Rick ended the call with a sigh of relief. He didn't feel at ease discussing the murder-for-hire over the phone, even if it was worded in code. Going back to his security post, he listened to Swagga's voice filling the studio. He figured he'd tell Swagga the news after he finished his session in the booth. Rick wanted Swagga to remain focused on his music and not the bullshit concerning hiring Fritz. Playing it safe, Rick pulled his phone from his hip and deleted Fritz's call.

~

Back at Club Taste Me, Trevon and Jurnee managed to slip out of VIP without being spotted by D-Hot. Down on the dance floor, Jurnee pulled Trevon along with her. Moving to the center of the crowded floor, she began to dance with him, using his body like a pole. Trevon enjoyed having Jurnee in his arms, and her moves defied her age of forty-one. Closing his eyes, he enjoyed the moment and his freedom. After staying on the dance floor through five songs, she motioned him to lower his ear to her lips. "Hey," she shouted over a new hit by 2 Chainz. "Meet me over by the ice sculpture in thirty minutes. I see an old friend at the bar."

Trevon looked up over the crowd toward the S-shaped bar. A bounty of beautiful women were socializing along the green LED lit bar. "Which one is she?"

"Stop being so nosey." She grinned. "Ain't forgot about our threesome, so let me do my thang." Before he could reply, she rose up on her toes and kissed him. When they parted, Jurnee danced her way off the dance floor, headed straight for the bar. She prided herself on her unique talent of being able to point out a bisexual woman at first glance. There were certain traits that couldn't be hidden nor overlooked by Jurnee's proven eye. In truth, she told Trevon a white lie. She didn't know any of the lovely women lined up along the bar. Jurnee was hunting, stalking for someone special that would cater to her erotic desire tonight. Twice she was stopped by men seeking her attention. She turned both of them down. The women in her view came in so many assorted sizes and colors. It was at the end of the bar near the waterfall when her intuition went off. Brazenly, she sauntered up to the gorgeous, doe-eyed, swarthy-skinned woman with an amiable, confident smile. "Care for some company?" Jurnee asked over the loud music.

The woman gasped when she got a clear look at Jurnee. "OMG!" The woman stood, staring at Jurnee with both hands up to her mouth.

Jurnee frowned. "Ummm, are you okay?"

The woman gushed. "Yeah! I know who you are, and if I'm wrong . . . But you're that porn star. Honey Drop, right?"

Jurnee couldn't recall the last time she was noticed in public by a female fan. "Yes, I'm Honey Drop and—"

"Oh my goodness! I can't believe this! I have *all* of your films and I'm like—your biggest, biggest fan! And to finally meet you in person! Gosh, you're so beautiful too!"

"So, I guess I can buy you a drink?"

"Not in a million years! But I'll buy you one."

Sitting at the bar, Jurnee ordered a glass of vodka and cranberry juice. Before the drink arrived, she learned her new friend was twenty-five and her name was Ariana.

"So, you're a fan of porn?" Jurnee asked.

"I love it!" Ariana confessed. "I bet it's so wild to have sex with so many well-endowed and good-looking men! And to be honest, I enjoyed those few girls on girl films you did a few years back."

"Really?" Jurnee beamed. "It's nice to finally meet a true fan and being that you're a female is . . . special."

Ariana was beyond star-struck. "May I please, please, please, get a selfie with you? I'd like to post it on my social sites."

"I don't think it would be a problem."

"And may I pretty please get your autograph as well?"

Jurnee nodded, showing no vain ego over her fame. "Relax, okay. Whatever I can do to make you happy tonight. Consider it done."

Ariana took a sip of her fruity cocktail in an effort to calm her excitement.

"You're a very beautiful woman," Jurnee said. "Have you ever thought about doing porn? You know I know the right people." She winked.

Jurnee was being completely honest with her suggestion. Ariana was on the slender side, but her small 5'3 frame was curvy.

Ariana blushed. "It's my fantasy," she admitted. "But it's something I could never ever do."

"Why not? Is there a boyfriend at home?"

Ariana sighed. "No, I'm single right now. But the real reason is because doing porn wouldn't mix too well with my career goals. I'm studying for my DVM–Doctor of Veterinary Medicine."

"So, you're intelligent and sexy."

"Thank you," Ariana said, starry-eyed. "Um, are you really done with porn? Like, I really, really enjoy watching you."

Jurnee shrugged. "Those days are over for me, sweetie."

"Do you come here often?" Ariana asked politely.

"Not much. How about you?"

"Oh, about once a month."

"Just to unwind, huh?"

Ariana nodded. "A girl still has her needs if you know what I mean."

Jurnee took a sip of her drink and crossed her thick legs. Just as she hoped, Ariana lowered her eyes to ogle her shapely legs. "Did you see the film I made titled, *Honey Drop for Two*?"

Ariana blinked. "It's one of my favorites! You and that other girl wore that one brother out!"

"Have you ever done a threesome before?"

"I did it in my dreams," Ariana said, fanning herself. "Like I mentioned, I live out my wildness by watching porn."

"Ain't no wrong in that, sweetie."

Ariana smiled. "Do you enjoy being with girls off the camera?"

"Yes, I'm bisexual, Ariana, and it's a part of my life that I don't hide. Does that answer your question?"

"Yes, it does."

"Have you been with a woman before?"

Ariana batted her eyes. "Why ask a question when you already know the answer?"

"It's not good to assume things."

"So, is it true?"

"What?"

Ariana touched the back of Jurnee's hand. "That you really taste like honey when you climax?"

Jurnee eyed Ariana up and down with lust in her eyes. "Would you like to find out for yourself?"

Ariana suddenly felt lightheaded. Calming herself, she nodded. "I would really, really, really, love to have sex with you."

"How about I make tonight really special for you?"

"You're already doing that."

Jurnee looked at the revealing dress Ariana had on. With its deep, plunging neckline, she was able to see the inner swell of Ariana's small, perky breasts. "I can make your fantasy come true."

"I just wanna have some fun with no strings attached. If you can help me with that, I'm down."

"Okay, before we leave, I'd like you to meet someone. That's if you don't already know him."

TREVON COULDN'T BELIEVE how his night turned out. He left the club twenty minutes ago and was now following Jurnee and her new friend, Ariana. When Jurnee arrived at the ice sculpture with Ariana in tow, he was speechless. The threesome got acquainted and Trevon was all smiles, Ariana proved she was a fan of his debut film. They recognized the sexual tension was heavy tonight, and they were willing to act on it.

Trevon slowed his A8 when the brake lights lit up on Ariana's burgundy Chevy Traverse. He was overwhelmed with uncensored sexual ideas as he turned into the parking area at the Betsy Hotel. Jurnee and Ariana went up to the room alone, leaving Trevon down in the lobby. Jurnee assured him that his wait wouldn't be long. She also explained how she wanted Ariana to be fully relaxed and ready before the threesome started. Trevon didn't mind the wait. He just hoped he would be able to please both women to their fullest content, while doing all he could to crush any and all thoughts of LaToria. About twenty minutes later, he received a text message from Jurnee.

Cum on up papi. We R ready 4 U

TREVON ENTERED room 37 at 12:25a.m. His eagerness to be with two women at the same time was heightened when he glanced around the spacious, dimly lit suite. The aroma of perfume teased him as he shut the door and quietly locked it. On the arm of a white and tan leather sofa he saw Jurnee's dress and thong draped across it.

He picked the thong up and fingered the smooth fabric. A fleeting image of Jurnee's sensational nakedness increased his heartbeat. Every aspect of Jurnee's short and thick figure filled him with an insatiable urge to be raw and hard inside her again. He glanced at the bed and saw it had not been touched.

The bathroom. He looked across the room and saw light spilling from the partially open door. As he neared it, he heard Jurnee giggle. Grinning, he pushed the door open. "Ladies, the third leg has arrived." He made his presence known.

Jurnee lowered a glass of champagne from her sensuous lips and set it on the padded edge of the Jacuzzi she shared with Arianna. "For a second I thought you changed your mind," she said softly.

"I took the stairs," he replied, enjoying an eyeful of Ariana's shiny, dark-skinned breasts that she didn't bother to cover.

"Come and join us, Papi," Jurnee cooed. "There's plenty of room and Arian is dying to see the real reason why you're signed to AEF."

Trevon unfastened his belt. "And what do I get in return?"

"Bring that masterpiece on over here and you'll see."

12

SHE CAME BACK

January 23
Monday, 10:30 A.M. – Coconut Grove, Florida

Trevon began the new day alone. Having returned home last night at 3a.m., he reluctantly went to bed without the warmth of a female. He had left Jurnee at the hotel with Ariana after he created his fantasy into a reality between the two of them.

Last night remained vividly in his head as he lay beneath the sweltering sun bench, pressing a 315-pound barbell with his shirt off. The explicit image of sexing Ariana doggy style on the bed was gratifying from start to end.

He exceeded his expectations by having enough stamina to maintain an erection that delivered what Jurnee and Ariana asked for. An orgasm. He had started with Ariana, pumping her gently at the onset while Jurnee waited feverishly for her turn.

He learned the importance of knowing what a woman preferred sexually. With Arian, she was in favor of multiple stimulations as he thrusted between her legs. She begged him to grope her breast or rub her ass while he slid in and out of her.

He wisely wore protection with Ariana; however, it was rightly tossed in the trash when Jurnee took her place beneath him. The culmination came when he stood behind Jurnee, gripping her waist as she leaned forward on the arm of the sofa.

Completing his last set, he sat up on the bench just as the chime of the doorbell turned his head toward the house.

KENDRA WAS HALFWAY down the driveway when she heard the door open behind her. Turning, her heart fluttered when she saw Trevon.

"Hey stranger," she said. "What's going on with you?"

"Just another day," he replied, knowing there was an issue between them since she had gotten back with Swagga.

"Bet you're wondering why I'm here?"

"Sumthin' like that," he said.

"I, um, thought I should give you a heads up on something."

"And that being?" He glanced at the AMG G63 and noticed she was alone.

Kendra lifted the shades off her eyes. "I'll be going back to work next week, and if you want me to, I can work some things out and get you back on my case load."

"Uh . . . that might not be a good idea since you're back with—"

"I'm not with Marcus anymore," she told him. "I'm done with him and his games, and he cheated on me for the last time."

"Well, only on the strength of your little girl not having a dad around. I'm sorry to hear that."

She smiled for the first time in three days. "That's a very considerate thing for you to say, Trevon. And if it's true, I'm sorry to hear about your breakup with Kandi."

"Damn. Where you hear that at?"

"It's all on the porn news sites. What? It's not true?"

"Yeah, it's true. But hell—it just happened three days ago, damn."

"They said it came from an unknown source that claimed they saw Kandi at a hotel with some other dude."

"Fuck it!" He shrugged. "It is what it is."

"Are you gonna be, okay? I mean, you won't have to move out again, will you?"

"I doubt it. But I'll know for sure when I go to see my boss later on."

"You still doing porn?" she asked as a bead of sweat trickle down the left side of his chest. She stared at it as it slid past his nipple. Though it was roughly three months ago that she had sex with him, the recollection of it triggered vivid memories.

"You ai'ight?" he asked.

"I'm okay. I was, um, thinking about something, and my mind got carried away. So, are you still doing porn?" she asked again.

"Yeah. I just gotta get back focused."

"That shouldn't be too hard."

"Um, you wanna come inside outta this heat?"

"I'm on a tight schedule as it is. But if you can make some time for a big girl, I might take you up on that offer on a later date."

He grinned. "You ain't no big girl, so kill that."

"This ain't small, baby." She laughed. "But seriously, do you wanna go back on my case load or not?"

He crossed his sweaty arms. "It depends. Will you be the mean ass probation lady that was trying to send my ass back to prison? Or will you be my little secret again?"

She couldn't resist the impulse to touch him. She slid her fingertips down his left shoulder. "I'll gladly be your secret again."

He easily recalled the few times he had sex with her. Remembering that night in her bed, a sense of worry filled him. He wondered if she was or had been currently having unsafe sex with Swagga? He also curious about whether or not she knew about Swagga and Chyna?

Before she left, she gave him her new cell number.

JURNEE TURNED the water off and settled back in the bathtub. Thinking of Trevon, she reached for her phone to call him.

"Hey sexy. What's up?" Trevon's voice emitted from the speaker.

"You, of course." She smiled. "I'm back home. Just got here about twenty minutes ago. Where you at?"

"At the office waiting for the boss lady to call me up. I see you and Ariana finally let go of each other."

"She's something special. We're planning to go out this weekend. Oh, she told me to tell you hey and, that she really, really, really enjoyed being with you." She giggled.

"Yeah, it was wild."

"Hmm, did you enjoy it?"

"That's a crazy question.

"No, it's not." She leaned back. "But I'll say this. You did your thing with us, and you're going to be even better when you do it for your film."

"I couldn't have done it without your sexy ass."

"I just want you to be happy and on top of your hustle."

"Shit, maybe you should be my manager or something?"

She laid her phone on the edge of the tub and turned up the volume on the speakerphone. "You serious about that?"

"Yeah, why not? You know a lot more about this business than me, and plus I know you'll push me to be the best."

"Run it by Janelle, and yes, she knows I'm here. I talked to her this morning."

"Did you . . . tell her about the drama between me and LaToria?"

"She already knew."

"Lemme guess. She heard it on the web."

"Uh-huh, how'd you know?"

He sighed. "I'll tell you 'bout it when I get home. But what did she say?"

"Nothing much. Just said she wanted to hear your side. I told her how it went down and all, and Janelle knows I'ma give it to her raw, and I did. I told her that Kandi is on some dumb shit, and that you shouldn't have to move."

"What she say?"

"She said I was right."

"Uh, what about us having sex? Did you mention that?"

Janelle isn't stupid. She asked me if we did it, and I told her the truth. We ain't got nothing to hide from nobody. And we didn't have sex yet. All we've been doing is fucking," she said, grinning.

"Did she trip?"

"Nope."

"You wild, yo."

"Hmph. You ain't seen nothing yet," she purred.

"What's the noise in the background?"

"I got the vent on in the bathroom. Don't want the place smelling like weed."

"You smoke!"

"Sure do. But I'm not a pothead."

"What else don't I know about you?"

"A lot."

"Well, we need to change that, don't we?"

"Sounds like a good move."

"Ai'ight. Do this . . . let's go out to eat tonight. No sex. I just wanna get to know you as a person. I can't let you be my manager and all I know about you is how good you are in bed, feel me?"

"You gotta point there."

"Hey look. Umm, you still want me to run the threesome idea with The Body XXX and Tori Taylor by Janelle?"

"Yes! Don't forget that. Oh, and here's another good power move for your career. I think you should do a film with someone that's a vet. I'm thinking like, ummm . . . Janet Jacme, Cherokee D Ass or Sinnamon Love."

"Or Heather Hunter?"

"That's if Janelle can convince her to come out of retirement."

"I'll see what she says."

"Listen, about last night. When I gave you that condom, it was mainly because of Ariana. I understand you're gonna be doing your thang, but you need to be safe. Now, I know how we've been doing it—but it's different."

"How?"

"Well, for one, you're the only man I'm fucking. But that don't mean you gotta commit to me. If and when you meet a girl you wanna fuck, do you. But save all of that raw dick exclusively for me."

"And why am I so lucky?"

"I'm feeling you, Trevon. Really, I wanna see you on top. Fuck the past. Stay focused on getting paid, and you better be saving your money for your future. I know you look young, but you can't see yourself doing porn for thirty more years, so move wisely."

"And you're gonna help me?"

"I give you my word. Take my advice. Live now. Love can come later."

"Was that your plan?"

"I don't believe in love no more. All I do now is care about those that mean something to me."

"You shouldn't be that way."

"Too much heartbreak has made me this way."

"Well, I ain't trying to cause you no more pain."

"I know." She smirked. "Right now, you make my heart smile."

"Good, let's keep it that way."

"Um, like I said. I'm all for the date tonight. But the 'no sex'. I might have an issue with that. I know I won't be forced to use my hands, will I?"

"Damn. You tryin' to wear me out." He laughed. "But yo, you know I'ma beat that back out if requested."

"Now you're talking."

"Ai'ight. How wild you wanna get tonight?"

"Remember how you fingered my ass last night? Well, tonight I wanna feel your tongue back there."

"That's all?"

"There's more. I want you to put that masterpiece in my ass tonight, and I don't want you to stop until you cum inside me."

"You won't have to ask me twice."

"Is your dick hard?"

"You know it is."

"Well, I can't—" She was interrupted by the doorbell. "Hold on, somebody at the front door."

"I heard."

Jurnee reluctantly out of the tub. "Let me go peek out the window right quick," she said. When she reached the curtains, she inched them apart, frowning at the sight of a dark silver M850i parked behind her Bentley.

13

BACK TO THE OLD ME

January 23
Monday, 3:13 P.M. - Miami, Florida

Trevon had to end his call with Jurnee before she was able to tell him who was at the front door. He was on his way up to Janelle's office after getting a signal from the third-floor receptionist. When he stepped inside the elevator, he nodded at a thick, dark-skinned female with purple hair. She had on a pair of heels and a form-fitting white body contour dress. Her large breasts stretched the thin fabric.

"The man of the hour," she said after the elevator doors slid shut. "Trevon Harrison, I finally get to meet you in person." She extended her hand. "My name is Brooke Vee." She smiled. "Ms. Babin gave me this name since I favor Brooke Valentine. I'm a new fan. I saw that film you did with my girl Kandi."

Trevon still had a way to go before he was used to his new fame. "Thanks, I'm glad you liked it."

She played with the tips of her hair extensions. "It's fucked up how Kandi peeled out on you."

He sighed. "She's old news."

"Shit happens," she said, checking out how he was dressed.

She gave him points on his grown man attire. Today he was dripped in all white. Gucci linen slacks and a button-down shirt with a pair of gators.

"You do porn?" he asked when he noticed she wore a similar rose gold necklace like his own. It also held a rose gold diamond encrusted AEF medallion.

"Yeah. But I'm just coming back from having a baby."

"Boy or girl?"

"Girl."

"So you're new here or what?"

"Nah. I got a year and a half in the industry."

"You like it?"

She nodded. "Wouldn't trade it for nothing. I don't lack for nothing, and neither will my baby."

"How many films have you made?"

"Nine."

"Guess I need to check 'em out and support you."

"That's what's up."

"Who knows . . . maybe we'll do a film together."

She smiled and fluttered her false, long eyelashes. "My contract is already filled, honey. But since Kandi done bumped her head, I ain't got no problem seeing you privately."

"You got a man?"

"No, I'm single. My baby's daddy is in the NFL and married. I'm okay with it because I knew the deal before I got pregnant." She shrugged.

"Ai'ight. I guess we can exchange numbers if you want to."

"That's what's up."

They exchanged numbers just as the elevator slowed to a stop.

"I'll get up with you," he said before he exited the elevator.

"Make sure you do that because if you don't, I will." She winked as the doors slid shut.

Trevon wondered if his life would be better off without Kandi. Maybe Jurnee was right about saying he needed to enjoy his freedom.

"Hey, Ruby. What's up, baby?" he said, playfully flirting with Janelle's personal receptionist.

"You, with your handsome self," she replied, grinning ear to ear.

"The boss lady ready for me?"

"Yes. And I'm sorry to hear about you and Kandi."

"I'm good. If it was meant to be. Well, you know the saying."

Ruby nodded, pushing her glasses up her nose. Trevon didn't waste his time asking how she knew about his personal life. He was learning firsthand about the power of Twitter and Facebook when it came to speaking to the public about other folks' business.

As always, even though Janelle was expecting him, he knocked on the door.

"It's open, Trevon."

Entering her office, he was instantly drawn to her stunning looks. If Keri Hilson had a clone, it would be Janelle. Today she wore a green blouse with an elegant pearl necklace. Her long natural hair was set in a spiral of large, bouncy curls that framed her round face. Smiling, she motioned him to sit. "You're looking better than the news that comes before you."

"Talkin' 'bout my issue with LaToria?"

She nodded. "I talked to Jurnee, and as shocking as it may be. It's life, Trevon."

"I'm learning that."

She drummed her glossy fingernails on the desk. "Mentally, are you okay? Do you need to take some time off?"

"That's the last thing I need," he said. "If anything, I wanna move forward. Yeah, I'm hurt over losing LaToria, but I can't let it drag me down. Ai'ight, you signed me because you really believe I can be a star, right?"

She nodded.

"Well, I think I need to do more than nine more films. I want to be the best! And Jurnee can be my manager."

She recognized the determination in his voice. If his ambition was set on his career and not love, then it was a change she endorsed. Her opinion of him and Jurnee being sexually involved wasn't a big surprise. Janelle knew how Jurnee could draw the line between business and pleasure. Making up her mind, she said. "If you're ready to make a career of doing porn, I'll back you one hundred percent."

Trevon thought about his future. He wanted his own money, plus the freedom to do what pleased him. True love and a family —he would have to store them away. Besides, LaToria demonstrated that love was just a mere four-letter noun. Moving off the hurt he still felt toward LaToria, he told Janelle he was ready to be a star. Keeping Jurnee's suggestion of a future threesome film in mind, he shared the ideas with Janelle. She said she would give them some thought.

"Ms. Babin, please forgive me. But there's an issue going on down in the lobby on the first floor!" Ruby's voice emitted from the intercom by Janelle's wrist.

"What type of issue? Isn't security on post?"

"Yes. But I feel you need to be made aware of who it is."

"Who is it?" Janelle asked, annoyed.

"It's the CEO of Bigg Dog Records, D-Hot. He's down there with his crew, trying to force his way up. I heard he's looking for Brooke Vee.

"I don't need this shit!" Janelle muttered. "Listen, call the police and get Brooke Vee in my office ASAP!"

"I'm on it."

Janelle rubbed her temple as Trevon stood. "Where are you going?"

"Down to the first floor. Sounds like your security needs help."

"Trevon, no—"

"Chill," he said, moving for the door. "Let me handle this."

Janelle did something she rarely did. She went against her better judgment.

"Just tell that 'Ho to bring me my fucking chain!" D-Hot shouted in the lobby with his entourage and personal security, backing him up. He stood chest to chest with three AEF security guards that were trying to end the tension peacefully.

"Sir," the middle guard said, holding his palms up as he spoke. "Please lower your voice and explain what—"

"The bitch stole my muthafucking chain!" D-Hot shouted even louder. "Now, somebody gonna bring that bitch down with my chain, or I'ma go up and find 'er my damn self!"

"How and when was it stolen, sir?" the guard asked.

D-Hot balled up his fist. "Muthafucka, I ain't come here to file no muthafuckin' report! I came here to get my shit! I know that stealin' ass bitch is here because her ride is out back! Right now, I ain't the one to be foolin' wit'!" D-Hot grilled the evenly height white security guard. "Oh, yeah." He sneered. "My crew got guns too, and I know you ain't trying to go there. Last chance. Get that bitch down—"

All heads turned to the elevator when it pinged. D-Hot stepped between the guards. But he came to a stop when Trevon exited the elevator.

D-Hot recognized Trevon right away. "Where Brooke Vee!" he shouted.

"She's around," Trevon said, walking up to D-Hot and his crew.

D-Hot shook his head. "Oh, you must be fucking that 'ho since you coming down here on some captain save-a-ho shit!"

"Nah, I'm just trying to see what's up. This is a place of business." Trevon crossed his large arms, staring at D-Hot's chubby face.

"Bruh, that Captain America shit don't hold no weight wit' me!" D-Hot laughed. "You ain't on the yard no more."

"It must hold some type of weight for you to notice."

D-Hot glanced back at his crew. "Y'all see this muthafucka here?" He turned back to Trevon and lowered his voice. "Yo, I aint come here to play no games. Yeah, I heard 'bout cha. But know this. I ain't that lame ass Swagga or his goofball Yaffa that you laid down. Now, that bitch gonna bring her ass down here, or there gone be some major problems."

"Bruh, I can't understand you 'cause I'm used to only females whispering in my ear."

D-Hot's nostrils flared. "Oh, you one of them smart mouth muthafuckas, huh?"

"Just trying to settle this shit, bruh," Trevon said, reasoning that D-Hot was bluffing. A man of his status wouldn't risk the chance of a bullshit charge over a chain. Trevon stood his ground with the security guards confronting D-Hot. Trevon was fully aware of the egos that had to keep their rank. D-Hot had to be the man. Trevon understands how some men foolishly strived to act like were built of concrete. He came down on the strength of Janelle, not Brooke Vee. Tension bounced back and forth, filling the lobby with the stench of bad vibes. Trevon uncrossed his arms. He would never underestimate the next man when it came to beef. He remained unflappable, keeping his temper in check.

"Yeah." D-Hot sneered, grilling Trevon. "This a place of biz. But we both know that 'ho can't hide fo'ever. Now, since you wanna jump in this shit. Don't holler when it starts to stink."

Trevon was done exchanging words. His entire body was ready to spring at the slightest provocation from D-Hot. One of the guards on Trevon's left laid a hand on his shoulder, giving him a concerned look.

D-Hot saw the exchange. "Yeah, you don't want no smoke, son." D-Hot eyed Trevon up and down. "But be sure to tell that bitch that I'll catch her around. And you can keep that in mind too, Captain Save-a-Ho." D-Hot sucked his teeth, backing away from Trevon and the three guards. When he was sure he had Trevon's attention, he lifted the hem of his large multi-colored Versace shirt, revealing the butt of a gun.

TREVON LATER SAT ALONE in Janelle's office while she spoke with the police on the first floor. D-Hot and his team had sped off two minutes prior to the cops' arrival in a caravan of three Range Rovers. Janelle didn't want Trevon to be questioned by the police. On her authorization, she made it clear to the guards that they were not to mention anything about D-Hot having a gun. She did not want any bad publicity raining on her company.

Trevon sat slumped on the chair, staring aimlessly at the wall. D-Hot had him unstable by flashing his heat in his face. He could feel his way of thinking edging back toward his *I-don't-give-a-fuck* mode. Day by day, he grasped the reality of how unpredictable life could be. Things were faster, and the risk ran deeper than his time spent in prison. D-Hot could have taken things to a level that Trevon very well knew he wasn't prepared to handle.

"Never again," he whispered with conviction. Sighing, he pulled out his phone call to Jurnee when Janelle barged inside her office.

"I can't believe D-Hot did this shit today!" She slammed the door. "I knew I shouldn't have let you go down there!"

"Now it's my turn to tell you to sit down and relax," he told her.

She grudgingly sat down on the edge of her desk, crossing her arms. "That was crazy what you did down there."

He shrugged.

"From what I was told, you had a lot to say to D-Hot."

"I was just trying to make things calm," he said with a deadpan expression.

"Next time, let's let the security do their job."

"I feel you."

"Don't get yourself caught up in no bullshit, you hear me. I can only imagine how you're keeping it all together up there." She tapped her head. "But you gotta do what's right for Trevon from here on out. Now, about you and Kandi . . . I'll leave that alone. Because from what Jurnee told me, I'm just at a loss of words on that. But anyway, you came here to speak on your future with

Amatory, and like I said before, I'll back you. Now, as for Jurnee being your manager, that's an excellent idea."

"Ai'ight." He nodded.

"So, you're serious about this, huh?"

"My choices are limited right now."

"Well, the ones you have in front of you are good ones. Trust me." She smiled. "Everything will work out for you."

Trevon had so much respect for Janelle. She was one of the rare females he could count on without the topic of sex being in the mix. Staying true to her always-on-the-grind determination, she brought the meeting to a close. Grabbing her iPad, iPhone, she explained about an out-of- state business meeting with Wahida Clark.

"What do y'all have going?" Trevon asked, as he followed Janelle out of her office.

"A movie deal," Janelle told him. "If I can reach a deal with WCP, AEF will turn a WCP sex-driven novel into a movie."

He raised his left eyebrow. "Be sure to keep me in mind for a part."

14

HAVING THE LAST WORDS

January 23
Monday, 5:07 P.M. - Miami, Florida

Trevon made a sudden U-turn along Miami Avenue –
changing his mind about going home – and subsequently
ending up in the neighborhood where he was raised. Liberty
City.

He cruised through the rough, poverty-stricken Pork & Beans
projects until he slowed and pulled to the curb behind a sinister
black Ford Bronco sitting high on a lift kit with all its four doors
removed. The tall, dark-skinned owner of the Bronco stared warily
at the A8 over his shoulder until Tevon opened the door and
stepped out. He grinned, let go of the Draco on his lap and jumped
out of his truck.

"If it ain't my muthafuckin' ace boon coon, Trev!" Twank
shouted.

Trevon was all smiles at seeing his classmate from high school.

"Damn, bruh. You look old as fuck!" Trevon joked, giving
Twank a thug hug.

"Shit. You just look young 'cause the pen kept yo' ass on ice.
But damn, it's good to see you. I heard you was out, and I see you

pushin sumthin' nice." Twank nodded at the A8 parked under a mango tree.

"I got a little gig going," Trevon replied.

Twank rubbed his hands together. "You know we go way back. So if you want some weight I—"

"Naw, bruh." Trevon shook his head. "I need something else if you can help me?"

"Holla."

Spending $350 cash, Trevon pocketed a Glock 22 .40. Twank assured him it was clean and fresh out of the box.

Trevon left Liberty City and struggled to suppress his apprehension on the likelihood of being pulled over by the police. Driving with the system off, he suddenly had an idea. LaToria was back on his mind. Knowing his iPhone number was blocked from LaToria's phone, he wondered if she did the same for the second number he used for the Bluetooth system.

"Call LaToria," he said. A second later, a small picture of LaToria's smiling face appeared on the central display touchscreen, along with her phone number. Willing the call to go through, he was startled when it started to ring. Gripping the steering wheel, his heart began to race after the third ring sounded from the hidden speakers inside the cabin. He slowed for a red light behind a late model Honda Accord when LaToria answered unexpectedly.

"Hey, Trevon," LaToria's voice rang into his ears. "I know it's you because you're real funny acting about letting people drive your car." Her tone was flat.

He had a million things to ask and a million things to say. "What's up with you? You gonna explain to me what's going on with us?" He exerted himself to maintain his poise.

She sighed. "It just wasn't working out."

"And you came up with that feeling overnight? What about the baby? Is it true you're going to have an abortion?"

"No."

"Oh, so it's just fuck me and on to the next, huh?"

"It's a lot of things that you don't understand, okay?"

"Yeah, I bet it is. But guess what? It doesn't even matter to me no more. All I care about is the baby."

"It's not like that," she said morosely.

"Then what is it? You act like I don't even matter to you, LaToria."

"Do you hate me?"

He frowned, staring at her picture. "Are you serious? You act like what we had wasn't shit. You fuckin' ran out on me for another man wit' bread and now—"

"Jurnee tell you that?"

"Why does it matter?"

"Is she with you now?"

"No."

"Maybe y'all need to stop assuming shit 'bout me and—"

"Ain't nobody assuming shit 'bout you! We speaking about the bullshit you doing."

"And you can't say much since you didn't waste anytime to go and fuck Jurnee."

"Well, least you *know* who I'm fucking!"

"Fuck you!"

His grip tightened on the steering wheel. "I don't even know why I'm wasting my time talking to you."

"That makes two of us then!"

Silence. Fuming, he stayed silent as the line remained connected. He couldn't find the resolve to end the call himself.

"Shit is crazy," she muttered.

"I guess you're just doing what makes you happy."

"You didn't answer my question. Do you hate me?"

He rubbed his forehead.

"Are you gonna answer me?"

"Why does it matter how the fuck I feel? Your ass didn't have that in mind when you left with Martin!"

"Martellus."

"Martin, Marshall, Michael, MacDonald, I—don't give a fuck what his name is."

"I can't make you understand."

"Ain't shit to understand, okay? You been cheating on me, so fuck it. It is what the fuck it is and trust me. You don't need to make me understand."

"It's not really like that," she tried to explain. "Please don't judge me."

"Whatever, yo," he said, glancing at the rearview mirror. His heart skipped a beat when he noticed a Metro-Dade police cruiser two cars back.

"I know what I did was wrong. But I—"

"It don't matter to me no more, okay? I don't care what you-"

"I have to go, okay? But you can't call me at this number no more."

"Like that's a surprise."

"I'll call you later on in the week with a new number, okay?"

Trevon, with all the hurt he held inside, matched it against the love he still carried for her. Frowning, he refused to be boyfriend number two.

"Nah, I'm good. Wouldn't want to make your *man* mad, so keep that new number to yourself. Or give it to somebody that wanna hear that bullshit you talking. I'm done." He jabbed a button on the steering wheel, ending the call.

JURNEE WAS CHATTING with her new friend Tahkiyah when she heard Trevon coming through the front door. Excusing herself, she met Trevon at the door.

"How did things work out with Janelle?" she asked, as he entered the security code to turn the alarm system back on.

"Good and bad," he replied.

"What happened?"

"Just some crazy shit with D-Hot," he said, turning to face her.

"D-Hot?"

"Yeah. But it didn't have nothing to do with me talking to

Janelle. It's all good on that subject, and she's down with you being my manager."

"Cool!"

"You got company. I see that BMW out front. Do I know 'im?"

"Yes, I got company." She nudged him. "But you don't know her."

"Oh, my bad." He grinned.

"Hell, I just met her today." She glanced over her shoulder.

"Who is she?"

Jurnee briefly explained that Tahkiyah was in the neighborhood to view the house across the street that was up for sale.

"She seems cool. C'mon and let me introduce you to her. She said she'll be moving in next month."

"Ai'ight. Just gimme a second. I need to use the bathroom right quick."

"Hurry up."

He reasoned it wasn't a good time to ask Jurnee about her talking to LaToria. After he hid the .40 in a shoe box under his bed, he joined Jurnee and his soon to be new neighbor in the living room.

"And here's the man of the house," Jurnee said when Trevon made his entrance.

Trevon was thankful that no one could read his mind. His first impression of Tahkiyah stimulated him instantly. *Damn, she fine as hell!*

"Tahkiyah, this is Trevon," Jurnee said, making the introductions.

Tahkiyah held out her hand as she stood to greet him. "This is a nice home you have," she said. *Whew! He is handsome!*

"Thanks," he replied, wondering what Jurnee had shared with the gorgeous stranger.

"Tahkiyah's from one of the northern states," Jurnee said when they were all seated.

"Which state?" he asked.

"Actually, I'm from D.C.," Tahkiyah replied.

"Too cold up there for me." Jurnee shivered.

"True, but it's something I'm used to," Tahkiyah said truthfully.

"She wants to know how the yard care is done," Jurnee told Trevon.

"Um, every other Thursday they have a crew to come out, but it's optional. Some homeowners like to do their own work."

"Which option did you pick, if you don't mind telling me?" Tahkiyah asked.

"I do it myself. But mainly it's because of badass over there." He pointed at the glass back door where Rex sat.

"He's just a puppy," Jurnee added.

"Yeah, and he don't listen." Trevon shifted on the sofa, lowering his eyes down the length of Tahkiyah's sexy legs. "So, you're gonna make Florida your new home?"

Tahkiyah nodded. "I think it's time for a new change of pace."

"You have any family?" he asked, noticing the big platinum ring on her finger.

"Just two kids, and both are grown and my husband, of course. If you see two energetic little ones in my yard, they're my grandkids."

"Grandkids!" Trevon noted how young Tahkiyah looked.

"Guess her age," Jurnee teased.

"Now you're being rude." Trevon glanced at Jurnee.

"Boy, I felt the same when she told me she's a grandmother. I know one thing. I hope I can look that good when I reach her age."

"I'm fifty-four," Tahkiyah told Trevon to prove she wasn't uncomfortable about her age.

"Hey, y'all excuse me for a second." Jurnee slid off the sofa and sauntered to her bedroom. Trevon's gaze followed Jurnee's heart-shaped ass out of the living room. Observing the way her ass moved, he knew she wasn't wearing any panties under her leggings. Being left alone with Tahkiyah had Trevon searching for a topic. Her beauty was undeniable.

"You got any more questions about the neighborhood?" he

asked as she crossed her legs, forcing the pencil skirt to tighten around her thighs.

"Not much. I see it's an upper-class area. And quiet."

"Yeah, it is."

"Jurnee told me you live alone now. She spoke briefly on your former roommate moving out just a few days ago."

Trevon's expression didn't change. "Yeah, and I'll be solo whenever Jurnee gets back in her own place."

"She told me that as well."

"What? Are y'all best friends already?" He laughed. "What all did y'all talk about?"

"Just women things—clothes, shoes, and men."

"Uh, if you don't mind me asking... what do you do for a living?"

"I own a public relations company up in D.C. And what about you?"

"I'm an actor."

She assumed he was teasing. "An actor? What movies have you been in?"

He wasn't sure if she would respect his line of work. In his assessment, she was a woman of sophisticated taste. Just as he started to explain, his iPhone chimed. Seeing an unfamiliar number, he was about to ignore the call until he realized it was Brooke Vee.

"Yeah, what's up?" he said after gesturing to Tahkiyah that he needed to take the call.

". . . Hello? May I speak to Trevon?"

"This me. What's up?"

"Hey. I need your help."

"What is it?"

"That fool D-Hot had one of his groupie hoes cut all my tires, and now I'm stranded."

"Where you at?"

"On South Beach. About a block away from the Marlin Hotel. Can you help me out?"

"Yeah," he said. "I'll be there in thirty minutes."

"Where are you coming from?"

"Coconut Grove."

"Okay. Just gimme a call back when you get on Washington Avenue. I'll be standing by my car."

Trevon ended the call just as Jurnee returned from the back. As he explained what was going on, Tahkiyah used the opening to make her exit as well. At the front door, he assured Jurnee that their date was still set for tonight.

TELLING lies was not a trait that Tahkiyah held close relations with. She hid her disappointment over LaToria's absence until she was back inside her car. She vented on the phone with Staton, the private investigator.

"She's gone!" she said, irritated. "I just left her house, but—"

"Slow down, okay. Where is she?"

"If I knew that I wouldn't be calling you!"

"Okay, what can I do?"

Tahkiyah drove behind Trevon's A8 toward the exit. "I need you to get some details on someone. You have a pen?"

"Yep. Go ahead with what you got."

Tahkiyah sat up against the steering wheel and read the Dade County tag on the A8. "All I have is his first name, and it's Trevon." She told Staton the details she knew about Trevon being LaToria's roommate.

"Okay, I remember seeing that car in the driveway, but I didn't know who drove it," Staton replied.

"How soon can you get something back to me?" she asked.

"Soon. I'll just reach my contact with the DMV and go from there."

"Please do that because I came too close to let go of this."

UP IN FORT LAUDERDALE, Swagga rolled from between the legs of his married hairstylist. He had fallen at first sight of her coke bottle figure. Like all the rest, she would remain a mere addition to the number of women he fucked just for the thrill. Reaching for his boxers, he stared at her ebony ass as she strolled to the bathroom. From the waist down, she was thickly built with an enormous ass.

Leaving her in the bathroom, he went down to the first floor to get a drink.

Rick sat in the living room with three other guards watching a Kevin Hart movie on the wall mounted plasma TV. Seeing Swagga coming down the stairs, he got up and met him halfway. Rick smelled the scent of sex, weed, and liquor on Swagga from an arm's distance.

"You look like shit," Rick said as Swagga nearly tripped over his untied retro hi-top John Varvatos Converse shoes.

"No, I don't." Swagga grinned. "I look like money."

"I got some news for you," Rick said.

"Whut up?"

"Martellus is back in Denver, and Kandi is with him." Rick followed Swagga into the kitchen.

"I knew that bitch was on some bullshit."

"Yeah, but my main concern was Martellus."

"Fuck 'em both!" Swagga said as he opened one of the stainless-steel doors on the refrigerator.

"I need to run something by you before you go back up."

"I'm listenin'," Swagga said as he reached for a bottle of Crown Royal Extra Rare.

"There was some drama down in Miami at the Amatory office."

"What kind of drama?"

"Trevon had some beef with D-Hot."

"And how you find that out?"

"Fritz was there. He's doing his surveillance, remember?"

Swagga nodded as he closed the refrigerator with his elbow. "So, what's that 'pose to mean to me?"

Rick didn't expect Swagga to see how things could be manipulated. "We can put Fritz to work early and turn that shit between D-Hot and Trevon into some major beef. Our buddy can be dead this week."

Swagga shrugged. "Make it happen an' make sure he suffers."

15

I'M LISTENING. SHE'S WATCHING

January 23

Monday, 7:27 P.M. - Coconut Grove, Florida

"Did you fuck Brooke Vee?" Jurnee confronted Trevon the moment he strolled through the front door.

"No. I didn't fuck Brooke Vee," he answered truthfully.

She smiled and kissed him on the cheek. "Good, because that means you'll have plenty of stamina for me after our date."

"Yo, what if I did?"

"I would just hope you used a condom," she said straight-forwardly.

He laid his hands on her waist and kissed her forehead. "I'ma always keep it real with you."

She circled her arms around his neck. "I need to tell you something."

"Speak your mind."

"I called Kandi the other day," she told him. "I just wanted to see what was up, but I lost my temper and told her about us. I didn't mean to start—"

"Listen, Jurnee," he said. "Fuck her, okay? Whatever you told her don't matter. I'm done lookin' for love. And since you waited 'til now to tell me. I'ma punish this ass tonight."

She jumped on him, crossing her ankles around his waist.

"Whoa, girl!" He laughed, carrying her weight easily.

"Am I heavy?" She giggled as he carried her to his bedroom.

"A little bit," he lied.

"You hurt my feelings," she said, rubbing his ear.

"Well, do something about it," he said, kicking his bedroom door open.

She looked over her shoulder at the bed. "What are we doing in here?"

"I want you to help me get all of LaToria's shit up outta here." He dropped her on the bed.

She tugged her shirt down, thinking of how quickly things had changed since she arrived. "You sure about this?"

"Yeah. Let's start now, and then we can shower and get ready for our date."

FRITZ WAS a man of trained patience when it related to his trade. Back at the one-bedroom apartment he was alone tonight, preparing his tools. He sat on a padded milk crate by the bed. He picked up a Bushmaster AR-15 fitted with a 12x50 riflescope and laid across his lap. He had cleaned it twice, taking it apart down to the firing pin. Two 30-round clips loaded with brass 5.56-millimeter rounds sat at the foot of the lumpy bed. On a bad day Fritz could knock a target down center mass at a distance of 500 yards with the AR-15. With the assault rifle fitted with a silencer, it made him a dealer of quiet death at a distance. Propped against the wall to his right was a Mossberg blue barrel 12-gauge pistol grip pump. Fritz favored the Mossberg when he needed to get his point across in close quarters.

His current essential item was a small GPS tracking system monitor. With it, he knew when and where his target traveled in his vehicle. If the opportunity presented itself tonight, Fritz would strike without hesitation. He received the message from Rick about making the target suffer. To Fritz, that was just an added bonus with no extra fee.

∽

AT 8:35P.M. Trevon stepped out of the shower.

"Good news and bad news," Jurnee said, leaning against the sink. She bit her bottom lip as she indulged in an eyeful of his stark-naked body. His hairless crotch and the way his wide upper body tapered to the V at his waist looked so titillating.

"Gimme the bad first." He reached for the towel to dry off as Jurnee shamelessly kept her eyes below his muscular stomach.

"I just got off the phone with Janelle."

"Damn, I don't want no bad news from her," he said, drying his biceps.

In a trance, she gazed at the shaft of his limp penis.

"My face is up here," he teased.

"Umm, we can't go out tonight," she said, snatching the towel from him.

"Why not?"

"She wants you to go on this live radio show tonight."

"What for?"

"Exposure. You're a porn star, and you have a brand to build. If you want to shine, you gotta stay on your grind."

"What kind of radio show is it?" he asked as she toweled off his chest and stomach.

"It's a late-night sex talk show called *Climaxx* hosted by this dude from Detroit. Last week he had Thicky Minaj up there talking about her sexual fantasies and stuff. Turn around."

"And I have to go tonight?"

"It's business. You wanna boost your downloads and DVD sales you gotta stay in the public. I think it's an excellent idea. Mmm, I love your sexy build."

"So no date tonight?"

"Nope. We have to be at the studio in Coral Gables by ten thirty tonight. The show starts at midnight."

"Ain't never been on—"

"I know," she said, caressing his ass with her bare hand. "I'm your manager now, and I'll walk you through the process. Just relax. Be yourself, and it will all be okay."

"Um, I think my ass is dry now," he said over his shoulder.

"Be quiet," she purred, reaching around his waist. "I know what I'm doing."

He felt her breasts mashed against his back as she circled her soft fingers around his penis.

"You like this?" She caressed his penis as it throbbed and grew in her grip.

"You know I do."

"I still want you in my ass tonight. I can't wait for it." She stroked the entire length of his penis. Just the thought of her ass being stretched by it had her clitoris bulging under her panties.

Wanting him to save all his vigor for later, she unwillingly released his dick to prepare for the radio talk show.

She switched into business mode as she coached him on a number of formalities related to doing interviews.

"If they ask you something stupid, let me handle it. And don't let them trick you into losing your cool and make a fool of yourself. If you do, this will be your first and last interview. And remember, you represent Amatory Erotic Films."

Following Jurnee's advice, Trevon later stepped outside wearing a tan sport coat, a linen shirt and a pair of denim jeans, all by Robert Graham. By habit, his head tilted toward the dark, star-lit sky. Moments such as now meant a lot to him. While in prison, he was forced to go inside before nightfall. For 15 years he had never been able to view the moon and stars in its true form. Seeing it from behind a Plexiglas cell window was not a moment to remember.

He turned back toward the house when he heard Jurnee's Jimmy Choo stiletto sandals clacking on the tiles.

"Did you feed Rex?" she asked, standing in the doorway. Tonight, she had her tantalizing frame poured into a blue bodycon dress that emphasized her ample hips.

"Yeah," he said as the wind rustled the pencil thin palmetto trees in the front yard.

As Jurnee locked the door and turned the alarm on, Trevon suggested they drive her SUV. Keeping his paranoid feelings of being followed to himself, he settled in the driver's seat of the Bentayga.

"You ready?" Trevon asked, as he started the engine.

She nodded, with a high gloss shine on her succulent lips. "Let's make history."

LaToria received the mass e-mail from Janelle's personal receptionist about Trevon's radio interview an hour before the show started. Dealing with conflicting emotions, she managed to slip away from Martellus by taking a bubble bath. Behind the closed door, she eased into the large tub with an iPad. She couldn't pass up the opportunity to hear Trevon's voice.

"Me say . . . yahhhhh! Dis yo' boy Grime comin' live fo' another night of the realest talk show swingin'. You're tuned in with me, Grime. Me say . . . yahhhh and my sexy co-host Chandra! Dis is the *Climaxx Late Night Talk Show,* and tonight is fo' my ladies. Wit' me in the studio, I have a special guest that I'll let Chandra introduce y'all to."

"Hey y'all. This your diva Chandra, and I wanna welcome everybody to another night of *Climaxx.* In the studio we have Trevon, who's an adult film star, and yes, I posted a link to his video on our site. Tonight, we're gonna interview him and find out what it's like to be a porn star."

"Oh, for the fellas," Grime jumped in. "I'ma post a few pics on my Instagram of his fine ass manager, former adult star, Honey Drop. Me say . . . yahhh!"

Trevon sat in the small studio wearing a pair of headphones. Jurnee watched him from a cozy sofa to his left. The studio was dimly lit with most of the lights coming from the switchboard that Chandra and Grime sat behind. Trevon sat facing them with a thick padded boom mic a few inches from his face.

"So, what's happening with you?" Chandra asked, starting the interview off.

"I'm good," Trevon began. "Just taking it day by day and enjoying my freedom and the job I have."

"That's how you view doing porn—a job?" Chandra asked.

"Shit. I get paid for it." He laughed. "But seriously, it's a job because at AEF that's how it's managed. Do I enjoy it? Hell yeah!"

"I watched your debut film on my phone, and whew. You got it going on!" She fanned herself.

"Thanks. And thank you for your support as well."

"You're more than welcomed. Okay, give our listeners a brief bio about yourself and speak up a lil' bit, baby."

"Uh-oh!" Grime said into the mic. "Bruh, she called you baby, so she might try to toss that big booty on you. Me say . . . yahhhhhh!"

"Grime, hush!" Chandra playfully shoved her co-host, then gestured for Trevon to speak.

"Okay, um, I was born and raised in Miami. Shouts out to Liberty City and them Northwestern Bulls. I'm thirty-three, I don't smoke or do any drugs and...I don't have any kids and, I consider myself to be humble."

"Ladies, this man does not look like he's thirty-three," Chandra said.

"I, um, did some time in prison, which isn't a secret. All you gotta do is Google it. Ah, I just got out of prison last year, and I was given this shot to do adult films by Janelle Babin."

"Okay, okay." Chandra smiled. "I see you're putting Liberty City on shine. Um, in your debut film... was it really the end of - was it really the first time you had sex since being release from prison, after fifteen years?"

"Yes, it was."

"Ummm, I wish I could've welcomed you home."

Trevon laughed, shaking his head.

"Okay. In your films, do you have any control over what kind of sexual acts you do?"

"At AEF, Janelle will not force anyone to do anything they're not at ease with.

"Can you see yourself still doing porn . . . say, five years from now?"

"It's possible."

"Okay, let's say if you were to have a private sex tape leak out with someone...who would it be?"

"Hmmm. I will have to say...Anansa Sims. It's just something about her sexy ass that gets me going."

"You heard it here first, y'all. Mr. Trevon Harrison has a thang for, Anansa Sims. Now, let's open up the phone lines and take a live caller. Is that okay with you, Trevon?" Chandra asked as Grime signaled that a caller was on hold.

"Yeah. I'm good with that," Trevon replied.

"Okay. Our caller is Nashlly from Fort Lauderdale. What question do you have for our guest tonight?"

"Yeah, I wanna know what the deal is on the whole issue with Kandi stepping out on you? Also, is it true that she's pregnant by you?"

Trevon cleared his throat. "First off, it's personal, but I'll address it since it's spreading like COVID-19 did on social media. As you all know, I did my debut adult film with Kandi. She also became the first woman I had sex with in fifteen years."

"So, she had you pussy whipped?"

"I won't put it like that," Trevon said, as Jurnee gestured for him to stop talking.

"So how would you put it then?"

"Nothing in life is perfect," Trevon said, as he signaled toward Jurnee that he could handle the call. "Yes, I had feelings for Kandi, and it was beyond just sex. Maybe I rushed it, or maybe I wasn't ready for a relationship."

"So, did you get her pregnant when y'all did that film?"

"No. All films produced by AEF are strictly safe sex, and if you were a true fan of AEF, then you would know that. What happened between Kandi and I was personal, and I don't regret one moment spent with her."

"One last question. How did you manage to avoid any legal issues for killing Swagga's bodyguard last year?"

Jurnee shot to her feet, wildly gesturing for Chandra or Grime to cut the line. Trevon shook his head, knowing it was best to face the facts before rumors took over.

"Nashlly, right?" Trevon said, composed into the mic. "Well, last year, I was cleared of all charges related to Yaffa's death. It's public record of a report filed by the U.S. Marshals and the Metro Dade Police Department that Yaffa's injuries were self-inflicted. Now, if you want to doubt their report, then that's on you."

"But—"

"Facts are facts," Trevon stated calmly. "I know I will always be viewed as an ex-convict by many. But I can't let my past, nor how people think of me, dictate how I live my life. Yes, it's true Kandi, and I were in a relationship, but it didn't work out. That's life and I hold no harsh feelings toward her."

"Good answer." Chandra nodded at Trevon. "That's what we get when we do it live and without a delay."

"Oh yeah. Nashlly, be sure to check out my DVD and do spread the word."

"'Cuse me for a second," Grime said, adjusting his mic. "We just got a question posted on our Twitter page by one of our listeners. But ah—I'm gonna have to let Chandra read it."

Chandra leaned in Grime's direction to read the question off his laptop. When she sat back up, she couldn't suppress her wide grin. "One of your new fans would like to know if you're up to allowing me to measure your dick right here in the studio."

"WHY THE FUCK YOU TELL'EM YO' real name?" Swagga barked at Nashlly as he followed her out of his master bathroom and into his bedroom.

"Because you didn't say not to!" Nashlly complained, stomping toward the bed. "It aint like they knew who the hell I was anyway! So why are you tripping? Hell, I didn't wanna do the shit in the first muthfuckin' place." She sat down heavily on the bed, frowning, with her arms crossed.

"Did you block your number? Or did I hafta tell you that too?" He paced in front of her.

Rolling her eyes, she sighed. "Yes, I blocked my number. Now can you tell me what that was all about?"

"No!' he snapped. "And stop askin' so many questions, damn!"

Nashlly who recently turned thirty, steeled herself to curb her attitude as she rose to her bare feet. "C'mere, baby," she cooed.

He ignored her, contemplating the idea of sending her back home in an Uber.

"I'm sorry, baby." She stepped in front of him and forced him to admire her brown-skinned breasts. "Let me make it up to you?"

He stared at her. "How?"

"I'm sorry, baby.' She stepped in front of him and forced him to admire her brown-skinned breasts. "Let me make it up to you."

She grabbed the waistband of his Gucci briefs. "Come to bed and I'll show you."

BACK IN MIAMI, Tahkiyah had everything in place for another one of her private moments. The lights were off inside her suite at Mondrian Hotel. Her nude body tingled with an insatiable compulsion to feel the euphoric excitement of an orgasm. She palmed her breasts. This was her secret ritual. Turning to her side, she flipped her laptop open. Within a few seconds, she was back on a porn site listed as <u>Black Sexxx.</u>

She scanned the list of fantasies she could indulge in.

<u>Theme</u>
<u>Videos</u>
<u>Theme</u>
<u>Videos</u>
<u>Anal sexxxx</u>

16

SADOMASOCHISM SEXXX

She clicked _oral sex_ and discovered a link to fellatio. All of the videos featured black on black sex. Rolling to her stomach, she previewed a 50 second clip of a video before she downloaded it. Tahkiyah's beautiful face was lit by the screen. She squeezed her thighs together and pressed her nipples against the soft, royal blue satin sheets. As soon as the download was complete, she touched the play icon to start the 20-minute video.

The film began with a topless big breasted black girl in a hot tub stroking a penis. Her breast wobbled with the slightest movements. She stared at the screen and watched the girl twirling her tongue all over the thick-headed penis.

"Ummmm, shit yeah! Suck that dick!" Tahkiyah moaned, staring at how the girl swallowed the penis. From a side view, the film showed a close-up of the girl engulfing the dick at a stabilized pace. She would give anything to have a black man in her mouth. Catching her totally off guard, Trevon slid into her erotic thoughts.

AFTER THE INTERVIEW, Janelle made a FaceTime call with Trevon to offer her congratulations. She informed him that his next film would be moved up to next week. The interview had proven to be a wise choice. Tonight alone, she was sure his video was downloaded around 800 times. Jurnee proved that she was serious about Trevon's career. Knowing he would begin his three-day film shoot next week, all sex was halted. Knowing how strong temptation could lure her in bed with him, she made the decision to sleep alone.

Trevon didn't make a big deal about her choice. Besides, there was always tomorrow.

LaToria felt a twinge of hope when she heard Trevon admit that he didn't hold any harsh feeling toward her. Listening to his voice rekindled her emotions for him. Hiding her hurt, she rushed from the tub and into her bedroom, where she dried off and slid under the thick green quilted comforter and sheets. Closing her eyes, she tried to hold back her tears. *God, please help me make things right with Trevon.* She wiped her eyes in the dark bedroom that she shared with Martellus. Not caring about Martellus' whereabouts, she curled up with the sincere thought of the only man she truly loved Trevon.

17

WATCH AND LEARN

January 24

Tuesday, 12:30 P.M. – Coconut Grove, Florida

Trevon stood outside waxing his Audi A8 in the driveway when Jurnee came out of the house.

"You finally got out of the bed, huh?" he said, squatting down to wax the front bumper. When she didn't answer, he glanced up at her.

She stood with a tight expression; her arms folded "You trying to go back to prison?"

He rose to his feet. "What kind of dumb ass question is that? And what's wrong with you?" he said, squinting from the sun in his face.

"Ain't nothing wrong with me!" she snapped.

"Gotta be for you to be coming at me all sideways and shit. Now what's up?"

She sighed. "I found that gun you got under your bed!"

"I need it, okay?"

"No! It's not okay!" she said. "I'm all for gun rights and stuff. But you're a felon and—"

"You don't need to remind me about that!"

"Obviously, I do, since you got the damn thing!" she stated. "If I didn't care about you, I wouldn't be having this conversation with you."

"My life isn't—it ain't all peaceful like yours, okay? I got shit I gotta deal with, and if it comes to me using a gun. Then it is what it is."

"Do you even realize what you're saying? Tell me. If you could do it all over, would you have killed that teacher?"

"Damn right I would! That muthafucka touched my little sister. So fuck him! And no, I don't regret it! I did my time. He's dead. So as far as I'm concerned, we fuckin' even!"

"You don't mean that."

"The hell I don't!"

"How can you become what you want to be by remaining what you are?"

"What the fuck am I, Jurnee?" He threw the polishing cloth on the ground. "Can you tell me since you wanna preach to me?"

"I'm not preaching to you, so don't try to play me like that. Hell, if you don't give a fuck about your freedom, then why should I?"

"Shit, I don't remember asking you to!"

"You know what. Ain't got time for this," she said, shaking her head. "Are you going to get rid of that gun or what?"

"No. I'm not gettin'—no!"

"So that's your decision?"

"Ain't gotta repeat myself."

"Fine! As long as you want to be a gangsta and all that, then you can do it by your damn self!"

"And what the fuck is that 'pose to mean?"

"How about I show you what it means!" She gave him a hard look before she turned and stormed back inside the house.

"Whatever! You wanna leave, burn the fuckin' road up!" he shouted. Balling his fist, he turned toward the street and cursed. Holding his head in his hands, he closed his eyes and took a few breaths to calm down. He needed his space, so he slid behind the wheel of the A8 and sped off, squealing the rear tires. Driving with no set destination, he was forced to think about his life and the words Jurnee had thrown on his troubled conscience. Cruising north on 22nd Avenue, he thought deeply on the man he was and the better man he wanted to be.

~

LATER, 3:32p.m. Trevon sat inside his A8 at Simpson Park when he received a call from Kendra.

"What's up, Ms. Probation Lady?"

"Somebody got some jokes today." She laughed. "How are you doing?"

"Surviving. Just taking it day by day."

"We're all doing that these days to tell you the truth."

"True. But some days shit just seems to get out of hand."

"You should just let some things be. Look. I was wondering if you can meet me at Halo's. It's a new soul food spot on Collins Avenue near the Marlin Hotel. The food is off the chain!"

"Uh, what time you trying to be there?"

"Five thirty. I hope you can make it."

"You paying?"

"Nope. You are. I paid for our first date, remember?"

He grinned. "I see you got jokes today."

"So will you be joining me?"

"It's a date."

"I was hoping to hear that. Oh, and Mr. Harrison. Don't be late this time, okay? If I have to come looking for you, you won't like it," she said, good-naturedly.

~

TREVON ARRIVED at Halo's at 5:20p.m. After he parked his car, he located Kendra's Mercedes-Benz AMG G63 near the entrance of the restaurant. He hoped he wasn't underdressed when he entered the cozy restaurant wearing a pair of wheat colored Timberland boots, black Gucci jeans, and a white tank top. Scanning the faces for Kendra. He was caught off guard when someone tapped on his shoulder.

"You walked right by me," Kendra said as Trevon turned around. "C'mon, I'm ready to place my order."

"How long you been here?" he asked as he followed her between the tables.

"Not long."

They took a seat at a green cloth-covered table near the tinted window. The wall behind Trevon was covered with framed pictures of prominent Black folks. Martin Luther King, Jr., Malcolm X, former President Barack Obama, Desmond Tutu, Maya Angelou and many others.

Kendra glanced up from the menu to see Trevon studying the pictures over his shoulder. "Who's in that picture above Nelson Mandela?" she quizzed him.

Trevon turned in the chair. "That's Frederick Douglass. He was a writer and fought to end slavery. In fact, he escaped from slavery." He turned back to the table. "Didn't think I knew that, did ya?"

"I must admit that you're correct." She smiled.

"Ai'ight, my turn. Who's in the picture that's below Kamala Harris?"

"Hmm . . . let me guess. Would it be the author of *Roots,* Alex Haley? Born in 1921 and laid to rest in 1992."

Trevon laid his iPhone on the table. "Okay, we both know our history and stuff. Now, let's order some of this good ass food I'm smelling."

He kept his fitness in mind by ordering the grilled chicken instead of a fried one. He explained his reason to Kendra by pointing out that the grilled chicken was loaded with protein but low in carbs. Along with the six-ounce grilled chicken breast, he ordered a side of steamed spinach and one baked sweet potato. Since Kendra wasn't too pleased with her size, she figured today would be as good as any to start eating right. She ordered the same.

Before the food came, they spoke about the topics of their life. Kendra admitted that she was ready to get back to work. She also told Trevon that she was officially done with Marcus, aka Swagga.

Midway through the meal, Trevon watched a couple entered with two small kids in tow. What he saw was an item that seemed out of reach. A family. He was still dealing with LaToria and the way she had left him. His choice of emotions was limited, sorrow or anger. He ran with the latter, having more comfort by not dealing with matters of the heart.

"You, okay?" Kendra asked, as one of the little kids waved at Trevon.

Shifting in the chair, he nodded. "I was just wondering what it would be like to have a child."

"It's a major responsibility," Kendra said. "The one heavy burden is trying to be perfect. You know. You trying not to do no wrong in front of your child."

"How's your little one doing? Did she like the canopy bed we put together?"

"She's doing great. Just wanting every toy, she sees on TV. And that bed, she treats it like a trampoline with her spoiled behind."

"You ever plan to have another baby?"

She glanced down at her plate. "I doubt it."

Clearing his throat, he leaned forward. "How well do you know Swagga?"

She looked at him, puzzled "Uh, he's my baby daddy. I know him very well. Why do you ask?"

"Look. All that shit that happened last year—"

"It's over with, Trevon," she said, becoming upset.

"Wait," he said, reaching across the table for her hand. "Just hear me out, okay? Please. I just need to share something with you."

"Something about Marcus?"

"Yeah," he replied.

She wanted to pull her hand back. However, his contact

reminded her of the passionate times they had together. She would never forget how satisfying it felt when he was inside her. Blinking, she pushed the sexual thoughts from her mind and told Trevon to share whatever he had to share.

He started from the beginning, telling her about what happened after he left her house last year. She showed no emotion as he admitted that LaToria had showed up unexpectedly at his front door.

". . . After we had sex, she went home to get some things so she could spend the night. Well, she left her phone at my place by mistake and when I found it, I saw a voice message from Swagga."

"And?"

"He was telling LaToria to turn over some footage of him and Chyna. He assumed LaToria was down with some type of scheme. Told her to leave her phone in the mailbox. Said Yaffa already killed Chyna and Cindy and she was—"

"I don't believe you, Trevon," she said, snatching her hand back. "Swagga ain't shit. I'll tell you that, my damn self. But he beat the case, and plus, where is the motive? Yaffa, he just—"

"I got the motive, Kendra," Trevon pressed. "All that bullshit that went down that night was because he didn't want his secret to get out, okay? He tried to burn LaToria alive for something she didn't even know about," Trevon said desperately.

"So how did her name come up, huh?"

"I don't know. Hell, LaToria don't even know."

"So what's the motive? What's Marcus got to hide that I don't know about?"

He turned his phone over and tapped the screen. "When Chyna and Cindy were killed, there was a guy in the closet."

"And you believe that?"

"This is what I believe." He slid his phone across the table. "He sent me three videos of Swagga and Chyna back on Christmas. You can see it for yourself."

She shook her head, refusing to touch the phone. "I don't care to see him fucking another woman, okay!" she asserted hotly. "Why would you even consider the idea of me wanting to see it?"

He slid the phone against her hand. "Chyna . . . isn't she."

Kendra averted her eyes to the ceiling, sighing. She held a ton of doubt toward what she heard. Since actions spoke louder than words, she picked up the phone to get to the bottom of whatever issue Trevon had with Swagga. With her mind twisting on what she was about to learn, she pressed *Play*.

18

I KNOW YOUR SECRET

January 24

Tuesday, 5:53 P.M. - Miami Beach, Florida

Kendra sat dumbfounded after she viewed the three videos of Swagga having sex with Chyna.

"Who else have you shown these to?" she asked, visibly shaken.

"Nobody but LaToria. I told Jurnee about it, but she wasn't pressed to look at them."

She pushed the phone back across the table with a look of anger and disgust twitching across her face.

"Did you know he was bisexual?" Trevon asked.

She tried to think back to any clues or hints that Swagga had a taste for men. "I can't believe this," she murmured.

"Were you, uhhh—having unsafe sex with—"

"No!" she replied. "He never proved to me he could commit, so even when I was back with him, we used protection. He was upset about it, but now I'm glad I didn't give in."

"That's good to hear," he said, hoping she was honest.

"What do you plan to do?"

He shrugged. "I was hoping you had some ideas."

133

"He's the father of my child," she reminded him.

"I'm aware of that. But all I'm sharing with you are facts."

"I...can't believe this."

"Look. He *did* try to kill LaToria for this shit, and now that I have it—"

"You think he'll do something to you," she admitted carefully.

"Something like that."

"What were you planning to do without me knowing this?"

He shrugged. "Everyone keeps telling me that Swagga being gay or whatever won't be such a big deal. Really, I'm thinking about deleting this shit and just moving on with my life."

"What's stopping you?"

"I hate losing."

"I have a question. Who's your favorite rapper?"

"Uh . . . alive, I'll say it's Future. Why does it matter?"

"And what if he came out of the closet? Would you still support him?"

"Sure. But if you're trying to compare how the public will feel about Swagga, he ain't gonna admit what he did with Chyna."

"Okay, you have a point."

"And that still leaves me at point A. Not knowing what the fuck to do."

"It's personal to me," Kendra said thoughtfully. "My life was at risk. What if he has STDs? That's my concern. I don't care about his rep or record sales. This is my life!" Tears began to well in her eyes. "I know he was unfaithful to me. But I—I never would have thought that he had gay tendencies." Her voice trembled.

"What do you want me to do with the videos?"

She wiped her eyes. "I need you to trust me."

"You've earned that already. So, what's up?"

"I need to download those videos to my phone," she replied quickly.

He struggled with her request. "Maybe I should just delete it," he said.

"Don't do that. Like I said, it's personal with me. Let me handle it. Please. He needs to learn what's done in the dark will one day stand in the light."

A SUDDEN RAINSTORM broke over Swagga's mansion in Fort Lauderdale and the lower parts of Broward County. Around 8:20 that night, a pair of headlights cut through the thick darkness at the unguarded back gate to the east of the mansion. From a distance of two hundred yards, Kendra saw the lit-up estate through the bars of the iron gate.

Since the back gate was rarely used, it allowed her to make a surprise visit. Using a remote, she opened the gate. Rain pelted the AMG G63 with wind-driven sheets as Kendra navigated toward the opulent mansion. Using a second remote, she pulled into the brightly lit climate-controlled garage contemplating on how she would confront Swagga. Slowing to a stop, she sat behind the wheel with the engine running. She sighed, knowing she had to face Swagga. Her resolve to do so was fueled by the possible danger she had unknowingly faced by sleeping with him. Exiting the SUV, she threw her heart on her sleeve and went inside to face a man she no longer respected or loved.

GROUPIES WERE a rapper's greatest delight in Swagga's world. It was verified tonight in the privacy of his grandiose master bedroom.

"Mmmm, right there! Ohhhh, keep pumping, baby!" Nashlly moaned with her baby oiled covered ass bouncing back against Swagga. Her breasts jerked beneath her as he thrusted his length in and out of her.

"Damn, dis ass so soft!" he moaned as he stood behind her shiny ass. The sounds of their raw sex was all the music Swagga needed.

"Yes!" She breathed, pulling the sheets from the head of the bed.

"Who pussy is it?" he asked, slapping her ass.

"Yours!" she cried. "Mmmm...harder!"

He sped up, gripping her hips. Her loose ass undulated like Jello. He picked up his pace, long dicking her until she tried to crawl away.

"Ooohhh, dis dick so good!" she shouted, coming up on her arms. "Mmmm, you better...not fuckin' stop!" she whined, looking back at him.

"Twerk that ass!" he shouted.

Nashlly did just that by switching her hips left to right. Swagga fisted his left hand in her fake hair. Going hard for another seven minutes, he turned her on her back. Sliding the crown of his dick up and down her gushy slit, he saw the hunger in her eyes. Hooking her legs over his skinny shoulders, he eased back inside her. She took the dick with her hands, clutching his ass. She assumed this was their make-up sex from their argument yesterday. As she humped upward, longed for him to stay inside her while he climaxed, 50 Cent said it best: *Have a baby by me, baby . . . be a millionaire.*

"KENDRA, WHAT ARE YOU DOING HERE?" Rick said, as he caught up with her.

"Uh, I live here, don't I?" she asked, standing halfway up the stairs.

Rick knew Swagga had company in his room, and he had a choice to make. Protecting Swagga from harm was his job. But as for the bullshit he was putting Kendra through, Rick had nothing to do with that. For the short time he had known Kendra, he had much respect for her. But it was clear that Swagga didn't know the meaning of respect. "I guess you're right," he said.

"Does he have a bitch up there?" Kendra asked bluntly.

"We're not having this little talk, are we?" Rick hinted.

"No, I guess I snuck by you on my way up."

Rick rubbed his face. "Yeah, he got company."

Kendra turned and started to head up to the bedroom.

"Hey wait!" Rick made his way up the stairs. When he reached the step below her, he glanced at Swagga's bedroom door. "Listen. Don't waste your time fighting that girl. I'll be close by, okay? And, um, we didn't have this talk."

She smiled. "Thanks, Rick. But I'm not here to fight any of his 'crab ass bitches. Now, if you'll excuse me. I have an ego to crush."

Rick admires Kendra, because most girls would put up with Swagga's blatant disrespect just because of his worth. He wasn't surprised by Kendra and the moral grounds she stood on. She might not be perfect, but the difference in his view was Kendra being a woman and not a girl.

SWAGGA WAS in the throes of his climax, moaning as he lay on top of Nashlly. She nibbled on his ear, locking her ankles over his ass, forcing him to spew every drop inside her.

"That was sooo good," she purred as he collapsed on top of her.

"Whew! Why you ain't warn me 'bout that good ass wet-wet you got?"

She unlocked her legs from around his waist. "It's your wet-wet now," she said, sucking on his neck.

"You keep doin' that, and I'ma keep ya ass here."

"That's what I'm hoping for."

He kissed her on the neck before he rolled to the side.

"Whatcha wanna do next?" she asked.

"Both of y'all need to carry your ass to the clinic!"

"What the—" Nashlly sat up quickly, crossing her arms over her perky breast as Kendra pushed from the wall; her eyes locked on Swagga.

"Bitch! Who the fuck are you?" Nashlly shouted and then turned to Swagga. "What the hell is this shit? Who is—?"

"My baby momma," Swagga said nonchalantly. "Yo, go clean yo' self up in the bathroom. This won't take too long," he told Nashlly.

Not caring how Kendra felt, Swagga playfully smacked Nashlly on the ass when she got off the bed.

"Who let you in?" he asked, lounging back with his hands behind his head.

"Didn't know I was locked out."

"Well, you see I'm busy. What do you want?"

"Definitely not your sorry ass. I can tell you that!"

He shrugged, flaunting his nakedness. "So, what the fuck you want? Ain't nobody tell yo' ass to dip out on me. What? Didn't think you could be replaced?"

"I wasn't never in your messed-up life to begin with!"

He laughed. "That's how you feel? I didn't care. But damn, why you gotta toss dirt on me? Talkin' 'bout going to the clinic an' shit."

She forced herself to sit on the bed. To her satisfaction, Swagga sat up and kept the distance between her.

"You know, I was so dumb when I fell for your bullshit when I first met your ass."

He fingered his locs from his face. "I can say the same fo' yo' thirsty ass! All you wanted was a baby by me!"

"Don't you dare bring Carmelita into this!" she warned, with a finger in his face.

"Fuck you!" he said, pushing her hand away. "It's a wrap fo' yo' fat ass anyway!"

She smiled. "Did you fuck that skank in the ass?"

"Why the fuck you worried 'bout it? If I did, so what! Sit here long enough and you can watch."

"No thanks. Besides, I already seen your nasty ass in action," she said coolly.

A silence gripped the room.

"Seen me where?" he demanded. "What the fuck you talkin' bout?"

"Around," she said, looking at her purple fingernails.

"So, you wanna play games?"

"Try to play me and watch what happens to your ass!"

"Fuck you!"

"Come up with something new 'cause that term is getting played out just like your dumb ass is!"

"Keep runnin' yo' mouth and get yo' ass fucked up!"

"Ahh." She grinned. "So, you do have an ass fetish." She looked across the room at the bathroom door. "It's she, isn't it?" she whispered.

Swagga suddenly realized what was going on. He slid off the bed and reached for his boxers. "You remember what happened last year, right?"

"A lot happened last year," she said as he pulled the boxers up over his ass.

Swagga moved around the bed, rubbing his hands together. "So, you seen me, huh?"

She didn't answer. Turning, she watched him move over near the dresser.

"You're right about that." He nodded. "Shit was like—crazy as hell. Motherfuckas were out to put dirt on my name and blackmail me," he said with his back toward her. When he turned, he had a chrome plated gun in his right hand.

She made no sudden moves. Fear gripped her, making her regret her choice to confront him.

"Look, yo." He smirked, lifting the piece and a cigarette to his lips. As he lit the cigarette with the gun lighter, he saw relief pouring into her face. "Why you lookin' all stupid and shit?" He laughed with the lit cigarette burning.

Kendra stood.

"Bitch, you ain't answer my fuckin' question yet, so you can sit yo' ass back down."

"Picture that!" she retorted.

"Don't push me!" he shouted.

"Then don't *shove* me, muthafucka!" she said, matching his tone.

He took a pull on the cigarette, and then he pointed at the door. "See your way out if you ain't got shit else to say."

"Why did you do it?" she asked after a moment's pause.

"Do what?"

"Chyna."

The cigarette quivered between his fingers. He crushed it out and stalked up in her face. To his displeasure, she didn't back down. "You sure you wanna play this game wit' me?" he warned.

"Is it true or not?"

"Fuck you, bitch!" He sneered. "You come here to blackmail me? Is that what dis shit all about, huh?"

"How could you put me at risk?"

He stared at her with contempt. "For the last time. What the fuck are you talkin' 'bout!"

"I'm talking about you having sex with Chyna! How *dare* you— do something like that and then you didn't tell me! I don't care if that's what you wanna do, I really don't. I thank God I'm not like that airhead you were just up in. You are so wrong, and you know it! Why didn't you tell me?"

His worst fear jumped in his face. *How?* Just like last year, his blame went straight to Kandi. Ashamed of his weakness, he lowered his eyes.

"Look at me!" she demanded. "I saw it, Marcus!" she shouted, with tears running down her face. "I saw you with Chyna."

Defeated, he had no more fight left. "Yo, lemme explain what happened right quick—"

"That's dead, Marcus!" She shoved him. "I gave you a chance to explain, so now I don't wanna hear shit you got to say!"

"C'mon, baby," he pleaded.

"Your baby is in the bathroom," she said, stepping away from him. "I don't know who you are anymore.

"Look, I fucked up. Okay? But let's let that shit stay between us and—"

"That's all you care about is yourself! Did you tell your groupie about Chyna? Huh? Answer me, dammit!"

"It ain't like that," he said, hoping like hell that Nashlly wasn't being nosey.

"Goodbye, Marcus."

"Kendra, wait! Please don't tell nobody 'bout this, okay?"

"And if I do?" she challenged. "Whatcha gonna do? Try to kill me like you did Kandi? I'm done with you. Do what makes you happy, because it's clear that my *fat* ass can't!"

19

BABY MOMMA DRAMA

January 25

Wednesday, 6:20 A.M. – Denver, Colorado

LaToria pretended to enjoy herself on top of Martellus. Tossing her head back, she lifted her hands to her breasts. In her mind, she was in front of the AEF film crew. Her actions were all for the benefit of the man that was inside her. A man she was losing touch with. Mad at herself, she moved her hips faster, grinding against him. Gasping, she fell over him. Biting her lip, she rose up on his erection and then slid back down. Shuddering, she did it again, only higher. Finding a steady pace, she bounced up and down, clutching the pillow under his head.

Martellus gripped her soft hips, guiding her up and down his slightly curved erection.

An hour and a half later, she watched him leave for work. She lay nude under the sheets, restless. With nothing much to do, she got up and pulled her iPad out of her tote bag. Surfing the web, she ended up on her Instagram page where she had 4.7 million followers. After thinking about it, she posted a message.

Freezing my ass off in Denver! Missing those warm Miami Nights soo bad.

Next, she randomly responded to a dozen of her followers, thanking them for their support of her films. After she was done, she logged on to her Facebook page. Again, she responded to messages and posts from her fans. Her heart fluttered when she came across Trevon's image. She had assumed he would have deleted her as a friend. She was torn with mixed feelings when she saw the change in his relationship status. *Single.* Out of his 5,725 friends, only a handful were men. She reminisced about the one time he was hesitant to accept friend requests from open gay men. That night she had pointed out his insincere actions and explained how his fans would cross the lines of all genders and sexual orientations. Going to his wall, she read his last post.

Ready 2 start next film next week! Hope U all will N-Joy. Shouts out 2 Jurnee!

1/249:15 a.m.

LaToria closed her eyes, fighting to keep her tears at bay. Holding her fragile composure together, she wondered what Jurnee was posting on her social sites. Just as she pulled up Jurnee's Facebook page, a knock sounded on the bedroom door. Knowing it was the housekeeper, she turned the iPad off.

"It's open," LaToria said from the bed. Mrs. Biathrow entered the bedroom. "Good morning, LaToria. Are you ready for breakfast?"

"Yeah, I guess," LaToria replied.

"Breakfast in bed, or will you be coming down to the dining room?"

"Uh, gimme a minute to put some clothes on and get myself together."

"Take your time," Mrs. Baithrows said. "I know you're worn out from what you did in bed with-"

LaToria gasped. "Excuse me! How do you know what we did this morning?"

"I—the walls are thin. I mean, I heard the two of you when I made my rounds this—"

"Get out!" LaToria shouted.

"I'm sorry, Ms—"

"Don't make me repeat myself! Get the fuck out. Now!"

"THIS IS SO STUPID!" Nashlly complained as she slid into the backseat of a Dodge Charger. "I told y'all dumb asses that I was gonna call!"

"Well, bitch, you didn't!" the driver shouted, twisting in the seat glaring at her.

"I was busy, okay! This shit ain't easy, Art!"

"Busy doing what? You had me and Veto sitting in the damn rain last night for almost three fucking hours!" Art shouted.

"Veto, tell Art that I woulda called if I had the chance to. Since his deaf ass ain't hear me the first time!" Nashlly said, raising her voice.

"Both y'all trippin'," Veto said, shaking his head.

"Nashlly, you need to tighten the fuck up!" Art said, turning back around. "You almost got us killed by not telling us his Cullinan was—"

"Art, how the hell was supposed to know that shit was bullet-proof, huh?"

"Better lower your tone!" Art warned, staring at her in the rearview mirror.

"Or what, motherfucker!" she yelled.

"That fly ass mouth is gonna run your ass down one of these days!" Art said, gripping the steering wheel.

"Well, today ain't the day! And I wish a motherfucker would!" she retorted.

Veto laughed at the two and sung out from the passenger seat. "Alright, alright, alright! You gon' learn today!"

Nashlly snickered with a hand over her mouth.

"Shit ain't fucking funny!" Art shouted.

"Look, I gots to go, okay? Swagga is expecting me back within the hour and I'm wasting my time fooling with y'all asses." She glanced at her watch and saw she would be cutting it close; 4:28p.m.

Art turned in the seat, grilling Nashlly. "Next time I call you better answer your fuckin' phone! I don't care what you might be doin' with Swagga. Now get the fuck out!"

Nashlly rolled her eyes as she shoved the door open. Slamming the door, she strutted across the parking lot, keying the alarm off her white Toyota Camry.

"I DON'T TRUST THAT 'HO!" Art told Veto as Nashlly drove off.

"You worry too much, bruh. Shit, we could've slumped Swagga if it wasn't for that damn tank he was riding in," Veto pointed out.

"Still don't trust her ass."

"You holler at your girl today?"

"Nah, not yet. She told me yesterday he supposed to swing by to see his seed, so you know how that shit go."

"You think she still fucking Swagga?"

"Truthfully, I don't care. I just know her skinny ass better break bread with that insurance money when we slump, Swagga."

Veto nodded. "The sooner the better."

AT THE SAME TIME, in West Palm Beach, Rick was back on the clock protecting Swagga. He hoped Swagga would pull a quickie with his baby momma, Jamilah.

Back in the bedroom, Swagga tried to keep his calm with Jamilah.

"Why my son ain't here? I told yo' ass last week that I wanted to see 'im."

Twenty-eight-year-old Jamilah smacked her thin lips. "You ain't been wanting to see 'im," she mocked. "How you gonna miss your *only* son's second damn birthday last month? Explain that!" She rolled her neck.

"I was busy. Damn! You know I had to beat them bullshit charges I had ova my head," he explained from the edge of the bed where he sat.

"Yeah, right." She rolled her eyes, leaning against the dresser. "I heard you wasn't too busy to be up under Kendra!"

"Where my son at?"

"My momma got 'im."

Swagga jumped to his feet. "You sent my son way up to Detroit without tellin' me!"

"Boy, you rich! Catch a jet. And I'm telling yo' ass now! Ain't my fault you ain't never around here!" She gestured wildly with her skinny arms, causing the four 18-carat white gold and diamond bangles to clink on her wrist.

"'Cause yo' dumb ass always on some bullshit!" he countered.

"Kiss my ass, Swagga." She frowned, with her hands perched on her hips. "And why you are looking at me all stupid and shit?"

"You got panties on?" he asked, closing the space between them.

She glowered. "You can dead that idea. You been done lost your rights to getting any of this pussy!"

He ignored her tantrum. "Oh, that's how you gonna handle me?"

"Go and be with Kendra, or your other baby momma Stephanie!"

Grinning with his locks hanging in his face, he reached for the first button on her silk blouse. "You look so much like Yung Miami when you get mad."

"You better get your hands off me," she said unconvincingly, reaching for his belt.

"I know you miss 'im," he teased. "G'head an' pull 'im out."

"Fuck you!"

"Can I get a taste of that good-good?" He unbuttoned her blouse.

"I can't," she whined, rubbing his growth through his jeans.

"Why not?" he asked, stroking her breasts. He squeezed the left one while circling his thumb over the other.

She took a deep breath. "I . . . got a boyfriend."

Before she said another word, he took her nipple between his lips. "Mmmm, mmmm." He sucked hard on her dark brown nipple while licking it. Knowing he had the green light, he grabbed the hem of her miniskirt and then hiked it up her slender hips and waist. A surge of lust overwhelmed him when he filled his palms with her tight, honey brown ass. She made no effort to impede him when he took a step back to drop his pants and briefs.

He jerked her around and bent her over the dresser. Even with her legs together, she still had a sizable gap. Bunching the skirt at her waist, he licked his fingers and spanked her ass. She rose up on her toes, shaking her ass to encourage him to spank her harder.

"Ahhhh. Maybe we shouldn't be doin' this—since you got a man."

"Boy, stop playing and put it in!" she said, pushing her ass against his penis.

"That's what I thought." Swagga shoved himself deep and hard between her skinny legs. Showing no love nor tenderness, he fucked her thoroughly and with a tight grip on her tiny waist.

As much as she hated Swagga, she was infatuated with his sex. She remembered the night she first met him at the King of Diamonds strip club down in Miami three years ago. Unlike many, Jamilah wasn't on no groupie love. Swagga had approached her while she was leaving the club with her friends. By the time she found out he was only playing with her emotions, she was four months pregnant with his second baby. Her dislike toward him increased when another girl he was messing with turned up pregnant two weeks later and gave birth to twin girls.

She moaned, "Swagga, please . . . don't stop!"

He kept pounding at her slender frame, trying his hardest to bend her spine. Stroke after stroke after stroke, he long dicked her against the dresser.

Her climax was triggered when he locked a grip around her slender neck. She mixed her juices with his. Satisfied, she folded down to the floor after he pulled his penis out. Resting up against the dresser with one breast exposed, she frowned when he rubbed his dick against her cheek.

"What the hell wrong with you!" she hollered, shoving him away.

"I cain't get no throat, baby?" he asked with his pants bunched down at his ankles.

"You better get that shit outta my face! Now move and stop playing so damn much!"

"Not even fo' a new Chanel bag?" He smirked, wagging his dick.

She kicked at his feet. "Stop playing, fool!" She rose, pulling her blouse closed.

"Why you actin' all silly?"

"Shut the hell up!" she said, tugging the miniskirt back over her ass. Shoving him aside, she stomped to the bathroom.

"Oh. I cain't get no throat but I can smash?"

Her reply came by slamming the bathroom door and locking it.

"C'mon, Jamilah, you ain't gotta be like that."

Silence.

He looked at the bed, then down at his wet dick. Waddling across the room, he picked up one of the pillows and used the pillowcase to wipe himself clean. When he was done, he put it back in place. "Dumb ass 'ho," he mumbled, pulling his clothes up.

"I'ma bounce, yo! And you better have my son here next week!"

The door eased open. "I need some money," she said with only her cute face showing.

"Get it from yo' punk ass boyfriend. Long as I pay that child support, I don't owe you shit!'

"I need new tires for my truck! Tires that are worn down from me taking and picking up *our* son from daycare."

". . . You better not be lying 'bout that shit! How much you need?"

"Sixteen hundred. And don't bitch about it, because you're the one that bought the rims and tires in the first place!"

Swagga moved his locks out of his face, then dug into his front pocket. "Here," he griped, tossing a thick roll of fresh one hundred-dollar bills on the bed.

"And how much is that?"

"More than enough. Use some to buy yo' broke ass boyfriend a hustle, so you can stop asking me for cash." He laughed.

She rolled her eyes. "Thank you."

"Yeah, yeah . . . I'm out."

"Um, where you going?"

"To the studio. Why?"

"Just asking. I might wanna see you again later tonight."

He popped the collar on his black and green Louis Vuitton shirt. "I might can swing through. Just gimme a call."

"And be careful, okay? I got worried about our son after you told me about somebody shooting at you."

He mellowed out, understanding her move to send his seed up to Michigan.

Jamilah walked Swagga to the front door of the modest three-bedroom house that was bought and paid for by Swagga. Standing in the doorway, they shared a brief kiss. She played her part flaw-lessly, waving goodbye as Swagga slid inside the back of his Memphis red Bentley Flying Spur.

Not a minute after they left, Jamilah paced on the mocha carpeted floor with her cell phone.

"Hey, honey," she said when her call was answered. "He just left."

"Did he suspect anything, baby?" D-Hot asked.

She smiled. "Nope. And just so you know, he's going to that studio in West Palm Beach."

❧

Swagga sat in the back of the Flying Spur in deep reflection. Gazing at the passing landscape along I-95, he wanted his focus to be clear before he hit the studio. His manager, Harry Storm was pressing him to get more studio time. Swagga needed to rediscover that drive and true hustle that had earned him three platinum albums.

Truth be told, the issue with Kendra knowing about Chyna had him fucked up in the head. When thoughts entered his mind about going to get tested for any STDs, he would balk and then dismiss the idea. Too much drama flooded his focus. Rubbing his forehead, he couldn't ignore his anxieties that dealt with Chyna and the shooting. When would the next hail of bullets buzz his way? Who else would learn of his slipup with Chyna? At one point along the trip, his mind drew a bead on the melic words bumping from the speakers inside the luxurious sedan.

Don't trust my lady, 'cause she's a product of this poison.
I'm hearing noises,
Think she fucking all my boys, can't take no more

20

I GOT A SECRET TO TELL

January 25

Wednesday, 4:25 P.M. - Coconut Grove, Florida

Trevon received a call from Brooke Vee.

"Hey. What's up?" Trevon answered behind the wheel of his A8.

"Um, it's me again," Brooke Vee said. "Whatcha doing, handsome?"

"On my way back home. I just left Chelsea a minute ago."

"The new white girl, right?"

"Yeah. We went over the script for our film and got to know each other a little bit."

"She's a lucky girl. Sure wish I could be in her position."

He grinned. "It ain't like this is my last film. But anyway, what's up with your sexy ass?"

She giggled. "Now I'm sexy, huh? You were so dang quiet when you picked me up the other day and took me home."

"Just had a bunch of things on my mind," Trevon replied.

"Hmm. Well, how about you swing by my place for a minute? My little one is with the babysitter. Maybe this time we can get better acquainted?"

Trevon wasn't looking forward to spending the evening alone. Jurnee was still tripping over the gun issue and wasn't speaking to him. "Gimme twenty minutes and I'll be there."

"I was hoping you'd say that. I'll see ya' when you get here."

BROOK VEE ANSWERED her front door of her upscaled apartment with a provocative smirk.

"Sorry I'm late," Trevon said, as Brooke Vee welcomed him inside.

She gawked at him, lusting at his handsome looks and muscular build. Everything about him appealed to her. His smile, the cleanness and sharp edges of his beard, and his somewhat thuggish outfit. It all stirred her appeal toward him. "Mmm, you look just like Gucci Mane."

"I've heard that before," he grinned, sliding his shades off.

"Well, it's true, baby," she said, wondering how long it would take for him to notice that she wasn't wearing anything under the green leggings she had on. "I heard you on that talk show a few nights ago. You really handled yourself well when that stupid girl called in the show."

Trevon shrugged as he followed Brooke Vee to the living room. It was impossible for him to remove his gaze from her ample ass. Being in his line of business, he already knew her alluring measurements. Barefooted, she stood at 5'6. Her measurements were 38DD-27-43.

In the living room, they took a seat on a peach sectional sofa.

She tossed obvious hints toward chim by brushing her breasts against his arm. "Would you like something to drink?"

"Nah. I'm good."

She settled next to him with her thick legs crossed. "Um, how do you feel about your next film with Chelsea?"

"Just ready to get it done and over with. The boss said it's a must that I do an interracial film."

"I hope she don't turn your ass out." Brooke Vee laughed. "Them white girls be going an extra mile on y'all brothers just to have y'all turn on the sistahs."

"I doubt that." He grinned, glancing at how tight the tank top accented her breasts.

"Okay, enough about her. How are things with you and Kandi? I don't wanna step on her shoes."

"It's just business between us."

"And none of this was planned? Like, y'all two got the porn biz buzzing with all types of gossip. I heard about the big spike in your DVD sales."

He shook his head. "Nah, it wasn't a publicity stunt. But I can see how you and others might view it as being one."

"Are you seeing anyone now?"

"Nah. I need to focus more on my career from here on out."

She nodded. "Can I ask you a personal question?"

"Sure."

She cleared her throat. "That, um, issue that went down last year between you and Swagga. Did D-Hot's name ever come up?"

He studied her with a puzzled expression. "Not that I can recall. Why? What's up?"

"Well, FYI. I've been fucking with D-Hot since last summer. I met him at a video shoot for one of Swagga's videos. Anyway, you know how some men's lips get loose when they fall up in some tight pussy. And one day he told me something."

"D-Hot was Swagga's producer, right?"

"Yeah. But do you know why they are beefing on the low?"

Trevon told Brooke Vee he had no idea of any beef between D-Hot and Swagga. In truth, he saw no concern in it. Brooke Vee went on to tell him what D-Hot had shared with her one night.

"I'm not in love with D-Hot, so don't get it twisted. But I'm not gonna allow no man to be in my bed and on the phone with another girl. Anyway, I got upset and asked him who the hell he was talking to. Can you believe it was Kandi?"

"And when was this?"

"Right around the time I first met him. Like mid-August. I was sorta jealous, but I didn't press the issue. He told me he was just in touch with her to see if she wanted to be in one of Swagga's video. I knew that was a lie because everybody knew how Kandi wasn't fucking with Swagga."

"Because he cheated on her with that white urban model. Um, what's her name?"

"Cindy aka Deja Pink. So I knew he told me a lie. But like I said, I didn't make a big deal about it. This was also the time when you got hired at Amatory and came into the picture. Well, D-Hot never stopped his little talks with Kandi."

"Why you say that?"

"He left his phone over here one night, and I found a bunch of text messages between him and Kandi. And it was a helluva lot more than texts for a damn video."

Trevon shifted uneasily on the sofa. "So whatcha saying? D-Hot was fucking Kandi while she was with me?"

"I won't go that far. But listen to this. That night Swagga was arrested at the airport. Guess who called the police and tipped them off?"

"D-Hot?"

She nodded. "I was down at D-Hot's mansion that night. It's down in the keys. Anyway, he was acting all weird and told me to stay in the bedroom because he was expecting company. Of course, I assumed it was another bitch, so I snuck out when I heard D-Hot talking."

"But it was Swagga?" Trevon guessed.

"Yep. And I heard it all. How D-Hot tricked Swagga into wiring a ton of money to his account."

Trevon took a moment to think about what Brooke Vee was telling him. He knew some of her words were true. But what worried him was the link between Kandi and D-Hot. "So, you're saying D-Hot tried to steal Swagga's money. And then he snitched Swagga out to the police that he would be at the airport?"

"I saw and heard it with my own eyes and ears. I still don't know why he was in touch with Kandi so hard. When I asked him about it a second time, he got upset so I fell back."

"Does D-Hot know you know about him snitching on Swagga?"

"Nope. But I'll betcha Swagga found out somehow."

"And why are you telling me?"

"Because I feel sorry for you," she replied. "And plus, I think Kandi hasn't been fully honest with you. Again, I don't know what she had going on with D-Hot, but something was up." She stood.

Trevon took a deep breath.

"I know this visit isn't what you expected," she said. "But I felt you needed to know what was going on behind your back."

He reached for her hand. "Thanks. But I didn't come here to talk about Kandi or D-Hot."

She smiled as he pulled her down to his lap. "Are you gonna tell me why you came?"

He slid his hand up her thigh when she was seated across his legs. She circled her arms around his neck and uttered a soft moan when his tongue traveled up her neck. Their lust for each other peaked when he discovered she didn't have any panties on. He palmed her ass through the leggings, practically molding it. He reasoned his actions with Brooke Vee would prove to himself that he was over the hurt from LaToria. He wanted sex with no emotions. Sex with no strings attached.

Brooke Vee positioned herself with her knees astride his lap, facing him. Lust was clear on her face as she pulled the tank top up over her head. Her fake breasts popped free in his face. She fed him her left nipple.

He sucked lightly on her cocoa butter scented nipple as his thick erection pushed up against his jeans. Her body was new to him, and it excited him. She ended the one-side foreplay and climbed off his lap.

"I've been wanting this dick since I first saw your film," she breathlessly moaned against his ear. "I just wanna fuck, baby. Can you break me off?"

Trevon removed all of his clothes, including his socks. Showing his strength, he scooped her in his strong arms and carried her to her bedroom. She turned the bedroom lights on with her pussy dripping. She began her pleasure with him by telling him to stand while she sat on the bed.

"I want to taste this," she said softly as she slowly massaged his ebony shaft.

He eased his dick inside her mouth. "Ohhhh," he groaned, as her lips circled his flesh. The warmth and wetness of her mouth sent a chill racing up his spine.

She didn't hold anything back as she sucked his dick as if a film crew were present. In and out, his penis filled her wet mouth. "Mmmm, mmmm, mmmm." Back and forth, she swallowed his turgid flesh. She salivated, slurped, licked and nibbled on his entire length. She couldn't believe how submissive her mind and body yielded for him. In her view, she realized she lived the reality that was desired by millions of women. While others could only watch Trevon in action, she had him in the flesh.

"Grab one of the condoms, baby," Brooke Vee said with the blunt head of his dick pressed against her cheek.

Trevon figured he would eventually do a film with Brooke Vee. However, today he intended to enjoy her on a personal level. When she positioned herself on the bed doggy style, he had to pause and admire her nude backshot. Like 90% of the women in porn, her pussy was bald. Staying on his feet, he tore the gold package open, and then rolled the condom down his throbbing shaft. Brooke Vee twerked while looking back at her jiggling ass.

"Don't run from this dick," Trevon teased, as he slid the tip of his erection up and down the length of her wetness.

"Ummm, fuck. Gimme all that dick!" she gasped. Balling up the sheets in her hands, she couldn't contain her whimpers as his long dick slithered in and out of her. Rocking back against his steady strokes, she found a smooth rhythm that had his name pouring from her mouth.

He was hypnotized at the sight of her ass bouncing back and forth. The bed squeaked each time their bodies collided.

Her husky moans reached a fever pitch when she felt an increase in the jarring tempo of his strokes.

"Ooohhh, Trevon!" She squealed as her ass recoiled back and forth. "I knew this dick was gonna be good! Yasss! Yasss-fuck me good and hard!"

He gawked at how her ass moved. "Ohhh, Brooke!" He squeezed her waist. "I'ma fuck you till you cum. I want you-you to cum, okay?"

"Don't stop!" She panted. "Oohhh, fuck! Feels sooo good like this!"

"Twerk that ass!"

She arched her back, pulled at the sheets and managed to twerk in pace with his hard-driving thrusts. Her loose ass held him deep in a trance. Their moans resounded in the bedroom as their unscripted sex scene continued.

21

SOMEBODY GOTS TO DIE!

January 25
Wednesday, 9:08 P.M. - Carol City, Florida

A low, dark gray cloud reflected off the glossy black hood of an idling Rolls-Royce Wraith. D-Hot sat behind the brown leather-wrapped steering wheel, leaning against the plush armrest. Sitting up, he looked up and down the dimly lit street. A block away, he saw a homeless man shambling across the street. Behind him, a few yards away, sat a Range Rover with two of his boys inside. Time was an issue tonight.

D-Hot realized his high-priced coupe looked suspicious in the shabby neighborhood. It wouldn't matter if he was black or white if the po-po rolled up. The Rolls-Royce would get stopped and searched, even if Tyler Perry was driving. D-Hot was clean. It was the Range Rover that had him stressed. Sighing, he leaned back against the headrest, and picked up a black polymer framed .45-caliber five-shot revolver, hoping he wouldn't have to use it tonight.

"Muthafucka better hurry the hell up!" he grumbled, just as the first sheets of rain speckled the windshield. He closed his eyes and hummed a new beat he was working on. The rain suddenly broke, pelting the roof. D-Hot jerked up and glanced at his phone. Only three minutes had slid by, testing his patience. He rubbed his face and scratched his beard. Just as he settled back in the seat, a pair of headlights appeared in the driver's side mirror. He paid little interest to the vehicle, but was able to determine the make, color, and model as it drove by under the pouring rain. D-Hot watched the taillights of the dark colored SUV fade out of his view. He was so busy looking ahead that he didn't notice the candy purple Dodge Ram creeping behind the Range Rover. His phone rang.

"Where the hell you at, bruh?" D-Hot said without raising his voice.

"Y'all sleepin'." Art laughed. "I'm right behind your boys in the Range Rover."

"What the—" D-Hot was made a believer when Art flashed his lights on and off.

"Yo, there's an unlocked warehouse not too far from here. Follow me 'cause it's too open out here," Art explained.

"Alright, man. Whatever—just hurry up so I can get this shit off me."

Six minutes later, D-Hot stood at the back of the Range Rover with Art and Veto. "Y'all better be happy with these." D-Hot pulled the towel off the assault rifles and handed one to Art. "It's a—"

"I know what the fuck it is!" Art retorted as he tested the weight and balance of the Smith and Wesson M&P15 M4 tactical rifle.

"Well, these babies had a lil' operation," D-Hot told them.

Art looked at D-Hot. "You sayin' these motherfucka's are fullies?"

"All the way," D-Hot answered as Veto picked up the second illegally converted M4 fully automatic rifle.

"You got ammo?" Art asked.

D-Hot leaned into the back of the SUV and pulled out a large backpack. "Here's four 30-round clips and 120 rounds. If y'all need more than this, then y'all fucked up."

"We gonna handle our end! Just make sure you handle yours," Art stated.

"We need to get on the road," Veto said, shouldering the backpack.

"Nashlly call you yet?" D-Hot asked Art.

"Yeah. They all still at the studio. Trust me . . . shit goin' down today."

"You mean tonight," D-Hot corrected him.

"Let's be out, Veto," Art said, glaring at D-Hot before he hurried back to the pickup.

Art sped off, leaving D-Hot and his Do-Boys behind.

"You ready to do this?" Veto asked from the passenger seat, loading the clips.

Art was silent for a moment. "Sumthin' ain't right."

"Speak your mind," Veto said, loading another brass round into the clip.

"Check it, right," Art said. "Jamilah wants Swagga out of the picture so she can collect some life insurance, right?"

"Uh-huh." Veto nodded.

"An' D-Hot is payin' us, what? Twenty thou' a piece, right?"

"That sounds 'bout right," Veto replied as Art switched lanes to hit a ramp for I-95 North. "So, what ain't right?"

Art's expression was hidden inside the dark interior. "Bruh, you know that big ass dookie green diamond chain that D-Hot got?"

"Yeah. It, um, got that Bigg Dog logo piece on it. What about it?"

Art shook his head as he picked up his speed. "Bruh, I found that chain in Jamilah's bedroom back on Monday."

"Damn! How the fuck—"

"Ain't say shit to 'er nor D-Hot about it."

"Alright, so what's up?" Veto asked after turning the police scanner on.

"We handle our biz, and then I'll get some answers 'bout this snake shit going on behind my back."

∾

FRITZ WOULDN'T CONSIDER himself a voyeur since he didn't experience any pleasure in viewing others in the act of copulation. Lowering the range finder binoculars from his eyes, he tightened the black poncho over his head and carefully adjusted his footing in the tree. The steady flow of rain wasn't helping Fritz, but neither would it hinder him. With the binoculars back to his eyes, he read the self-illuminating LED display that showed he was 275 yards away from his target. Scanning the upscaled apartment complex, he location his target's car 300 yards away, the distance of three football fields.

He smiled, thinking of a name change for the benefit of his trade. "The Mailman" seemed suitable to him since he could strike come rain, snow, sleet or hail.

∾

"YO RICK! You got a call on line four." A studio assistant with a blond Mohawk shouted from the front desk down the hall.

Rick was down on the first floor, chatting with a cute Haitian receptionist in the lounge. "Take a message," he said, figuring if it was somebody important, they would have had his cell number. "So how long have you been working?"

"Yo, they said they got some info on that I-95 shooting."

Rick quickly excused himself from the receptionist and hurried down the hall to the front desk. "Hello, who this?"

"Uh, ain't gonna say my name, but I got some info for you."

Rick didn't recognize the dude's voice. "What kind of news? And what do you know about that I-95 shooting that wasn't on the news?"

"Listen, and this all I'll say about it. I know about that trip you and Swagga made up to West Palm Beach before the shooting, and *that* wasn't on the news."

Rick motioned the assistant to step out so he could have some privacy. "Okay, I'm sold. What's this info you got for me?"

"Here's your warning. Two hittas in a purple Dodge Ram are somewhere near the studio waiting for y'all to leave, and they ain't playing the radio."

"And it's real?"

"Ya think? Damn right it's real! Ignore this warning . . . I guess you'll be out of a job by tomorrow because you can't guard a dead man, can you?"

"Alright. I need more—Hello? . . . Hello?" The line went dead. "Shit!" Rick slammed the wireless phone down and then ran to the elevator, making a call on his cell phone. He couldn't afford to ignore the warning, even if it wasn't his life that was on the line. As the elevator took him up to the third floor, his call was connected with a bodyguard up in the studio with Swagga.

"Whut up, Rick?"

"Yo, Tweet! We gotta code black. I repeat, code black!"

"Ai'ight. I'm moving now!"

Rick made a second call to one of the two bodyguards that were down in the parking lot.

"Yo?"

"Hey Rock, we gotta code black an' this shit is real. Tweet and the boys are moving Swagga as we speak. What y'all holdin' tonight?"

"Uh, me and Bobo packing two Glock nines apiece, and I got a Draco too!"

"Ai'ight. Be on point, and y'all know what to do! If it's the same two from the first time, we gotta be heavy 'cause they had an AK last time."

"Okay, dawg. We moving!"

Rick made his last call just as the elevator reached the third floor. He called 911.

Swagga was in the middle of recording a track when Tweet

bullied his way inside the recording booth. "What the fuck! Don't you see me—"

Tweet uttered two words and grabbed his arm. "Code black!" From day one, Rick had preached to Swagga about the dire seriousness that could initiate a code black. To make sure Swagga knew what to do in such a predicament, Rick had explicitly stated, "Don't ask no questions! Just shut the fuck up and move! Let me and my men do our job, simple as that."

Swagga was sandwiched between two of his bodyguards as they rushed toward the fire exit. He knew the threat was serious when Tweet paused to check the fire exit with a black 9-millimeter that was fitted with a laser beam under the barrel. Rushing down the stairs, his heavy chains and diamond pieces bounced off his chest and stomach. Reaching the second floor, Tweet shouted for Swagga to hustle faster. Fear overwhelmed Swagga. He wasn't ready to die. Not tonight.

Fritz was in his element. Hunting the prey, clad in black boots and matching cargo pants and fitted a shirt, he crossed the lit parking lot with his head down. He was aware of the surveillance camera positioned to his left. With the pouring rain, it would help distort his features. He walked with a fake limp, knowing the footage would later be reviewed by the police. Even without the fake limp, he would be a ghost, coming and going. Out of the range of the camera, he reached his target's high-priced car. Without pausing in his steps, he reached inside the rear left fender and removed the quarter-sized GPS tracking device. He dropped it in his front pocket and then moved into the shadows. From his concealed position, he had an unobstructed view of the front door, where his target would soon exit.

Fritz ignored the rain that flowed down the bridge of his crooked nose. This was luxury in comparison to the last locale where his talents were needed.

Down on one knee, he turned stone like, only his eyes moved. Waiting. Not a minute later, he saw two silhouettes in the living room window. The tendons in his legs tighten. He waited. Moving only his right hand, he removed the silenced pistol from a custom holster fitted under his left arm. His breathing slowed as he thumbed the safety off.

He rose out of the puddle he knelt in. Still in a squat, he watched his target exit the apartment with a dark colored umbrella. *Perfect!* Fritz thought. The rain beating on the umbrella would most surely cover any sounds of his approach.

His target moved briskly down the sidewalk, keying the alarm and remote starting his car. Fritz remained, hidden in the shadows behind his target. Easing his finger on the trigger, he moved with a purpose. He sped up when he saw the interior light come on inside the target's ride. He darted between two cars, making his approach from the rear. His target slid inside the car, pausing to close the umbrella. Fritz reached him just as he swung his legs inside the car.

"Excuse me, sir," Fritz called out.

His target jerked up in the seat, startled by Fritz's sudden appearance. "Yeah, what—"

Fritz struck. His target moaned in agony after two hollow-point bullets pierced his crotch. Blood pooled from the fatal wound. Fritz watched him, writhing in pain and gasping for a breath that he would never take. He nudged his target with the silencer. His target coughed up blood, not understanding that he couldn't move his leg because he was paralyzed from the waist down. Fritz knew he could walk away and leave the chances of survival of his target up to whatever higher power he believed in. *If* he survived, he would never walk again. Fritz held the Glock steady, nudging his target once more. A heartbeat later, their eyes met. Fritz nodded at him. Then he shot him three times in the face at point-blank range. The body went lifeless, slumped across the center console with three holes above his left ear and cheek. Fritz was closing the door with his elbow when a scream cracked the silence. In a moment's breath, he saw the girl his target had been with. She stood a few feet away on the sidewalk, holding an umbrella. A cell phone fell from her hand. A phone that apparently belonged to his target. She was filling her lungs to scream again. Fritz took it all in, and then coldly shot her twice, once in the forehead and once in the throat, before the cell phone clattered to the wet sidewalk.

22

I WILL CRY FOR YOU

January 25

Wednesday, 10:50 P.M. – Boca Raton, Florida

Art and Veto rapidly increased the distance between themselves and the studio. The decision to call off the hit made sense after they heard the APB over the police scanner. Art was heated as he left the scene. His eyes remained checking the rearview mirrors, praying against all hope that no blue lights would appear. He knew he had some bullshit traffic violation warrants over his head, but that wasn't shit compared to having a fully automatic assault rifle. As for Veto, he was shitting bricks just the same.

Art sped south, leaving the city limits of West Palm Beach. After driving for several minutes on edge, He reached for his phone.

"We should get rid of these guns before we get pulled," Veto suggested.

"Bruh, chill!" Art shouted, checking the speedometer to make sure he wasn't speeding. "We good. Just . . . sit back and chill."

"Look, man. You're the one talkin' 'bout shit ain't right. Now look what the fuck just happened! Who the hell called the po-po and gave 'em the description of your truck?"

"'On't fuckin' know, bruh! Who I look like? A fuckin' psychic or sumthin'! Just . . . we good. Lemme call this bitch right quick."

Veto frowned as Art made a call.

"Yeah, hello? Who's calling?" a female answered.

Art sucked his teeth. "Yo, lemme talk to Jamilah."

"Who's calling?"

Art sighed. "Art! Now put Jamilah on the phone!"

"Damn, Mr. No Patience. Hold on?"

Art turned on the high beams as he drove down a back road, leaving Palm Beach County.

"Hey, baby," Jamilah answered a minute later. "What's up with you?"

"Bullshit!"

"Huh?"

"Look, you know I can't say too much over this phone, right?"

"I'm listening." She sounded worried.

"Somebody talking."

"How! Do Swagga know—"

"Nah, just listen. Yo, somebody called the police before we could, ah . . . go see our boy."

"Uh-huh."

"And they knew what I was driving."

"Ohh fuck!" she groaned. "Where are you now?"

"I just made it to Broward County."

"Where Veto?"

"Right here with me. Look, get my car and meet me at my aunt's house in Hialeah. And yo, where Nashlly?"

"In the kitchen playing cards."

"She made any calls in the last thirty minutes?"

". . . Ah, not that I know of, baby. I hope you aren't suggesting she called—"

"I just don't trust that 'ho!"

"I don't see her doing that, Art. But damn, somebody had to call."

"This shit is all fucked up, so I'ma lay low for a minute."

"What about Swagga?"

"Jamilah! Didn't you just hear what the fuck I said! Somebody tipped the police off!"

"But—"

"But—my ass! I already did that dumb shit the first time and damn near got ran off a fucking bridge! Listen, whatever plans you had wit' Swagga, don't change it."

"Baby, I'm scared. What if—"

"Hold up! Don't start that shit, so stay calm."

"I'm trying."

"Look. I'll see you later. And make sure my gas tank is full."

"Okay, bye. Baby, wait. Do you want me to tell Nashlly what's up?"

"Uh . . . no. But bring her with you."

"Okay. I'm leaving now."

Art ended the call as Veto adjusted the settings on the police scanner. "We going to my aunt's crib," Art said, wishing he had a cigarette.

"And then what?" Veto sat up, waiting for an answer.

"Between you and me—fuck all this shit. Fuck Jamilah, fuck Swagga, and fuck D-Hot! I'ma hit the stash, gas up my Charger, and go visit my fam' up in New Bern, North Carolina. Ain't 'bout to risk my life or freedom, so fuck it. So, what you gon' do?"

Veto scratched his ear, grinning. "Shit, you ain't leaving me down here. I'm goin' with you."

ARIANA SOFTLY NUDGED Jurnee on her shoulder, waking her.

"Your phone is ringing," Ariana muttered.

"What time is it?" Jurnee asked with her head under the covers.

Ariana sat up, rubbing her eyes before she focused on the digital clock across her bedroom. "Um . . . three twenty-two."

Jurnee mumbled a few words before she tugged the covers off her head. She answered the call without checking the ID.

"Hello?"

"Uh, Jurnee, this is Ruby. I'm glad you answered. I was told to call you and inform you that there's been a shooting—"

Jurnee sat up. "Who was shot?"

"All I can say is that you're to meet Ms. Babin at the police station downtown."

"Ruby! Who was shot? I need to know, dammit!"

Ariana sat up on the bed when Jurnee gasped and dropped her cell phone.

JANELLE WIPED her teary eyes as the white female homicide detective entered the small office. After they shook hands and introduced themselves, the detective offered Janelle a cup of coffee, which she declined.

"Thank you for making the time to talk to me," Janelle said. "I'm sure it's been a hectic night and all."

"Just the weather," the detective replied, nodding at the rain-streaked window behind Janelle.

"Can you tell me what you're at liberty to discuss?"

"Two victims. One female shot twice in the face. The male we found inside his car was shot multiple times, and the crime scene is still being processed."

"Do you have an assumption of how it happened?"

The detective nodded. "I think it was a possible robbery attempt that went wrong. It's possible the suspect was caught in the middle of the act and killed the girl. But what I find interesting is no one heard any shots."

Janelle wiped her eyes again. "I...have Brooke Vee's next of kin information that your partner asked for."

"Thank you." The detective replied. "And I personally want to apologize for having to get you involved. However, we were only able to identify Brook from one of her DVD'S we came across."

Janelle nodded. "It's...okay. I understand. It's...I just don't know-"

Jurnee knocked on the door and stepped inside the office. Janelle stood.

Crying, Jurnee asked. "Is it true?"

23

GUESS WHAT HAPPENED?

February 8

Wednesday, 2:30 A.M. - South Beach, Florida

Two weeks later . . .

The sultry sun claimed its dominance over SoBe (South Beach). With the temperature in the high 80s, Janelle and Jurnee lay out tanning on the sand. Both were topless, wearing skimpy bikini bottoms. After attending two funerals in the past nine days, both were open to a more upbeat mood.

"How's Victor doing?" Jurnee asked Janelle about her fiancé.

"Working on a new novel," Janelle replied.

"Tell him he better put me on the cover of his next book."

"I will," Janelle said as two Asian women walked by.

"Been a rough year, huh?"

"Yeah, and it's just the beginning," Janelle added morosely.

"Um, about Trevon."

"Don't wanna talk about it," Janelle retorted, brushing sand off her elbow.

"Okay. So, you were telling me about that last call you got from Brooke Vee."

Janelle smoothed out the edges of her orange beach towel.

"She called me like—an hour or so before they said it happened. She said D-Hot was over and that he came to say he was sorry for that stunt he pulled at the office."

"Really?"

"Yeah. Said something about him finding his chain, and she even put him on the phone to apologize to me. I told him it was okay and that his main concern should be Brooke Vee since he accused her of stealing his chain."

"I heard what you did for her baby."

"I was there when her baby was born. The least I can do is make sure Brooke Vee's mom won't have any problems financially raising that child."

Jurnee's face suddenly lit up when she saw Ariana waving at her from the rollerblading path. They had been inseparable since the day Jurnee left Trevon back on the 24th of last month.

"I see you and Ariana are doing well," Janelle commented as she slid a wisp of hair off her cheek.

Jurnee beamed. "She's a breath of fresh air," she said, waving back at Ariana before she took off down the crowded path, rollerblading.

"Are you bringing her to the party tonight?"

Jurnee shrugged. "It depends on if we can get out of the bed."

"You are such a big freak." Janelle laughed.

"Hey! Did you hear about Swagga being shot at?"

"When?"

"Last month. Ariana told me about it. She said there was a small story on *TMZ*."

"Girl, if it don't land on my desk, I don't know about it. But since you mentioned him, he's been keeping a low profile."

"I think it's because Future and DaBaby are tearing up the airwaves. It might be over for Swagga."

"His problem. Not mine," Janelle replied.

～

"Don't raise your voice at me, Anthony!" Tahkiyah said firmly as she packed her suitcase.

"Baby, you've only been home for twelve days and you're going back down there! It doesn't make any sense!"

"That's because you don't understand, okay?" she replied as she continued packing.

"I don't want you to go."

"We've already discussed this."

"Well, I'm not done discussing it, okay!"

"Listen," she said, looking at him across the bed, "In the next few minutes, I'm walking out that door, and I'm getting in my car and I'm going back to Miami! In truth, it was never up for discussion."

"Why!" he shouted, turning red. "Because you've turned this matter into an *obsession*!"

She snatched her glasses off. She stared at the man she cared for. She had knowledge of the gossip that her co-workers and employees would remark behind her back about her and Anthony. *"Oh, she like a little cream in her coffee", "If it ain't white, it ain't right for Tahkiyah", "She got money, so only a white man will suit her."*

Tahkiyah had a *reason* for not dating Black men, a *reason* that was a pain only she knew. Eyeing Anthony, she spoke clearly. "Are you saying I'm being compulsive and unreasonable about this?"

"No. I just—"

"Yes, you damn well did! Look up the meaning of the word! And while you're at it, look up the word finished because that's what we are! Now if you'll excuse me, I have to pack for this *obsession* that is driving me crazy."

"Okay, I get it," he said, pointing at her. "You want to be with a Black guy."

"What?" she shouted. "What makes you think—"

He snatched her laptop off the bed. "I saw the videos you downloaded, Tahkiyah. The black sex porn? You didn't have to hide it behind my back! You lied to me about everything!" he rebuked her, shaking the laptop.

"Anthony, I—"

"Save it!" he shouted, with an odd grin on his face. "I know what this . . . little trip is all about," he said, walking around the bed. "Before we got together, you were dating another white man. Warren, the VP of Integrated Marking for that automotive magazine. And before him it was that college professor, white as well. And I know of your past love life because you've confided in me, baby." Dropping the laptop on the bed, he smiled, easing his hands on her waist. "You don't have to leave, okay? If you're missing what it's like to be with a black man, bring him here. Let me watch him with you. Is that what you want?"

She smiled. "Are you sure?"

Reluctantly, he nodded.

"But, baby," she wooed, sliding her hands up his chest. "What about that old adage that people always say?"

"What adage?" he asked as she toyed with his silk tie.

"You know . . .." She grinned. "The one about once you go black, you never go back. Since you've seen the porn. Can you measure up?" She shoved him. "What the hell is wrong with you? Going through my shit behind my back! Fuck you!" she said furiously.

"But, baby, I thought—" he began to plead his mistake.

"You thought wrong, *white* boy! This is one cup of coffee you can cancel ever tasting again! Now do this Black woman a favor and get the fuck out of my house!"

AT THE SAME TIME, across the vast Atlantic Ocean, Swagga accelerated along a stretch of Autobahn Expressway in Germany. He sat behind the wheel of a black and orange McLaren Senna with Nashlly in the passenger seat. In the wake of the Senna was a purple Ferrari 812 Superfast driven by Rick. The trip to Germany was a needed vacation for Swagga.

Swagga had grown accustomed to Nashlly's company and her super climatic sex. Just two days ago, he had purposefully flaunted her in Paris, France, just to get the paparazzi riled up and to keep his name buzzing. She ate up the attention and kept her lips or legs wrapped around him every chance she got.

Swagga's mind was elsewhere. He tried to conceal his stress from everyone, including Rick. For some reason, he couldn't find peace. Peace of mind is what he seeked. He just wanted to rap and make music. As he sped toward the horizon, he tried to put the bullshit behind him. For starters, his conscience was afflicted ever since his successful plot resulted in D-Hot's murder. Swagga had discovered through his legal team that D-Hot had snitched him out to the U.S. Marshals.

Swagga's plane was never going to Morocco that night. D-Hot had returned Swagga's money, yet that didn't settle the beef for Swagga when he saw the disloyalty in his motion of discovery. As for Brooke Vee being murdered, Swagga felt somewhat responsible for it.

BACK IN FLORIDA, at a hotel on South Beach, Kendra stood in the shower with Trevon. They had rekindled their secret sexual bond, and neither had any objections about it.

"I was just thinking about something," she cooed, rubbing the soapy rag over his chest. "Remember when we did it at my house that night? Why were you so trusting of me to not use any protection?"

Trevon was caught off guard by her serious question. "Shit, I guess I just got caught up in the moment."

"Has that happened before? I'm bringing this up because that mess Marcus did behind my back scared me."

Trevon removed his hand from her wide hips. "Um, since I've been outta prison, I've only went raw with three women. You, LaToria, and Jurnee."

"You're not afraid of the risk you're taking?"

He sighed. "Everything just moving so fast for me. I come

home and find myself living a life that I only thought was a dream. LaToria and I hook up, and then we breakup over some bullshit."

"And I popped up," she said, grinning up at him.

"Hell yeah!" he said. "My sexy ass probation officer, that's thicker than water. One minute you're trying to send me back to prison-"

"And the next I'm riding your dick like it's my mission in life." She beamed.

"That sounds about right. But to be honest with ya, I've made a bunch of mistakes since I've been out."

"Including me?"

"Picture that," he said, palming her ass.

"I'm happy to hear that. And I'm glad you respected my decision about using protection when we hook up."

Kendra managed to have Trevon reassigned to her case load two weeks ago. She would show up at his door no less than four times a week. When she was with him, he made her feel desired. Her stance was still the same. Sex with no emotional strings attached.

"I can't believe what I'm about to do with you," she said, stroking his soapy penis.

He licked both of her swollen nipples as she continued to work her grip along his manhood. "You sure you want this to happen?"

She nodded. "My friend thinks I'm a square when it comes to sex. Doing a threesome has always been a fantasy of mine."

"Who's it really for? You or her? I don't want you to start tripping on me if we do this."

She squeezed his dick. "You're not my man," she reminded him. "Tonight, is my night. And it's only gonna be a one-time affair. Just the three of us, okay?"

He was down to be a part of her fantasy. It was Kendra's idea to invite her BFF Dani to join her with Trevon. She explained to him how Dani had showed her an unedited copy of his first film.

Telling the truth was easy for Kendra. She openly told Trevon that his first film changed her attitude toward him. Not only would Kendra do a threesome. She wanted to film it!

Trevon wasn't surprised when Kendra informed him about the rules.

1. *Safe sex.*
2. *No anal sex.*
3. *No girl on girl.*
4. *Leave the lights on.*

When Dani later showed up at the door, she was star-struck and tongue-tied. Kendra felt a surge of sexual prowess when it was her and not Dani that started things off. After downing two glasses of gin and juice, Kendra acted out her fantasy as a sexy plus-size vixen. With the camera rolling, she shamelessly wrapped her pink glossy lips around Trevon's fully erect penis. Tonight was eventful and special for Kendra. As she eased her lips back and forth along his dick, she was relieved she had the willingness to do what she had only fantasized about. Everything snapped to reality when Dani finally broke from her trance to join Kendra at Trevon's feet. Kendra held not a stitch of jealously as she watched Dani slurping her lips up and down Trevon's glistening penis.

He sexed both women tirelessly in front of the camera. Dani turned out to be a screamer. Her loud moans and stuttering praises of Trevon's dick was an event itself. She yanked at the sheets as her big ass bounced all over the place.

He gave his all to both women, showing them the difference between making love and fucking. His focus was on the latter. Jurnee had taught him well.

He later found himself relaxing alone in the tub. Kendra and Dani had left twenty minutes ago. Trevon had his eyes shut, ruminating on his life since he was released from prison. He didn't have much to complain about. He had a big body ride, a nice home, and money in the bank.

Porn was his root, his foundation. The women he had been

with crossed his mind. LaToria, Linda, Kendra, Jurnee, Ariana, Dani, Chelsea, Brooke Vee and Cindy. He wavered to claim Cindy since she had drugged him.

So in truth, he had sex with nine different women since being released out of prison on August 17 of last year. A spasm of sadness moved him when he thought of Brooke Vee. From what he was told, she was murdered not even two hours after he left. He felt guilty that he knew nothing about her. *Damn. I don't even know the name of her little girl.* He thought. Sighing, he realized that life could hold no promise of tomorrow. Above all, he was through dealing with matters of his heart!

Wanting to clear his head, he left the hotel at 6:53p.m. He saw the world through a pair of light green shades, and he realized that 90% of the women that looked his way was his own doing. The wet candy paint, the big rims and glossy thin rubber band tires, and the dumping sound system. It all screamed, "look what I got!"

For those reasons, he collected eight new phone numbers from ladies that waved him down. He didn't mention anything about his *job*. All they saw was a Black man balling. As the starlit sky blanketed Miami, he noticed a lava red McLaren 765LT at an intersection along Alton Road on Miami Beach.

Grinning, he flicked the headlights a few times, and then made a call.

"Hello, Trevon," Janelle answered with Lizzo playing in the background.

"I see you're out ballin' tonight. Switched up your Lambo for the McLaren."

"Where are you?"

"At the red light to your left. Behind the white Lotus. What are you up to tonight?"

"I'm still mad at you for changing that script. But since I like you, I'ma let it slide, again."

"You know you can't stay mad at me. But yo, where you headed?"

"Nowhere fast. Just cruising."

"Me too."

"You coming to my party?"

"Wouldn't miss it for nothin'."

"Good, because I want you to meet your next costar for your next film."

"Ai'ight I'll be there, boss lady," he promised.

JAMILAH WAS MOVING TO ATLANTA, and Swagga would be the last to know. Her little insurance scheme was a dead issue, pun intended due to D-Hot's murder. She was alone since Art had bounced out on her without a kiss goodbye. Too much was on her shoulders to deal with. *Does Swagga know I was in on the two hits? Who killed D-Hot? Am I next?* To make matters worse, she had taken a call from Nashlly three days ago. In the simplest terms, Nashlly told her that Swagga was unaware of the stunt *they* tried to pull, and it would stay that way. She also admitted that she had her cousin to call Rick to warn him about Art and Veto's second attempt in West Palm Beach. As for why? This too she was direct and blunt with.

"Swagga is *my* money ticket now, so y'all bitches can step back!"

24

DICED PINEAPPLES

February 8

Wednesday, 8:47 P.M. - Bay Harbor Islands, Florida

S ince the weather permitted, Janelle's RSVP party was held outdoors under the faint lambent full moon. Greenish lights lit up the palm trees that lined the infinity edge pool, creating a serene ambience. Men and women of nearly every nationality were in attendance at Janelle's Bay Harbor Islands mansion.

Lounging by the pool sipping a lemon daiquiri, Jurnee stood with four other women. She constantly received admiring looks her way by flaunting her shapely figure in a gold sequined and mesh dress that clung high above her knees. Her skin had a soft, radiant glow of gold that matched the new highlights in her hair. Without being vain, she *knew* she was on top of her game tonight.

Five men and two women had approached her in just an hour of her arrival. They were all politely turned down. DJ Kay Slay had the classic sounds of *"Fucking You Tonight"* by Biggie Smalls and R. Kelly playing at a respectable level for the swanky partygoers.

You must be used to me spending,
and all that sweet wining and dining,
well, I'm fucking you tonight . . .

And another one . . .

Jurnee held the women's attention with a story about a blunder that happened to her once during a film when one of the women nodded at someone behind her.

"Excuse me, ladies." Trevon snuck up behind Jurnee, easing his hands down to her soft, prodigious hips. "I need to speak to my manager for a second."

"Hi, Trevon," two of the women cooed in unison.

Trevon didn't speak until he was alone with Jurnee. "You still giving me the silent treatment?"

"I've been in touch by e-mail and Facebook Messenger," she replied nonchalantly, without bothering to turn around. "Plus, I sent you a text yesterday."

"You still trippin' off that gun?" he asked, brushing his lips against her ear. "Huh?"

"We still cool." She shivered from his closeness. "But I meant what I said. As long as it's under your roof, I won't be visiting you."

"Nah, your sexy ass is just stubborn, that's all."

She shrugged, taking another sip of her drink.

"I got rid of it," he said as he moved around her.

"When?" She looked at him, shifting her stance in the strappy Manolo Blahnik heels.

"After the funeral," he replied, adjusting his silk and black-green tie.

Jurnee pushed a curly wisp of hair off her cheek. "I might need to check for myself." She smirked, wondering if he realized how severely she missed him.

"Ai'ight, we can make that happen as soon as we leave."

"And who said I'll be leaving with you?"

"I did," he proclaimed with a grin, tugging the corners of his lips. "Where your girl Ariana at?"

"Home. She has a big test coming up."

"Stay with me tonight," he said.

"You miss me?"

"Hell yeah," he groaned, easing his hands back on her hips. "I wanna wake up with you in my arms. How that sound?"

"It's not *how* it sounds . . . I'm more concerned about *how* it's gonna feel to have you back up in me. And since it's been a while, I want it all night long."

"Um, you sho' know how to make my dick hard." He bit his bottom lip and squeezed her wide hips. "You like that song that's on right now?"

She nodded.

"Good, 'cause that's what I'ma do to your sexy ass tonight."

"Show me better than you can tell me," she said, as her nipples stiffened.

Disregarding their public presence, their lips met in an open-mouthed kiss. She relished the kiss, tilting her head and sucking on his tongue. A soft breeze caressed her exposed arms and legs. Their brief titillating moment ceased when the deejay got on the mic. He kissed her lightly on her nose with his yearning for her written all over his face.

She noticed a few eyes turned their way as she stepped back from his intimate embrace.

"You taste as good as you look," he said.

"C'mere." She licked her thumb and then wiped off a smudge of lipstick from his lips.

"Where's Janelle?" he asked.

"Somewhere with Victor," she told him. "Um, look over by the rock garden. See the girl in the white backless dress?"

He nodded. "Who is that sexy lady next to her in that black dress?" he asked, rubbing his hands together. "You know I gotta taste for older women."

Jurnee rolled her eyes. "She's married, so stop lusting."

"Who is she?"

"That's Janelle's homegirl."

"Damn, she's fine as hell! What is she doing here?"

"She's doing an interview on Janelle for her porn e-magazine. Now pay attention. The girl in the white dress."

"What about 'er?"

"How does she look to you?"

"Gorgeous, kinda slim, but sexy. Nice little ass. And, um…she looks like Sasha Lane a lil' bit. Why you pointing her out?"

"That's Glaze, and she'll be your next costar for your third film. And before you ask, yes, I'm still working a deal out with The Body XXX and Tori Taylor. Oh, and Skyy Black is someone else I want you to do a film with."

Trevon reached inside his suit for his phone.

"What are you about to do?"

"I'ma go ask Janelle's homegirl if I can take a selfie with her to post on Instagram."

Jurnee laughed easily and reached for his hand. "Let me introduce you to Glaze."

"And Janelle's homegirl," he said.

TREVON WAS THROWN for a surprise when he was introduced to Glaze. Along with her sexy petite frame, she had a strong British accent that added to her sex appeal. Unlike Chelsea, Glaze wasn't an amateur, and her unique talent was centered on her lissome body. Glaze could easily lock her legs behind her head. He also learned that she had a man, and she took her relationship seriously. The only time he would see her nude would be on the set.

By 9 PM, Jurnee nursed on her fourth martini while sitting by the pool under a row of blue assorted paper lanterns. Her eyes were on Trevon as he enjoyed himself across the pool, dancing on the white and blue checkered patio. A new hit by Chris Brown had the crowd buzzing. As long as Trevon was happy, Jurnee's mood was content. She laughed at the sight of him *trying* to keep up with the current dance moves with Chelsea and Glaze.

"Looks like he is having a ball."

Jurnee looked up from where she sat as Janelle took a seat next to her. She had her hair down, rocking a white blouse and a pair of skinny jeans.

"Hey, girl!" Jurnee said.

Janelle sighed, lifting a glass of vodka mixed with pineapple juice to her lips.

"What's on your mind?" Jurnee asked.

Janelle lowered the martini to her lap. "Thinking about Brooke Vee. I told DJ Kay Slay to do a moment of silence for her before the party is over."

"That's a good idea," Jurnee said as three bikini-clad porn stars slid into the pool.

"I see Trevon has met Glaze," she observed, lifting the martini again.

Jurnee crossed her legs. "I see a bright future for him. I really do."

"I'm thinking . . . eight films in the next six months," Janelle said.

"Think we can get the paperwork done for a film with him and Cherokee D Ass?"

"How does he feel about it?"

Jurnee giggled. "I think he's infatuated with her big butt. But yes, he's all for it. Oh, let's add Skyy Black to the list."

"Send Ruby an e-mail tomorrow."

"Alright. Um, you gonna make Trevon and Chelsea retake their last scene?"

"Nah," Janelle decided. "I viewed the footage, and it's good."

"What exactly did he do?"

Janelle plucked the olive out of her empty glass and then slipped it past her lips. "The script called for him to do the money shot as Chelsea gave him some head. But our Mr. Harrison thought it would look better to continue the anal scene."

"He had her outside on the picnic table, right?"

"Uh-huh. He kept the anal penetration going but pulled out and came on her breasts and stomach after he took the rubber off."

"Were the camera angles good?"

"Yeah, there were two cameras rolling simultaneously, so we got a nice close-up of his climax."

Jurnee set her glass on the round table and then glanced up at the moon. "Five years from now, what do you hope is different in your life?"

"God's will . . . I pray that I'll be married and with one or two kids," Janelle replied.

"Really!"

"Yep." Janelle smiled. "I kinda already started on having a baby."

"And I got dibs on being the godmother."

"You know I gotcha on that."

They smiled at each other.

"Heard from Kandi lately?" Jurnee asked.

"Not since the funeral. I surmise you two still aren't talking?"

"It's her doing, not mine," Jurnee retorted.

"You need to put whatever issues you got with her aside and call her."

"And why should I do that?" Jurnee frowned.

"Because you're still her *friend*, and I think she needs one in her life."

Jurnee crossed her arms. She had too much concern for Kandi to pretend not to care. "What's going on with her?"

Janelle stood. "Call and find out yourself, and you better do it."

Jurnee twisted her lips.

"I'll see you later, girl. I got my man waiting on me."

Jurnee giggled. "Okay...and take care."

Alone again, Jurnee began to feel the effects of the drinks she had knocked down. Smiling, she placed her eyes back on Trevon. She wondered if he ever pictured himself living such a life while he was in prison. *I probably care more about his behind than he does himself,* she thought as the party continued.

Her heart fluttered when he later strolled toward her with that sexy grin.

"I'd like to get er'body attention right quick. Jus' wanna do a moment of silence for our girl, Brooke Vee. She will be missed and never forgotten, so y'all need to keep your eyes dry and your heart easy." When DJ Kay Slay lowered his head, a hush settled over the party.

Jurnee stood in her four-inch stilettos as Trevon lower his head. After the moment of silence, *"I'll Be Missing You"* by Puff Daddy, Faith Evans, and 112 closed the party on a sad note.

"C'mon, baby. Let's go home," Trevon whispered in Jurnee's ear.

"AAHHH, TREVON," Jurnee moaned as she strained against the satin restraints that bound her wrists together. Her movements were limited with the bond tied to the center of the headboard.

She was on her knees with her face buried sideways on a green satin pillow. Blindfolded, she was denied the chance to see what treats he had in store for her. His hands palmed her velvety butt cheeks open as his tongue stimulated her oversensitive ass. She whined softly; his electrifying tongue feasting famish-like. Without pause, he picked up a cold diced pineapple off the food tray to his left. He licked up her right ass cheek and caught her off guard by inserting the diced pineapple inside her pussy. She squealed, moaning his name as he pushed two more diced pineapples inside her dampen vagina.

"Papi, please!" she gasped when he pulled his face from her juicy ass.

He spanked her cheeks. Again, he reached for the food tray and picked up a bottle of Dom Perignon. With apt plans to blow her mind, he slid the chilly neck of the bottle all over her ass. When she couldn't stand it any longer, she heard the bottle pop.

He deliberately poured the suds onto her velvety ass, palming her right cheek open. He poured a small amount down her crack.

"Trevon, I—"

"Shut up!" He slapped her ass again. "Raise that ass up! Higher!" He drank from the bottle while rubbing and slapping her ass. "Who ass is it?"

"Yours, baby!" she moaned.

Positioning himself on one knee, he grabbed his erection and laid it between her warm butt cheeks. "Be still!" he said before he trickled a small amount on her ass again. He shivered when the cold bubbly drizzled down his shaft. Closing his eyes, he moved his hips to slide his penis along the valley of her ass. He could tell she wanted his dick in her ass by the way she twerked her hips.

"Papi, please, please put it in," she whined.

"Not yet, stop begging."

She tugged at the bonds when he moved his dick off her ass. She was a breath away from begging when she welcomed his tongue against her wet pussy. The tip of it traveled along her outer folds.

"Mmmm . . . yess! Ooohh, Papi . . . ahhh shit! Awww fuck! Awww fuck!" She pushed herself against his mouth as his tongue sought out the fruit inside her. She squealed when he slurped and sucked the first pineapple out. He chewed it and swallowed it. No man, nor woman, had *ever* freaked her this good before. She swore she was going to faint as his tongue chased the second pineapple around and around and around. She felt it slip out of her hole. Like the first, he ate it, pausing to lick the pineapple juice that flowed down her inner thighs. The instant he went in search of the third pineapple, she lost control. Her body shuddered as he foraged laboriously inside her pussy. She felt his hands massage her ass. Suddenly, her breath became stuck in her chest. She bared her teeth, toes curled. Her release came in a teaspoon of creamy fluid that pushed the fruit out. Trevon slurped at her slit with two fingers, working gently on her clit. Her nectarous release dripped from his bottom lip and left his beard wet.

"Mmmm," he groaned, licking the outer folds of her pussy.

Jurnee collapsed to her stomach and muffled her moans against the pillow. Goose bumps spread across her sumptuous ass checks as Trevon removed the blindfold and the satin restraints from her wrists.

Making the end of their short issue over the gun, they reconciled with actions opposed to words. She straddled him with nothing separating them. She rode him with an impassioned purpose, expressing her need of him.

25

OMG!

February 9

Thursday, 10:40 A.M. – Coconut Grove, Florida

Trevon's mood was upbeat, with Jurnee back under his sheets. She had sexed him before sunrise, bouncing on his morning thickness until he came inside her. After a quick shower, she cooked breakfast and then rolled off in her Bentayga to handle some business.

Trevon was outside, shirtless in the driveway, rinsing the suds off his A8. He was thinking about having lunch at Hooters when he heard a car turn into the driveway across the street. Tahkiyah took over his thoughts when he glanced over the roof of his sedan.

Curious, he watched a clean-cut, casually dressed black man step out of a BMW 750i. As he strode across the manicured lawn, Trevon lifted the spray nozzle over the roof of his car. When the man removed the *for sale* sign out of the front yard, Trevon loosened his grip on the plastic spray nozzle. He was compelled to cross the street to get some information from the guy. The dude with the sign greeted Trevon with a friendly smile as the trunk of the BMW popped open. Trevon spoke first.

"Hey, I live across the street." Trevon thumbed over his sweaty shoulder. "You just sold this place to a couple from D.C., right?"

The man placed the sign in the trunk. "Ah . . . no. Actually, it's a couple from Tampa."

"Tampa?" Trevon said with a confused expression. "Tahkiyah told me she was from D.C."

"Ah, that name doesn't ring a bell, and I'm sure about that."

"Uh, she's a Black female with—"

"Whoa!" The man smiled, closing the trunk. "Now, I'm sure there's a mistake. The couple that purchased this home is white."

"So you *never* spoke with a lady name Tahkiyah about buying that place?"

"Positive, bruh." The man shrugged. "Sorry, I can't be of any help."

Trevon thanked the man for his time. *Maybe she spoke with another agent or something?*

JURNEE STRODE GRACEFULLY across the marble floor inside the Turnberry Isle Spa and Fitness Center. Reaching the front desk, she gained the attention of the short Kenyan receptionist.

"Hi. I'm Jurnee Cruz, and I'm here to meet my friend Janelle Babin. Could you check to see which treatment room she's in?"

The 25,000 square-foot luxury spa boasted all the amenities to pamper the elite women in South Florida. Footbaths, full body massages, aromatherapy, a gym, a cardio room, the list went on.

Jurnee inhaled a strong scent of rosemary when she entered the treatment room. "Hey girl, I got your text," she said as she walked by the bed and out on the balcony. Breezing through the sliding glass doors, she stepped around a chaise longue. "Why didn't you—" Her words came to a halt when she saw Kandi sitting at a table.

"Hey. Betcha surprised to see me?" Kandi said with a glass of tea in front of her.

"Where's Janelle?" Jurnee asked with an attitude, crossing her arms.

"She's home. She helped me set this up. I figured you wouldn't have come otherwise."

Jurnee remained on her feet as the lush tops of the palm trees swayed in the breeze behind her. Reluctantly, she sat down. "You got ten minutes, so talk."

Kandi showed clear signs of her pregnancy. She was still a diva, rocking a white Prada dress and heels. With the sun warming her skin, she glanced at Jurnee. "Did you sleep with Trevon last night?"

Jurnee sighed angrily. "I know you didn't go through all the trouble just to ask me that! Shouldn't you be concerned about *your man*, Martellus?"

"I'm not with him anymore," Kandi replied flatly.

"Oh, so now you want Trevon back? Spare me, okay."

"Will you at least listen to me?"

"I am! You're talking, but you ain't saying nothing. And since you want to know so bad. Yes, I slept with him last night."

A twinge of jealousy shot through Kandi's heart. "Do you love him like I do?"

Jurnee's mouth dropped. "You call your treatment of him, love!"

"I made a mistake."

"Ya think!" Jurnee scoffed.

"Look, I don't want you nor Trevon to hate me. I just need y'all to know the truth," Kandi confessed as a cloud slid in front of the sun, throwing a blanket of shade over the balcony.

"Truth about what!" Jurnee asked with anger laced in her tone.

Kandi drew in a deep breath before she spoke. "About the baby."

Jurnee's face softened. Whatever beef she had with Kandi; she couldn't include the child. "Okay, I'm listening. What's wrong?"

"Please don't judge me," Kandi murmured, tears welling in her eyes. "Remember when I asked if you ever did something you regretted?"

Jurnee nodded.

"Well, I did something I deeply regret doing." Kandi's voice broke. "I loved Trevon so much, and you know that. But I'm not mad at you, Jurnee. I know I caused all of this trouble myself. A part of me died when I left Trevon."

"Please tell me what's going on."

"I was planning to have an abortion," Kandi admitted as she wiped her eyes.

"Why? Why were you going to—"

"I didn't want to live a lie," Kandi told her. "I couldn't do it to Trevon. Not after I learned the truth."

"Learned what truth?"

Kandi glanced down at her lap. "I was already a month pregnant before I had sex without a condom with Trevon."

Jurnee gasped.

"It was a mistake. It wasn't supposed to happen," Kandi continued. "I was going to have an abortion, then lie to everyone and say it was a miscarriage. I just couldn't tell Trevon the truth."

Jurnee shook her head, filled with disbelief. "Why?"

"I . . . was so lost. I didn't mean to hurt Trevon like I did. When I was with him, I was true to him. If I had known the baby wasn't his, I would have never put him through this," Kandi cried softly. "When I went to the doctor back in late November, I found out I was fourteen weeks pregnant. I knew right then that Trevon wasn't the father. I didn't know what to do. He was so happy about being a dad."

"So, you've told no one else about this?" Jurnee said as she came to grips with the pain that Trevon would have to face.

Kandi shook her head.

"And you think you've made your issue better by leaving Martellus? You know he'll put up a fight for the baby. Kandi, you need to get your shit in order because this is a mess. I mean—"

"Martellus isn't the father, either," Kandi interrupted.

Jurnee slid to the edge of the chair. She stared at Kandi, wondering how badly things had turned for her. "Who's the father?" Jurnee asked.

26

SWAGGA LIKE US

February 9

Thursday, 1:49 P.M. - Miami, Florida

"What in the hell is wrong with you, Marcus? What gave you the idea that it's okay to make a surprise visit to my job!" Kendra said as Swagga sat across her desk.

"I just got back from my vacation. Just wanted to see what you up to," he said with five different colored diamond chains around his neck.

"And somewhere in that head of yours you figured my place of work would be a good spot? Who are you trying to impress by barging up here with your clique?"

"Ain't nobody wit' me but Rick and a few of my bodyguards," he said, taking off his gold sunglasses. "Do I look high?" He grinned, glassy-eyed.

"What do you want? If you want that SUV back, you_"

"Ain't worried 'bout that, okay?"

"Alright. Speak what's on your mind." She leaned back, crossing her arms.

"Yo, that bread I wired you last year. Why you give it back to me?"

"Marcus, I told you why already. I was not with you for your fame or money. I gave it back because I assumed you would need it for your legal fees."

"That was some real shit you did. I thought I was gonna be broke until I got my bread back from D-Hot. Yeah, he did some grimy shit, but I hate what happened to 'im," he said in a sullen tone.

"Speaking of which, why didn't you tell me about what happened last month?"

He frowned. "A lot happened last month, so—"

"The issue you had on the road. The shooting where somebody tried—"

"It ain't shit to stress ova'. Just some hatin' ass folks. And I *couldn't* tell you because you ran out on me, remember?"

"I know we're not on the best of terms, but I want you to be careful out there, Marcus. And when are you coming to see your daughter?"

"This weekend if you'll let me."

"I'll never stop you from seeing your daughter and you know that, so stop trippin'."

Swagga glanced at his new $22,000 Corum Golden Bridge timepiece. "What time do you get off?"

"Later, around six. Why?"

"Maybe we could go out to—"

"No. We are *not* going back down that road again, okay?"

He nodded slowly, realizing she was one in a million. She was special. "It's about the videos you saw, huh?"

"Listen, Marcus. I don't trust you no more. Even if it was a onetime thang or whatever. It happened, okay? The fact is that you didn't tell me you had sex with that she-male. You weren't supposed to keep things like that from me. How could you put me at risk?"

He didn't have an explanation that would make any sense. He was about to tell her about his doctor's appointment set for next week when the phone on her desk rang. He stayed quiet, watching a woman that he knew *had* love for him. With Kendra, he became familiar with the true meaning of making love, which was different from sex and fucking. In truth, he couldn't explain his spontaneous urge to see her. Maybe he could fix things *if* his HIV test came back negative. Nashlly crossed his mind for a second. *If* his test was positive, she would be given a rude awakening for her gold digging ambitions. His daze of thoughts stopped when Kendra stood up, smoothing her shirt in place.

"I need to run down the hall right quick. Can you wait here for a minute or two?"

"I'll wait." He settled back in the chair.

She nodded and then made her way around the desk. Once the door was shut, he combed his fingers through his locs. If he could be with one woman, it would be Kendra. Glancing back on her desk, he saw her iPhone beside her coffee mug. *I wonder if she still got the same code?* Knowing he was in the wrong, he leaned up and picked up the pink iPhone.

When the five-digit code unlocked it, he immediately touched the video icon. There were only five videos.

My baby's B-day party

Future @ Club Liv

Untitled

Untitled

My fantasy cum true

He touched the icon to view the first untitled video. He only needed to view five seconds before his stomach tightened at the sight of him and Chyna. The second untitled video was the second time he was caught on film with Chyna. *I wonder how the fuck she got this shit.* Moving fast, he pulled out his new cell phone and quickly downloaded the videos. And just for the hell of it, he also downloaded the fantasy video. Placing the iPhone back how he found it, he tried to relax so Kendra wouldn't be suspicious of anything.

When she returned minutes later, he made a comment on her

lemon scented perfume. She ignored him, keeping a wall up around her emotions.

"Marcus, for future reference. Please don't visit me at my job again, okay?"

He slid his sunglasses back on. "Fine. I won't. Shit, why you slavin' at this bullshit job anyway? Ain't like you need any money."

"I was working when you met me and—"

"Yeah, yeah, I know. You're an independent woman." He rose, adjusting his palm-sized Gucci belt buckle. "Here." He dug inside his front pocket and pulled out a band of cash. "Put this unda' my princess' pillow." He dropped four $100 bills on the desk. He knew she would never turn down any money for their daughter. As he turned to leave, he paused at the door. "Um, yo." He looked back at her. "For all it's worth. I'm sorry fo' all the bullshit I put you through."

She refused to take any emotional steps backward. What she had with Swagga was a done deal. All she could do was maintain her position to ensure he had a relationship with his daughter. That was the best she could do. When he left, she thought of his secret. Like she told Trevon last week after she confronted Swagga, exposing him was pointless. Damn near every month or so, a rapper or some celebrity was coming out of the closet. Being politically correct, she took a lax view on gay relations, but it was *not* okay for her private life. She had no need or want to be with a bisexual man. And it didn't matter if he was out of the closet.

SWAGGA'S EXIT from the probation office building was coordinated by Rick and his security team. They escorted Swagga out the back door and right into the newest vehicle in Swagga's fleet.

Swagga climbed into the side of an idling black armored Mercedes-Benz Sprinter van and took his seat on a leather reclining chair as Rick slide to the middle of the "J" lounge seat to his right. The luxurious limo-van could seat up to 10, but today it only carried 4, Swagga, Rick, the driver and a guard riding shotgun up front.

As the Sprinter pulled from the office building, it was followed closely by the rest of Rick's team in the F-250.

"What Kendra talking about?" Rick asked.

"Same old shit," Swagga replied, staring pensively through the tinted window.

Rick could see the troubles weighing down on Swagga. "I know you're not worried about that D-Hot problem. We clean on that. We got nothing to worry about, trust me."

"Fuck that snitchin' ass bama!" Swagga mumbled.

"Your mind right to hit the studio?"

"Yeah, let's go. I'm good."

Swagga dwelled on the issue of Kendra holding the Chyna issue over his head. When they reached I-95, He pulled out his cell phone. He looked at the *sender's* information on the first video of him and Chyna. A 305-number showed up. He also learned that Kendra had received the video on the 24th of January last month.

His stomach knotted on the thought of someone else other than Kendra knowing about his secret. Pulling up the second video, the *sender's* information was the same. He came up with an idea. He could block his number out and call the sender's number to find out who the third party was. Taking a deep breath, he made the call. Instead of a ring, the sound of Lost Boyz' "Me and My Crazy World" filled his ear. A short loop of the late '90s hit played twice before the voicemail kicked in.

Yo, whut up? Yes, you've reached Trevon Harrison, but I'm kinda busy at the moment. Ain't nothin' changed, so leave your name and number, and I'll get back atcha. Peace.

Swagga hid his boiling emotions from Rick. Ending the call, he laid his head back on the headrest. His grip tightens on the phone. He could deal with Kendra having the videos, but with Trevon *back* in the picture, it was a different story. *So that bitch Kandi had the fuckin' videos all along! Knew I shoulda killed that 'ho when I had the chance to!* Swagga thought. *Okay, so she fuckin' wit' Trevon. He gave her the videos, which he got from Kandi. They must have a reason to be keeping 'em.* In the end, he knew their reasons for keeping the videos would only turn to embarrassment for him. Moving past his boiling anger, he looked at the third video he had downloaded off Kendra's phone.

The scene started with a clear shot of Trevon sitting on a bed, wearing a pair of briefs.

"Dis muthafucka again!" Swagga said under his breath. *Okay, so this bitch gotta fuck flick of Trevon on her iPhone. Ain't no big deal. He's a porn star,* Swagga reasoned as the video continued. *Wait a minute. That's Kendra's purse on the nightstand!* Swagga noticed when Trevon stood.

He averted his gaze from the scene as Trevon slid his briefs off. For a few moments the scene was unchanged until a second person ambled into the shot.

Swagga jerked upright in the seat, his eyes bugging out.

"Yo, dawg. You, okay?" Rick asked.

Swagga sat dumbstruck. A sour bile bubbled in his stomach at the sight of Kendra deep throating Trevon like a true bitch in heat.

27

THE TRUTH

February 9

Thursday, 2:10 P.M. - Miami, Florida

Jurnee finally pulled her shocked emotions in check. She sat on the bed next to Kandi in the treatment room. *Why, why, why!* bounced off the walls in her head. "Of all the men, why him?" Jurnee asked, with a wad of tear-soaked tissues in her grip.

"He was convenient at the time, and it was just a spur-of-the-moment thing," Kandi told her with the intentions to come clean about everything. She was tired of trudging alone with her burdens. By telling the truth, she was optimistic that Jurnee would understand.

"How did it happen?" Jurnee pressed with the need to know.

"I drove over to confront Swagga at the studio, but he wasn't there. I was just so mad at him for cheating on me. Anyway, D-Hot was there, and I was on some bullshit."

"How?" Jurnee asked impatiently.

Kandi looked down at the floor. The memory of what she did remained regrettable. "I knew how tight Swagga and D-Hot were. Both business and friendship. I just wanted Swagga to feel my pain. I knew by me just fucking D-Hot wouldn't hurt Swagga. So I gave D-Hot something that Swagga never had."

Jurnee shook her head. "And that was to let D-Hot do it without a condom?"

Kandi nodded. "I was gonna throw it all up in Swagga's face, but I changed my mind. Plus, D-Hot wanted it to remain just between us. He didn't want any beef with Swagga."

"How many times did y'all do it?"

"Just once. He was the one that tipped the police off. He told me everything when Swagga was arrested."

"He did it for the baby?"

Kandi nodded. "It's all a mess."

"So, nobody knows—"

"We kept it a secret."

"And now you got Trevon thinking the baby is his. But in truth it's D-Hot's, and he's no longer with us."

"I didn't want this to happen, Jurnee. I didn't expect to fall in love with Trevon and not know I was already pregnant. I wanted Trevon to be happy with me, but I screwed it all up."

"It ain't what I thought," Jurnee admitted. "I thought you were just on some bullshit. I mean, I can't even imagine having to deal with your problems. I know what I'm about to say is, well . . . easier said than done. But you should've told Trevon the truth when you first learned the baby wasn't his."

"I couldn't, Jurnee. That man was beyond happy. I just couldn't shatter his world like—"

"You crushed him when you left. You took the easy way out by running and not dealing with it. It was *my* shoulder that he cried on because of you," Jurnee stated, unconcerned if Kandi's feelings were hurt.

"You're right," Kandi said. "But...I don't think I can face him with-"

"That ain't an option. You *have* to woman up and tell him the truth, okay?"

"And what about the fact that I'm still in love with him?"

Jurnee stood and paced the floor.

"I did all the wrong things for all the wrong reasons," Kandi said with tears building in her eyes again. "I didn't know what to do, okay? I never had a *real* mother to teach me this . . . shit! All I wanted. All I needed was Trevon, and I messed it all up." She broke down, crying into her hands.

Jurnee wanted to comfort Kandi, but she couldn't. Knowing the truth had filled Jurnee with compassion. Kandi had simply made some dumb life-changing decisions that she didn't think all the way through.

"Where are you staying?" Jurnee asked.

"At the Mondrian," Kandi said, wiping her eyes.

"So, it's really over with you and Martellus?"

"Hell yeah," Kandi murmured. "Go ahead and say, 'I told you so'."

"About what?"

"I caught the housekeeper suckin Martellus' dick in the garage. I needed a reason to leave his ass, and he gave me one."

"And what if you hadn't caught him? Would you still be with him?"

She shrugged. "I never stopped loving Trevon. I just want to make things right."

"You have to face Trevon. He needs to know the truth, okay?"

"Will you help me?"

Jurnee had to set aside her own emotions and deal with the truth. Kandi hadn't meant to hurt Trevon. It was just a fact of life that stood true through any type of issue. Life is only what you make it. "Yeah, I'll see what I can do."

Kandi stood. "I don't wanna be alone, okay. Please help me."

Jurnee left Kandi behind with a promise that she would call her later. Jurnee cried silently when she got inside her Bentayga. Again, she fought to pull herself together, and she did. Driving away from the Turnberry Isle Spa, Jurnee tried to picture how Trevon would react to the heart-crushing truth about the baby. Realizing that assuming, wondering, nor hoping would give her the answer, she knew what had to be done. If Kandi didn't like it, she would have to deal with it.

~

Trevon stepped out the front door on his way to Hooters when Tahkiyah pulled up behind his A8. She waved at him. He was caught off guard by her sudden appearance. When he reached back to lock the door, she stepped out of her BMW M850i.

They met at the rear of the Audi.

Tahkiyah had her hair down, adding a pinch of flavor to her sex appeal. A pair of gold wishbone earrings adorned her ears. Gold trimmed aviator sunglasses hid her eyes. She was dressed modestly in a black embroidered silk-chiffon top and a flesh-clinging blue, silk pencil skirt. Her award-winning legs and calves were enhanced by a pair of Gucci pumps.

Trevon kept it causal today, wearing a fresh pair of wheat colored Timberland boots, True Religion jeans, a white tee and a Gucci bucket hat.

"Uhhhhh, Tahkiyah, right?" he asked, giving her a quick once-over. *Damn, ain't no way she fifty something! She fly as hell.*

"Yes." She smiled.

"Ah, what brings you around today?"

"I was just in the area, so I thought I'd drop by."

"Where you coming from?"

"I have a suite at the Mondrian."

"Oh. You and your husband?"

"Actually, I'm not married." She watched his reaction closely. When he crossed his big arms, she read the doubt he expressed.

"Is there anything else you lied to me about?" he asked.

Tahkiyah casually removed her gold sunglasses. She didn't feel comfortable being untruthful. "I was never moving in across the street."

"And?"

"I only have one child—"

"I know you're not moving into that house across the street. Wanna tell me why you lied about that also?"

"It's, um, really complicated."

"Telling lies isn't complicated from what I'm starting to see about you."

She looked at him, matching his unsmiling expression. "What if my reason for...not being honest with you are justifiable?"

He shook his head. "Since I know you're not... just in the area. I think it's best for me to ask you to leave, okay?" He glanced down the road, wondering how she had even managed to get past the security booth.

"I'm..." She took a step towards him. "Okay...I'll be straight up with you. I did all this because I wanted to meet you. Can fault me for being attracted to you? I thought Jurnee was your girl and then I-"

"Wait a minute. Are you stalking me?"

She shook her head. "Don't get too full of yourself."

The idea of having sex with her diverted him from keeping his distance. He shifted his eyes from her lovely face and lusted at the decent size of her breasts. Are you working undercover or something?"

She laughed. "No, handsome. I'm not the police or working for any state or federal agency."

"Lemme see your ID."

"Really! You're going to card me?"

"Damn right. You may be fine and all that, but it ain't good to lie."

She turned and breezed back to her car and reached through the window. She pulled out a quilted white leather shoulder bag. "Let's make a deal," she said as her fingers brushed against the 9-millimeter in her bag.

"What kinda deal?" he asked as she removed her license.

"If my license proves something you think I lied about, I owe you one wish."

He thought it over for a second. "And if I'm wrong?"

"Hmm. Then you owe me a nice, private massage," she said seductively.

He viewed the bet with her as a win-win situation. "Ai'ight. You *said* you were fifty something. Prove it."

"Mmm." She grinned, handing him the license. "I hope you're good with your hands."

He looked at the information on the D.C. driver's license. Her date of birth showed she was fifty-four.

Tahkiyah Lloyd Bradford. HT: 5'4" WT: 120* Eye: Hazel * Race: Black **

"A bet is a bet, Trevon." She smiled, sliding her sunglasses back on.

"How do I know you're not crazy?"

She laughed, strolling back to her car. "If somebody is going to be crazy, it might just be you," she said over her shoulder. When she slid behind the wheel, she motioned him over.

"And what will I be going crazy over?"

"I'll let my actions speak louder than words." She lifted the sunglasses off her eyes and boldly looked between his legs. "But I'm willing to bet *again*." She smiled. "That this sugar is so good and sweet that you won't last no longer then . . . five minutes."

He had never met a woman that intrigued his interest so deeply. He couldn't back down.

"Come to the Mondrian. I'll leave a note for you with my room number. And *if* you're man enough to show up and honor your bet, I'll be waiting." She revved the engine twice and backed out of the driveway, leaving him speechless.

At 3:39 P.M., Trevon's lust and increasing inquisitive nature toward Tahkiyah had him in the lobby at the Mondrian. A perfume envelope was handed to him when he reached the front desk. Inside it was a folded sheet of paper with a room number and a red print of a pair of lips.

TAHKIYAH ENDED the call with the hotel concierge that gave her notice of Trevon's arrival. Her body tingled with excitement over the possibilities of what could happen between herself and Trevon. She moved quickly, spraying perfume in her wake. *I have to go through with this,* she thought for the hundredth time. By the bed, she checked to make sure the ice hadn't melted too much in the shiny bucket. The bottle of Moscato wasn't her top choice of drink, but today it would suit the moment. The wineglasses were spotless, the bed was made, the curtains were shut, the lights down low and most important, Tahkiyah wanted to cater to her sexual needs. She viewed Trevon as an object. Being with him would simply be mixing her mission with pleasure.

The knock at the door filled her with a grip of nervousness. She held her poised composure and sauntered barefooted across the carpeted floor to let him inside.

Trevon knew straightaway what would likely occur when he laid his eyes on Tahkiyah. He viewed her as a temptress that he couldn't resist. Her body was coated with a red sheer negligee, black lace trimmed panties, and a black garter set that connected to some black thigh high fishnet stockings. Even her glasses added to her charm and sexiness.

"I see you came," she said softly.

He nodded, knowing his skepticism toward her was dwindling under her enchanting sex appeal.

"Well, come in." She motioned him inside.

He hesitated for a breath before he entered and stood by the TV as she locked the door. He couldn't take his eyes off her pert, light brown ass and how the panties bit enticingly into her flesh.

"Do you know the key to pleasing a woman, Trevon?" she asked, crossing to where he stood.

"Yeah, communication," he said, playing it cool.

She came to a stop in front of him. His size alone made her moist. "Good answer. And can you explain it?"

"All women don't like the same thing. Some like it rough, some like it nice and slow."

"Continue," she said, reaching under his white tee. What she felt was a rippled sea of hard muscles.

"Knowing what a woman wants makes it easier to take care of her needs."

"And which is more important? The want or the need?" She trapped his nipples between her fingers.

"The need," he said, knowing he should push her hands away.

She pulled his white tee up. "Oh, my gosh!" she moaned, licking her lips at the sight of his chiseled stomach. Unable to control herself, she licked his left nipple.

Not once did her age cross his mind. She moistens his hairless chest with licks and kisses. Her hands explored his chest, arms, stomach, and back. His white tee came off.

"I'm not a fan of wearing bras," she moaned as he inched the hem of the negligee up her waist.

The passion between them moved to another level when he rubbed her throbbing vagina through the thin panties. She was hot and damp. Her knees shivered as he massaged her vulva while sucking her ear.

"Mmmm," she moaned, reaching down into his jeans, "Take a shower with me first."

"PICK UP THE PHONE, TREVON!" Jurnee muttered as she sped west along Dolphin Expressway. When his voicemail picked up, she ended the call by voice command. Switching lanes, she mashed the gas, rocketing past a SUV in the right lane. The throaty exhaust note matched the W-12 600 horsepowered engine under the hood. Jurnee wheeled the attention-grabbing Bentley SUV over the posted speed limit without thought. At her speed, the chrome rims turned into a blur, giving an illusion of spinning backward. Her state of mind didn't register the speedometer creeping past 90 miles per hour. She kept pushing the speed, jumping lanes without using the turn signal. Horns sounded in the wake of the speeding Bentayga. Trevon consumed her troubled thoughts. A tear broke from the corner of her eye. She gripped the wheel, her foot still adding pressure to the gas pedal.

"Call Trevon!" she shouted at the voice activated Bluetooth system. Tears blurred her vision. *I have to tell him,* she thought. *If I don't, I'm no better than Kandi, and he—*

Before she could finish her thought, two things happened simultaneously that broke her concentration on the road. First, Trevon answered her second call. And with his voice in her ears, a Florida State Trooper appeared behind her with its light bar flashing. Jurnee glanced her at speed. For the 2.3 seconds that her eyes left the road traveling at 98 miles per hour – the Bentayga traveled the length of a football field. When she looked up, she saw a vehicle ahead and panicked in that flash of a moment when it registered that a crash was imminent. She stood up on the brakes and screamed before she rear-ended a panel truck.

AT THE SAME TIME, Trevon didn't think much of it when his call with Jurnee suddenly dropped. Shrugging, he pulled his socks off and joined Tahkiyah in the shower.

UNBEKNOWNST TO KANDI, she was two floors above Trevon and Tahkiyah at the Mondrian Hotel. She felt apprehensive about having to face Trevon. Jurnee was right. Running away from him wasn't the answer. Sulking alone in the suite, she lay back on the large bed, gazing at the ceiling. Needing *something* to do, she reached for her iPad on the bedside table. As soon as she turned it on, she saw a new e-mail waiting to be read.

. . .

To: Kandi@aef.com
   From: Tbradford@BradfordPR.com
   Subject: You and I
   Date: Feb 8 11:10 p.m.

*B*E *it God's will this message will reach you. I've been meaning to sit down and send this ever since I got your e-mail. There are things I need to tell you face to face, and all I seek is your understanding, for we all make mistakes that we have to live with. In my case, I lived with mine for too long. I hope to hear from you soon. Here's my # 202-530-2023*

Tahkiyah Bradford

28

I AIN'T A KILLA . . . BUT DON'T PUSH ME

February 9
Thursday, 4:27 P.M. - Miami, Florida

Fritz looked at his Swiss Hublot timepiece when a knock sounded at the door of his suite. His guest was on time, not a minute late.

Getting up from the table, he picked up a black 9-millimeter pistol. The gun he had used on D-Hot, and Brooke Vee was in three pieces at the bottom of Biscayne Bay. He treated his used weapons like used condoms. They were only good for a single use. To his surprise, he saw Swagga standing alone in the hallway. Just to be sure, he looked through the peephole again. Clicking the safety off, he waited to open the door until a middle-aged couple cleared the hall.

"Where's Rick?" Fritz asked Swagga as he motioned him inside with the gun.

"We don't need 'im," Swagga replied, looking at the gun Fritz held in plain view.

"What's in the bag?" Fritz closed the door.

"Money."

"Get against the wall so I can pat you down and I won't ask twice."

"Chill, yo! Whut the fuck!" Swagga complained, shoving his hoodie off his head.

Fritz pushed Swagga up against the wall. "Drop the bag and *don't* move." Fritz held the 9-millimeter against Swagga's spine. "Why did you come alone?" he asked, frisking Swagga with one hand.

"I can handle my own gotdamn business. And yo, I thought you was from the islands. Where yo' accent?" Swagga asked with his face against the wall.

"I'm bi-accented," Fritz said sarcastically. "Turn around and keep your hands on your head."

Swagga turned to Fritz, masking his face with a scowl. He stiffened when the tip of the silencer dug into his throat. It stayed in place as Fritz thoroughly patted Swagga down. Once he was sure that Swagga was unarmed, he relaxed.

"Dis how you do business?" Swagga said, fixing his clothes.

"How much is in the bag?"

"Thirty bands."

"Dump it on the bed. If it's all there—*then* we can talk business."

"And if it ain't?"

"Then I'll consider you a threat, and you won't live to see tomorrow."

Swagga snatched the bag off the floor and stomped over to the bed. He stayed under gunpoint up until the money was counted and spread out over the king-size mattress.

"Okay, have a seat at the table," Fritz said.

Swagga adjusted his headband as Fritz joined him at the table.

"I had a flight leaving tonight," Fritz began. "But I must assume you need something taken care on an urgent notice, huh?"

Swagga nodded. Sure, Fritz looked like a preppy dude in the dress shoes, black slacks, and a green linen shirt, but Swagga wasn't fooled. "It's a guy by the name of Trevon. He's a porn star."

Fritz nodded. He picked up a black felt humidor. "Would you enjoy one?" Fritz opened the humidor, revealing six cigars.

"Hell yeah!" Swagga picked one out, looking at the square cut on both ends.

"It's a cheroot. By the way it's cut is why it's a cheroot. For example, if it was tapered at both ends, it's a perfecto," Fritz explained.

"You know your cigars, huh?"

"Every man has his joy. And yours?"

"Instagram models and strippers," Swagga said as the headband slid down his forehead. "So whut up? Can you help me?"

Fritz reached for a gold lighter. "When do you need it done?"

"ASAP," Swagga said, nudging the headband back up as Fritz lit his cigar.

"Why the rush?" Fritz pushed the lighter across the table.

"I'll pay extra if needed." Swagga lit his cigar. He leaned back in the chair, filling his lungs.

"What has this man done to you?" Fritz asked, surrounded by a thick cloud of smoke.

"A lot. I just need 'im gone. Done wit'. Period," Swagga said with the cigar in his mouth.

"If you want it done tonight, it will be ten thousand extra." Fritz tapped the cigar over the ashtray.

"Not a problem. Just let me know when and where to break you off wit' the rest. Hell, you can still catch your flight tonight." Swagga held the cigar out. "I think I need to invest in these."

"We can do a bank wire for half on my laptop," Fritz suggested.

"Say no more. Let's do it," Swagga replied.

Fritz placed his cigar in the ashtray and got up from the table. When he left the room, Swagga reached behind his head and under his locs.

Fritz returned to the table about a minute later with a thin laptop. He sat, placing both hands on the table, looking directly at Swagga.

"You ai'ight, yo?" Swagga asked, smoke flowing from his nose and mouth.

Fritz picked up the silenced 9-millimeter he had left behind. "There was a hit on me once. A guy came to see me, sorta like this. I left the room and left my gun on the table."

"And what happened?"

"He was armed, but he figured he would get more . . . how you say—street rep by killing me with my own gun."

"He missed?"

Fritz grinned. "My gun didn't work. I allowed that mistake to ride him for three seconds before I killed him with my second gun that did work."

"Man, I'm here to do *bidness*," Swagga explained. "Fuck all that other shit."

"I see that now," Fritz said, opening the laptop. "I'll need your account number. Do you have it?"

"Yeah. Lemme get my wallet."

Fritz typed on the laptop as Swagga slid back from the table. "I'll need your—" Fritz paused and looked up from the screen.

Swagga stood across the table with a tight grip on a Smith & Wesson .22 caliber pistol.

"Where did you hide it? Oh, the headband." Fritz slowly raised his hands. "Behind your head. Under your hair. I'll have to keep that in mind for next—"

Swagga lunged across the table, popping four quick rounds into Fritz's face. With his adrenaline thumping, Swagga ran to the bed and stuffed his money back inside the leather bag. He tried not to look over his shoulder at the body slumped face down on the table. On his way out, he paused to snatch up the box of cigars.

"Won't be no next time, muthafucka!" Swagga pulled the hoodie back over his head and slipped out the door with the bag slung over his shoulder.

Swagga scared the piss out of Nashlly when he yanked open the passenger side door of her Camry.

"Boy, damn!" She jumped as he slid inside and threw the bag in the back.

"Let's roll, baby," Swagga said with his hands shaking.

He settled low in the seat as Nashlly pulled out of the Fontainebleau parking lot. He was buzzing off that new taste of power. That rush of being invincible had flowed through him when he popped Fritz's top. Killing Fritz would tie up the loose ends. Fuck the bullshit of having to worry about Fritz coming back to blackmail him. Swagga was done with paying others to do his dirt. Yeah, Fritz had taken D-Hot's grimy ass out of the scene, but that was over with. If you wanted shit done right, do it yourself! Swagga assumed things would've been done differently had he done shit *his way* on that Chyna bullshit last year. Bringing Yaffa in the fold had fucked everything up.

Swagga kept Nashlly in the blind about killing Fritz. He threw her off by telling her he was hustling that *white* girl on the side. Swagga snapped his fear of pulling a trigger. Next on the menu, Trevon.

29

IF HE ONLY KNEW

February 9
Thursday, 4:47 P.M. - Miami, Florida

Back at Mondrian Hotel, Tahkiyah lay nude on the Egyptian bed sheets with a content smile.

"That was wonderful," she cooed as Trevon slid his magical hands across the back of her shoulders. "Are you sure you're not a professional masseur?" she quipped.

"A bet is a bet," he said, staring at the perfection of her lovely ass.

"Um, you can go lower if you want to."

"Nah." He slid off the bed. "I think it's time for you to come clean with me."

She turned to her side and looked up at him. "Yes, you really want to know the truth?"

He nodded. "Considering I just took a shower with you; I figure the least you can do is stop bullshittin' with me."

"I'm surprised." She sat up.

He glanced at her breasts. "About what?"

"That you didn't try to have sex with me in the shower. Are you, um, gay?"

"Hell no."

She looked at the large imprint his penis made under his briefs. "Can you take those back off?"

He crossed his arms. "Look. This is some weird shit, okay. I don't know who the hell you are – am I being set up – is this some kind of-"

She slid off the bed. "I wanna have sex with you, okay? You want the truth, that's it."

"And why me? How do you know?" he asked, suspecting she was a star-struck fan of his debut film.

Tahkiyah knew any lie she told would be discredited. She could not tell him the truth. She wondered how he would look at her if he knew she had not been with a Black man in twenty-four years? She couldn't tell him about the affair she had while she was married. An affair that resulted in her getting pregnant by her lover.

She couldn't tell him the deceitful motive of her creating a false strain to leave her husband. She left him before he knew she was pregnant by another man. She couldn't tell him how she gave birth, in secret, to a child she didn't want. She couldn't tell him how she returned to her husband and tried to reunite with him after a year. She couldn't tell him how she hid the childbirth from her husband. The marriage failed two months after she came back. Her husband had heartlessly left her for a white girl.

And for that, Tahkiyah's only way to vent was to come to detest Black men. However, being around Trevon had awakened her desires to experience the lovemaking that only a Black man could sate. She had grown dissatisfied in using black porn to get herself off.

Her nipples throbbed when she tentatively reached for his hands. She couldn't tell him the truth about anything. But she would act on the urge she knew he wanted.

Lifting his strong hands up to her breasts, she asked. "I...saw you were hard in the shower." She let go of his hands and, to her excited relief, he began to caress her breasts. She moaned, lowering her hands to his crotch.

She knew the art of seduction.

Rubbing his robust erection through the briefs, she felt light-headed when his hands roamed to her ass. She tugged his briefs down and gawked at his impressive penis. She touched it. Stroked it. Squeezed it. Caressed it.

He moaned as she manipulated his penis from tip to shaft with her slender hands. Her natural sexiness overpowered him. He wanted her.

"Let's do it, Trevon." She pulled him back to the bed. "Please. I really want you, bad."

He slid his briefs off.

She handed him a condom off the nightstand. He put the condom on.

She got on all fours. He positioned himself behind her. She gasped as he slid inside her. "Ooohhh, yessss!"

Gripping her tiny waist, he added her to the list as her breathy moans resonated inside the room.

Nearly an hour later Tahkiyah sat in the hot tub with her eyes closed. Naturally, Trevon preoccupied her thoughts. Not even five minutes after he left the room. She could still feel the stretch of his lengthy penis. She could still feel the grip of his hands on her breasts. She sucked her bottom lip into her mouth, thinking back to how he had sensually thrusted in and out of her through the peak of her orgasm. She moaned, remembering how it felt when his-

A chime from her laptop on the bed interrupted her vivid replay. Reluctantly, she climbed out of the hot tub, knowing it was an e-mail she needed to read.

She smiled when she discovered a romantic gesture left

behind by Trevon. On one of the pillows was a single rose and a small card. She sat on the edge of the bed and opened it.

<u>You're the best I ever had!</u>

She definitely didn't have any regrets about having sex with him. Setting the card aside, she picked up her laptop and saw she in fact had a new email.

To: Tbradford@BradfordPR.com

From: PIstaton@Unseen.com

Subject: Trevon

Date: Feb 9 7:55pm

Sorry for my delay. His name is Trevon Harrison, age 33 no known aka. DOB 7/25. He has a criminal record and is currently on probation. Did 15 years for 1ˢᵗ degree murder. I dug deep, and I found something that's best for you to see for yourself. I found his connection to LaToria.

See Attachment file

The rose fell to the floor. *Murder . . . I slept with a convicted murderer! This can't be true. And what's this connection with LaToria?* Sitting at the foot of the bed, she moved the cursor over the *open* icon to view the attachment file. Her heart pounded in her chest as she waited for the file to open.

"What the hell?" Tahkiyah murmured when an opening credit scene for an adult film filled the screen. She quickly assumed that it was a mistake on Staton's part. Her mind went numb when Trevon's face popped up on the screen. In a minute's span, her world was turned upside down by the sight of Trevon and LaToria, aka Kandi. She exploded off the bed, losing the contents from her stomach before she reached the bathroom.

30

THIS CAN'T BE TRUE!

February 9

Thursday, 8:27 P.M. - Coconut Grove, Florida

Trevon picked up his phone after taking a shower and he noticed that none of his recent texts to Jurnee had been read. Sitting at the foot of his bed, he called Ariana as Rex lay at his feet.

"Hey, Trevon!" she answered after the first ring. "What's going on?"

"Nuthin' much. Ain't wake you up, did I? I know you got a bedtime since it's a school night," he said with a grin.

"Nah, you're good. But it's close to me turning in."

"Um, you seen Jurnee?"

"Not since she left for Janelle's party last night."

"Hmm. I just tried her number right before I called you."

"Nothing's wrong, I hope?"

"I'ma call her again and leave a message this time."

"When did you see her last?"

"This mornin'. She said she was gonna swing by to see you after she took care of some kind of business.

"I'm worried."

"Chill with the negative thoughts," he said, trying to quell his own uneasiness. "She knows damn near everybody in Miami, so ain't no telling where she at. Well, lemme get off this phone, and *when* I reach Jurnee, I'll make sure she calls you. So don't be stressin' yourself out over nothing, ai'ight."

"Okay. But promise to have her call me. No matter what time it is. I'll leave my ringer on."

"Ai'ight, and you do the same if you see or hear from her before I do."

"I will. Bye and good night."

"Ai'ight, take care."

Trevon tried Jurnee's number again. Just as the first ring sounded, the door chimed. Rex, as always, sprung to his feet and shot out for the front door, barking. Trevon was right behind him with his iPhone ringing. *I know it ain't Jurnee 'cause she got a key and the code to get in,* he thought as Rex barked aggressively at the door. Trevon's heart dropped in his stomach when he saw the red and blue light flashing through a gap in the curtains.

He ended the call when Jurnee's voicemail kicked in. *What the fuck the police doing here?* He stared at the door, his heart racing. The dread of going back to prison stressed him to the point of having nightmares. Rex kept barking. The doorbell rang again. Trevon felt like his feet were mired in thick mud as he moved to the door. *I know I ain't done shit. God, I hope it ain't nothin' 'bout Yaffa.* "Rex, sit!" he said, peeking through the curtain. *Shit. Ain't but one police at the door. Fuck it.* Trevon grabbed Rex by his collar and tugged him back to the bedroom.

After he left Rex in the backyard, he hurried back to the door with his worst fears forming in his head. Taking a deep breath, he turned off the alarm and then opened the door. The female Coconut Grove police officer greeted him with a curt nod. "I'm looking for Mr. Trevon Harrison," she said with a stoic expression.

"Uh, I'm Trevon."

She glanced down at a notepad she held. "Do you know a Ms. Jurnee Davon Cruz?"

"Yeah, I know her. What—"

"Sir. She was in a bad car accident, and we need—"

"Where is she!"

"Jackson Memorial. She's in critical—"

Trevon ignored whatever else she had to say. All that mattered to him was reaching Jurnee. *C'mon, baby, hold on! Hold on! God, please let 'er pull through this.* He sped off in his A8, hoping his prayer was heard.

An hour later, Swagga lay relaxed in bed with Nashlly, preparing to call it a wrap for today. He sat up, watching old reruns of *Martin*.

"Dude, funny as hell!" He laughed, with a bottle of Moet beside him.

Nashlly ignored Swagga as she sat engrossed with her face glued to her phone. She was topless, wearing only a pair of blue cotton panties.

"How much longer you gon' be on that shit?" he asked.

"Just a minute," she replied without looking up.

He leaned over, trying to see what held her attention. "You been on Instagram for almost an hour," he complained. "Here, post this. In bed wit' da KOM, Swagga." He laughed, thumping her nipple.

"Oww!" she said. "And you better stop before I post it for real. And then all your groupies gonna get mad. And what does KOM mean?"

"King of Miami. Hell, I might need to buy the rights for that. But yo', take them panties off."

"Wait, baby." She reached between his legs. "You know I'ma handle my business in this bed, so relax. It's just some big news that's going viral."

"'Bout what?"

"That porn star, Honey Drop, was in a car accident today.

Fucked up real bad. People posting info that she might not make it."

"Word?" Swagga said, losing interest with the TV.

She nodded, hiding her sigh of relief when he rolled over to get his own phone. "Swagga, the bottle!" She caught it by the neck just as it started to spill.

"My bad, yo," he said, grinning.

Swagga was easily drawn into the news about Honey Drop, aka Jurnee. He saw Nashlly had told the truth. All the big names were posting heartfelt messages in support of Honey Drop. When he saw messages from DJ Kay Slay, Rick Ross, Uncle Luke, Trina, Megan Thee Stallion, and Gucci Mane, he knew it was time to add his two cents.

@ Home hopin' that Honey Drop will pull through

He wasn't sincere about a single word; he merely wanted his name in the mix. The worry and concern increased when a picture of Jurnee's crumpled Bentayga was posted. All of the AEF porn stars were showing their true support for Jurnee, while a few mentioned something about the unsolved murder of Brooke Vee. Swagga was about to log out when a post from Trevon popped up.

@ Jackson Memorial showing love for Jurnee. Pray!

His face balled up instantly. "I need to use your car!"

"Huh? Where you going?" She looked up as he jumped off the bed.

"Don't ask too many questions."

She laid her phone down as she slid off the bed. "I'm going with you!" she stated.

"No, you ain't," he said, reaching for his hoodie.

"Why?"

"'Cause I fuckin' said so, bitch!"

"Why I gotta be all that?"

"Listen," he sneered. "Get dressed and get the fuck outta my crib!"

Nashlly was about to get fly at the mouth but held her heated words when Swagga pulled a gun from the bag he was toting around all day.

"You think I'm playin', yo?" he said, placing the .22 in his pocket.

"This is fucked up. I know you're going to the hospital to see your ex!"

"Fuck you talkin' 'bout?"

"I just saw the post by your ex-bitch, Kandi! She's on her way to the hospital."

Swagga flopped on the bed to put his boots on. "You don't know what the fuck you talkin' 'bout, so shut the fuck up!"

"So you gonna do me like this!"

He reasoned he could knock off two birds with one stone. He wouldn't pass up the chance to catch Trevon and Kandi at the same spot. All his troubles would end tonight! Fuck any talking— wasn't shit else to say. Since they wanted to hold that Chyna shit over his head, they would die for it. When he was on his feet, he stared at Nashlly. "Don't be here when I get back!"

Nashlly saw her future of living the *ballin' life* fading quickly. "Swagga, wait. I'm sorry, I'll—"

"Bitch, it's over. Get yo' shit and get missin'!" He started for the door.

"Swagga!" she called after him.

She was left alone in his bedroom, shocked at how fast things had turned from sugar to shit. The leather bag sat on the bed. She waited a second, thinking he was coming back to see if she was leaving. Instead, she saw the light flick on outside the huge window. *I know this dumb ass fool ain't leaving for real?* she thought, rushing across the floor to look outside. She stood at the window, looking down at the multi-port garage. He couldn't take her car because the keyfob was on the dresser. A minute after he slipped inside the garage, she saw him pulling off with no lights on behind the wheel of his Flying Spur.

"This fool done crossed the wrong bitch!" She fumed, turning from the window. She made a quick dash for her phone on the bed. Clinging to a hope that he wasn't serious, she called him to see what was really up. Hell, she could deal with the shit talking and his bitches on the side as long as he kept her laced up. *But nooo, this muthafucka trying to bump me to the curb! Oh, really!* She stood by the bed, waiting for him to pick up.

"What the fuck you want, bitch!"

"Baby, why you buggin' out on me? Listen, we can have some freaky sex when you—"

"Yo! Why are you asking like I care or need your ass? It's two things ain't ever seen. One is a UFO and two, a bitch I need!"

"So, you gonna flex on me like this?"

"Bitch, you don't even exist to me no more!"

Nashlly opened her mouth to reply, but he ended the call. Steaming mad, she got her shit together and snuck out past Rick with a tight grip on the money-filled bag. She had a trick for Swagga, one that would put his ass on blast and viral!

TREVON SAT ALONE inside his A8, FaceTiming with Janelle. "Ain't nobody telling me anything!" he said frustrated. "All they keep saying is that she's still undergoing a bunch of operations and shit! I don't even know if she's breathing on her own or not. She had to be airlifted from the accident, so I know her condition ain't good," he said.

"Trevon, listen to me," Janelle's voice broke from the pain she was dealing with. "I know what we *do* for a living isn't viewed as righteous. But tonight, it's really based on what you and I believe in, okay? We have to pray for her, and I mean *hard*." She sobbed. "We are all the family she's got right now, so we have to stay strong. But know that whatever happens it's for a reason and it's God's will, so—"

"She's gonna make it," he stated firmly, refusing to listen to any negative talk about Jurnee not pulling through.

"I know she will."

"How soon can you and Victor catch a flight from New York?" he asked, wiping his eyes.

"I hope by noon tomorrow. If I can get a sooner flight, I'll take it."

"Ai'ight 'cause I'll be here. Ain't goin' no fuckin' where till I can take Jurnee home."

He was patient with himself as he struggled to control his emotions. He was unconcerned about the bullshit he thought was so important. He didn't care if his rims were shiny. He didn't care which model had the biggest ass. He didn't care about fucking a new female. *All* he cared about was his friend, Jurnee.

A car across the parking lot pulled off, its headlights briefly filling the dark cabin of his ride. He saw the wetness around his eyes in the rearview mirror. Shedding tears wasn't helping Jurnee. He reluctantly made his way back inside the hospital.

He was drained, walking with his head down. He couldn't forgive himself for being in bed with Tahkiyah while Jurnee was fighting for her life. He had learned from the police that her last phone call was made to him. He was on the phone with her at the point of impact. All he could do was hate himself. Stopping at the front desk, he spoke to the male RN. Tonight, he wasn't going for that 'no news is good news'. Leaving the front desk, he ended up in the waiting area. He sat down in a corner seat, dropping his head, alone.

KANDI SWALLOWED the lump in her throat when Trevon walked by her. *He didn't even notice me,* she thought with her eyes blurred. Part of her wanted to sit and just stay silent. *I have to do it.* She shouldered her black leather tote bag, then rose up in her ankle strap pumps. She left her tears in place as she closed the space between the man she so deeply loved. He sat with his head down, his shoulders slumped.

"... Hey, Smooch," her voice broke.

He didn't move. She waited, her heart jumping. After what seemed like forever, he looked up at her. His face showed no emotion. Each time he blinked; it sent a new line of tears down his face. She shifted her eyes away, hoping he didn't hate her.

"What are you doing here?"

She fidgeted with the strap on the tote bag, unable to look him in the face. "I'm . . . here because of Jurnee," she whispered.

"I guess your *man* put you on a private jet, huh?"

"I'm not with him anymore," she replied quickly, and then added, "I've been here since yesterday."

His expression stayed the same. *Beefing with her now ain't the time nor place,* he reasoned.

"Do you know anything about Jurnee's condition?" he asked.

"Not much. I just got here about ten minutes ago."

He scratched his beard. "You can sit down if you wanna."

She had all types of feelings still locked inside her heart for him. If she could, she wanted to just be in his strong arms again and just be. Just be one, together. As it stood, her life was turned upside down with the blood speeding to her head with a dizzying quickness.

Silence came to rest between them as they sat inches apart. Out of the corner of her eye, she saw the pain in his slack posture. She couldn't stomach the act of adding more hurt in his life by telling him the truth about the baby. That's what she wanted to do. But in truth, going off her talk with Jurnee, she knew she *needed* to tell him the truth. She had to do it, even if it ran the risk of him hating her.

"Trevon, can I talk to you?" she asked nervously.

"You ain't gotta explain nothing to me."

"Yes, I do," she said. "Do you remember when I said you couldn't understand why I—"

"I remember everything you told me! I remember you said it's over, so why try to—"

"Trevon, please!" She laid her hand on his knee. "Just listen to what I have to say, okay? I *never*—I swear, I never meant to hurt you."

"Well, you did. And like I said, it is what it is."

"It's not what you think—"

"It never is!" He finally looked at her. "You wanna talk. G'head and tell me why I deserved this shit you put me through. *Make* me understand!"

She held her useless tears at bay. "I didn't cheat on you, okay? I was already a month pregnant when we met, and I didn't know it."

"So what you saying? The baby ain't mine!"

"I swear to God I didn't know I was pregnant when we met."

"This some bullshit," he muttered. "How the fuck—yo, this shit here is—"

Cutting him off, she told him everything. She left nothing out, speaking the truth, just as she did with Jurnee. He didn't know how to feel when she explained how she planned to have an abortion. "I was wrong. I should've told you back in November after I learned I was fourteen weeks pregnant." She wiped her eyes.

Trevon had to face his reality. D-Hot was the father, not him. Did it hurt? Yes, a hole cratered in the center of his chest.

"Please don't hate me." She sobbed quietly.

Finding the right words to say eluded him. He didn't hate her. He couldn't hate her. Staying silent would not solve any issue.

"So, you thought I would . . . not love you had you told me this last year?"

She nodded weakly.

He sighed. "Life ain't perfect. If you had told me back then, yes, I would've been crushed just like I am now. But it wouldn't have changed how I felt for you."

She looked up. "I'm so sorry, Smooch. I just didn't know—"

"How's the baby?"

She blinked and glanced down at his hand on her belly. All she could do was cry. He sided with staying calm. What good would come from a reaction seeded with anger? Nothing. What shook him were the memories of all the good times they shared. Their issue was defined easily. A mistake on LaToria's part that they would have to settle together. He was in love with her for the present and the future. He could not judge her. Not tonight, not tomorrow, never.

On the strength of keeping it real, he eased his arm around her shoulder. "Stop crying, okay? We gon' talk about this, but right now we gotta be strong for Jurnee."

She nodded, thanking God that he didn't hate her on this heartrending Miami night.

31

BUSTIN' SHOTS

February 9

Thursday, 10:03 P.M. - Miami, Florida

Back at the Mondrian hotel, Tahkiyah moved a step closer to uncovering LaToria's whereabouts. By visiting the AEF webpage, she came across the news about the accident involving Honey Drop. Tahkiyah, at first, didn't make the connection of Honey Drop being Jurnee until she came across her picture. On a hunch, she then logged into her business Instagram and saw the last post posted by Kandi. She didn't waste any time getting dressed to make a ride to the hospital. On her way out the door, she turned back and added one item in her purse. Her mind was set, and there would be no other alternative other than finding and facing LaToria. Once she was seated inside her BMW, she checked the 9-millimeter inside her purse to make sure it was loaded and ready.

SWAGGA TURNED the headlights off after he found the closest parking spot to Kandi's black Escalade. From his position, he could see the front end of her SUV to his left. He had also seen Trevon's A8, but it was too close to the hospital entrance to do anything crazy. He would wait and form a plan with the .22 on his lap. He sunk lower in the seat when a Metro Dade police van rode by. *A plan! I need a fuckin' plan! Ai'ight. Cappin' that bitch out here might get my ass life. Gotta snatch her ass up somehow.* He picked up the .22 just as it dawned on him of his fuck up. "Damn!" he grumbled, popping the clip out. He only had six rounds left. In his rush to catch Trevon slipping, he had forgotten to reload the .22. *Shit! Three for Trevon and three for Kandi. Fuck it.*

KANDI WAS BACK on Instagram making an update when a frugally dressed middle-aged man shuffled into the quiet waiting room. It was easily seen that he was homeless.

"'Scuse me," he said with his hands in his pockets.

No one bothered to look his way and make eye contact with him. The only reason Kandi looked up was due to the funky smell coming off his body. She moved her purse under her seat with her foot, ignoring the white bum like everyone else. She looked past him, hoping that Trevon would return with some good news about Jurnee's status.

"Um . . ." the bum continued. "Anybody in here drive an, uh, black Escalade truck?" He pointed over his shoulders. "Been a little fender bender, and the other—"

"Sir," Kandi said. "Did you say a black one?"

He nodded. "Yeah, an' it got dem big ole chrome rims. Real nice-looking."

Kandi muttered a curse under her breath, *Damn! Of all nights, this is the last thing I need!*

BACK IN FORT LAUDERDALE, Rick was shoved out of his sleep by Tweet. He sat up with his eyes heavy. "What's up?"

"Dawg, we got major problems!" Tweet exclaimed.

"Talk." Rick shoved the covers off as Tweet looked over his shoulder back at the door.

"Feds at the front gate."

"Feds!" Rick jumped up and grabbed his six-shot Sig Sauer sub-compact 9-millimeter.

"FBI, and they ain't playin'."

Rick rubbed his face. "Fuck! Where Swagga?"

"Uh, that's another problem. I checked all over the place, and he ain't here."

"Fuck you mean he ain't here?" Rick shouted.

"He bounced. And the same for Nashlly."

"Call—"

"I already tried calling Swagga like . . . five times. He ain't picking up."

"Yo, let the Feds in. . . . They might . . . shit—just let 'em in. I'ma be down in a sec."

By the time Rick reached the first floor, the Feds were stationed around the living room. A tall, suited, dark-skinned agent greeted Rick at the bottom of the stairs.

"Your name, sir?"

Rick looked at the bodyguards on duty with Tweet. All four were seated on the sofa with worried looks. "Uh, Rick."

The FBI agent frowned. "Your government name."

"Rickey Terrell."

The agent glanced across the room at an agent standing by the lamp. They exchanged a quick nod that went unnoticed by Rick. "Ah, repeat that please."

Rick sighed. "Rickey Terrell."

"Mr. Terrell. I have a search warrant for this property."

"Can I see it?"

Rick was shown a legalized federal search warrant that he couldn't dispute. The only thing that seemed odd was the fact that the warrant didn't list what the Feds were looking for. When Rick took it upon himself to ask, the agent said he would soon find out. Shit got weird when one of the agents pulled out a small handheld scanner. Once he turned it on, he waited a few seconds and then left the room.

"Mr. Terrell, can we step into the kitchen?" the suited agent asked Rick.

"What's this all about?"

"I'll explain in the kitchen."

Rick knew he had no choice. *Fuck! I hope Swagga ain't leave no weed or nothing lying around.* Rick tried to play it cool with the agent following him to the kitchen. Once they were seated at the table, the agent introduced himself.

"My name is Lorenzo Thompson, and I'll get to the point, okay? I have a picture of a man I'd like to show you. Here's the first one." Agent Thompson reached inside his jacket and removed two 4 x 6 glossy pictures.

Rick's stomach dropped to the floor when the agent slid a picture of Fritz across the table. It was clear the picture was taken without Fritz knowing it.

"His *real* name is Ronald Bleibtreu. Born in Germany and he has a *very* interesting military background, which I can't speak on. He's fluent in six different languages, and you might know him simply as . . . Fritz."

"Never seen him before." Rick slid the picture back.

"Are you positive, Mr. Terrell?"

Rick nervously scratched his neck. "Yeah, I 'on't know dude."

Agent Thompson slid the second picture across the table. It was a closeup of Fritz lying face down on a table. "We found him at the Fontainebleau today. He was shot four times, close range with a small caliber."

Rick stared at the picture. *Shit, I'm good! Ain't kill the muthafucka.* Rick started to relax a little. "I don't know him."

Agent Thompson adjusted his brown tie and then sat back, crossing his arms. "The FBI has been aware of Ronald for quite a while . . . five years, to be exact. He's an expert at taking care of things. Making people take permanent naps, if you know what I mean."

"Nah, I don't."

"Anyway, our agency got word that Ronald had created too many enemies abroad. We heard he was bringing his *talent* to the U.S. By then we had a nice thick intelligence file on Ronald, and with that, we came up with a plan."

"Yo, why are you telling me all this? I don't know the dude." Rick was irritated.

"I'm almost done. Well, one of our agents met Ronald in parts of Portugal and gave him a gift. A gift we *knew* he would keep. See, we couldn't allow him to roam freely in the U.S. knowing what we knew about him. We allowed him to move as he pleased because we were *always* on him."

Rick cleared his throat. "Yo, this is a waste of time because—"

"Do you know the charge for conspiracy to commit murder, Mr. Terrell?"

Rick shifted in the chair. Things took a turn toward a fucked-up situation when the agent with the handheld device entered the kitchen with a bagged object. Agent Thompson stood as the second agent handed him the evidence bag.

"This look familiar to you?" Agent Thompson asked.

What the fuck! That's Fritz's black cigar box! How the fuck that shit get here?

"It was in the master bedroom," the second agent told Thompson.

"Who sleeps in that room, Mr. Terrell? Care to tell me?" Agent Thompson pressed.

"I don't know." He shrugged.

Agent Thompson was tired of the games. "Look, this cigar box is the gift we gave Ronald. It's a tracking device *and* a listening device, okay? Now, do I need to repeat word for word of you talking to Ronald about hiring him to kill David Reed, aka D-Hot on January 21 of last month at the Fontainebleau?"

Rick knew the deal and how the FBI got down. "Ain't got shit else to say. I wanna call my lawyer." Rick eased back from the table.

Agent Thompson nodded, giving the signal to arrest Rick, just a split second before Rick took his fate into his own hands.

~

TREVON COULDN'T HIDE his letdown after his brief talk with one of the doctors. No new information was being released about Jurnee's status. Rounding the corner to the waiting room, he saw a face that slowed his steps. *What the hell is she doing here? And where is LaToria?* He walked by a row of occupied chairs to where Tahkiyah stood by the water fountain.

"You following me?" he asked.

"Trevon!" she said. "I see we meet once again." She forced a smile, her hazel eyes darting around the waiting room.

"You looking for somebody?" he asked.

She pushed her glasses up on her nose. She had to come clean and tell him what was really going on. "Indeed, I am," she told him. "I'm looking for—"

She was interrupted when Trevon's iPhone started ringing.

"Uh, hold on for a sec. I gotta take this call." He turned his back to her and answered LaToria's call. "Hey. Where are you and why did you—"

"What up, playboy!"

Trevon took the phone from his ear to double check the caller ID and number. As clear as day, LaToria's name, number, and a small image of her face showed on the screen. He recognized the voice, and it turned his stomach inside out.

"Don't get all quiet on me!" Swagga jeered. "Shit gonna *almost* be like a déjà vu fo' yo' ass tonight! Only this time, ain't gon' be no tricks, feel me? Well, I don't know if you still care fo' this 'ho, Kandi or not. But yeah, I got 'er and you know what I want!"

"What type of shit you on?" Trevon's temper came sudden, like a lightning strike.

"I'ma be on this bitch's *ass* if you don't do what I fuckin' tell you! And trust me, dawg, I don't give a fuck 'bout this bitch being pregnant!"

"Look, just tell me what you want. Ain't no need to do anything to harm her."

"Bitch, didn't I just say it's gonna be a déjà vu! I want them videos you got since you an' yo' bitch played me the first time. Don't know how the fuck you got 'er off the boat, but shit goin' my way tonight!"

"Swagga, I'll give you whatever you want, ai'ight? Just don't hurt—"

"Listen up! You gon' see me tonight. See, I can play games just like you. I guess you think shit just gon' fly 'bout you fuckin' Kendra! Nah, muthafuckas takin' my kindness fo' a weakness ends tonight!"

Trevon wasn't in a position to agitate Swagga. "Yo, I hear ya'. Just tell me what to do."

"Oh, so you do care. Even after this bitch been fuckin' around behind your back! You's a sucka fo' love ass bum. Listen, and I won't say it twice. I want you to come alone to the same spot where this shit went down between us last year."

"The warehouse?"

"Right. Come alone so we can talk. Settle this shit like men. Just you and me."

"What time?"

"Midnight. That will gimme some time to have fun with this big booty 'ho I got wit' me. Shit, I know you don't mind me runnin' up in it. Not with how you fucked Kendra an' her fat ass friend."

Trevon glanced at his watch. It was ten minutes to eleven. Every second LaToria was with Swagga would tear him apart. He felt helpless, having no one to turn to. Calling the police would only make matters worse.

"Midnight, muthfucka!" Swagga said.

"TAKE ALL your clothes off and hurry the fuck up!" Swagga shoved Kandi on the small bed inside a cheap motel along 12th Avenue in Hialeah. He moved along the green wall with the .22 aimed at her. "And I mean er'thang. I'ma have me some fun, and bitch, you can bag them tears because they don't move me."

She hated him so much that she couldn't even look at him. She removed her shoes and then reached behind her back to unzip the dress.

Swagga sat down on a dingy brown chair beside the night table. He watched her tugging the expensive dress down her super thick frame. Seeing the swelling of her belly had him boiling with envy. *How she gonna let a broke ass jailbird bust raw over me?* His bitter thoughts grew as she slowly took her bra off. *Damn, that bitch bad. Titties big as hell. Hmm, look at that cat!* "Turn around and take them drawers off. And do it slow. Show that phat ass!" he said, undoing his belt. He wanted her to feel like shit. When he had his dick out, he fumbled with his cell phone. "Act like your ass at the strip club, bitch."

She trembled, feeling humiliated as he played one of his songs from his phone.

"Dance, bitch! And keep that ass facing me. That's all I wanna see. Now, do what it do and bounce that ass." He laid the .22 on the table. All the love he once had for her was twisted in hate.

She kept her eyes shut, moving her wide hips off beat. She couldn't find a rhythm, no matter how hard she tried.

"Now turn around," he said, midway through the song. "And open yo' eyes! Look at my dick. Yeah, now rub your nipple and rub that pussy." He stroked his dick at the sight before him. "Now, get down like a dog—"

"Swagga, ple—"

"Now, bitch!" he sneered as he grabbed the .22.

She held her stomach with tears streaking down her cheeks. Sobbing, she got down on all fours.

"Now, crawl yo' ass over here and suck my dick. C'mon, bitch. Ain't got all fuckin' night!" He gestured with the gun. "You do it fo' a livin', but tonight it's fo' free."

Fear of not seeing tomorrow gripped Kandi's soul. She was afraid of Swagga. She saw the deranged expression etched across his face.

"Don't look away from me!" He pointed the .22 at her. "Shit aint gonna turn out in your fuckin' favor like it did last year! I promise your phat ass that it won't! I should make you choke on this dick! But since I don't wanna leave no DNA behind, yo ass in luck tonight! Stupid ass gonna learn tonight." *I gotta dead this 'ho soon. Ain't no need to take any kind of chances tonight.* Swagga thumbed the safety *on* then *off* then back *on*.

"Hurry up, 'ho! Put yo' shit back on. We 'bout to take a ride."

AT THE SAME TIME, a manhunt was in its early stages for Rick. He managed to kill the two FBI agents in the kitchen before he hauled ass out the back door. It was true of a person being able to hear bullets whizzing by. Rick could personally attest to it from the close rounds that nearly popped his top. The remaining Feds had opened up a barrage of lead on him. A Florida Highway Patrol helicopter was the first to respond to the Feds' frantic plea for assistance. Swagga's mansion resembled a police convention with local, state, and federal law authorities amassed on the property.

Rick had run north until he shook the Feds in the dense woods. He knew they wouldn't cease chasing, so he wouldn't cease running. As he sprinted across an open field, he tripped and stumbled in the dark. Rolling to his back, he struggled to catch his breath. The starlit sky gave him no sense of peace. Pulling out his cell phone, he called Swagga. *Dis fool better answer!*

"Yo, whut up?"

"It's over, dawg," Rick said, rolling to get up.

"Whut the hell you—"

"Man, shut up and listen!" Rick took off at a jog as he gave Swagga the scoop. "We fucked up. Feds been listening since day one. And if you can't explain how you got Fritz's cigar box without poppin' him, it's over for you." Rick sped up when he heard the dogs barking in the distance. "Swagga! I need your help—" Rick took his phone from his ear. "Bitch ass muthafucker!" he vexed at seeing how easily Swagga had turned his ass around for him to kiss.

The call had ended.

32

FEEL MY PAIN

February 9
Thursday, 10:27 P.M. - Hialeah, Florida

Kandi trembled uncontrollably as Swagga shoved her back inside the trunk of the Flying Spur. Her hands were tied and her panties stuffed in her mouth. The ripped bed sheet Swagga tied around her face kept her quiet. All she thought about was the baby and Trevon. She was afraid that both would suffer because of her. She was thrown against a hard object when the Flying Spur sped out of the motel parking lot. She cried hard, finding it easier to give up. Just as it seeped into her mind, she forced that thought out.

Minute after minute, mile after mile, her trip in the trunk increased. Something wasn't right. When she cleared her mind, she realized the trip to the warehouse should have been short. Focusing on the sounds around her, she judged she was speeding along a highway. The sedan had been rolling nonstop for at least ten minutes. She wasn't going to the warehouse.

TREVON DIDN'T KNOW what to do anymore. Showing no fear of Swagga, he had driven to warehouse 1017 at two minutes to midnight. His sedan sat with the engine running and the lights off. He waited, feeling it was pointless to pray since he was a sinner. When the time on his phone showed 12:20 a.m., he stepped out of his car.

He dialed LaToria's number. It wasn't answered, not even a voicemail. At the end of his rope, he looked at the ground and struggled not to cry. "Why God?" he raged. He tried her number again. Nothing. Sliding down to the ground, he leaned his head back against his car. He was defeated. If Swagga were to walk up and catch him slipping, he wouldn't care. Jurnee crossed his mind. He couldn't do shit for her, and it pained him that it stood the same for LaToria. Just as he gave up all hope, his iPhone chimed.

RICK WAS WINDED, pausing for the eighth time to catch his breath. Leaning up against a tree, he wished he could redo his past. He ruined his life over $20,000! "Fuck!" he muttered, kicking at the high weeds.

Suddenly, he heard voices to his left. He ducked, moving around the tree with the baby 9-millimeter gripped tightly. With only four shots left, a shootout was suicidal. He peered in the direction of the voices, hoping like hell they hadn't heard him. His heart thumped in his ears. He eased down to one knee, his finger on the trigger. The voices grew louder but dropped silently not a second later. Rick stayed motionless, only moving his eyes. Remaining in one spot was not aiding his escape. He *knew* someone was close, but he couldn't take the risk to give his position away.

"Rickey Terrell!" A loud voice came from his left, followed by a bright spotlight. "This is Broward—"

Rick let off two quick shots over his shoulder and took off running. He made a life altering choice by falling for Swagga's plot. He allowed Swagga's troubles to become his downfall. Running hard, he intentionally stayed in the spotlight. This time he didn't hear any bullets whizzing by. He didn't hear the sporadic shots of gunfire behind him. Closing his eyes, he sensed the final period of his life. It came a split second later in the form of a 5.56 full metal jacket round that punched him an inch below the base of his skull.

THE TEXT MESSAGE Trevon had received led him to an abandoned trap house in Carol City.

He parked behind Swagga's Flying Spur and a brown van. The trap house was unlit and located at the back of a dead-end street. He stepped over broken wine bottles and crushed beer cans. A tightness pained his heart when he neared the Bentley. Under the faint cast of the moon, he saw streaks of blood on the trunk lid and bumper. He was numb, yet he went on.

Taking a step on the concrete and wooden porch, he prepared himself to face whatever awaited him. Pushing the creaky door open, he saw blood at the entrance. A light was on, a single lamp without a shade over it. He stepped inside the funky smelling house. To his right sat a black couch with several tears in the seat cushions. All of the windows were covered with black curtains that reached the floor. Drug use was apparent by the broken needles and empty clear vials. The piss-stained colored walls were bare, marred with ragged holes along sections of the baseboard. His attention fell to the smear of blood trailing from where he stood that marked a path down the dark hall.

"LaToria!" he called out. Dreading the silence, he took a deep breath and then moved along the line of blood. He would not accept thoughts of any harm befalling on her. He refused it. There were three doors along the narrow hall. Two were on the left and one on the right.

The blood continued past the first door on the left, only to turn and go into the second. A light was on. All he wanted was for LaToria to be safe. He was not a man of great need. He called her name again. No reply. Sliding a hand down his face, he opened the door. What he was met with sent him stumbling back against the wall. His eyes told the truth, but his mind couldn't accept the reality of the sight.

33

BAPTIZED IN ETERNAL FIRE

February 10
Friday, 1:23 A.M. - Carol City, Florida

"Who the fuck are you?" Nashlly asked Trevon, with a black .380 at her side.

"Trevon," he replied.

She glared at him with a spiteful expression. "He good, Art. You can put it down."

Art lowered the pistol grip Remington 12-gauge pump from Trevon's face. "Anybody else come wit' you?"

"Nah," Trevon said, shaking his head. "You the one that sent me the text?"

"Yup," Art said with the pump pointed to the floor. "Yo." He turned to Nashlly. "I'ma go outside and make sure we don't get no unexpected visitors."

She nodded without taking her eyes off Trevon. "C'mon in." She waved him inside the small bedroom. "Watch out for that puddle of blood," she said, wiping a sheen of sweat off her forehead.

He stared at the bed and the dingy, bloody mattress. "Where's LaToria?"

"In the bathroom. She's okay and lucky."

"I want to see 'er!"

Nashlly frowned. "Tonight ain't a good time to be lifting your voice at me. If it wasn't for me and my dude, your girl woulda—" Nashlly paused when the bathroom door to her right came open.

"LaToria!" Trevon rushed across the room, taking her in his arms.

Nashlly watched them, wishing she had a man that would love and care for her. *Nah, fuck that shit!* she thought.

"What the fuck is going on?" Trevon asked with LaToria sobbing against his chest.

"We both got smoke with Swagga," Nashlly said. "I had a little issue wit' him today. Long story short, we followed him and just waited for a chance to kidnap his punk ass. We caught him slipping at a motel. He had your girl tied up in the trunk. After she told me what was up, we called you here."

"All this blood?" He looked at the floor.

"It's from Swagga," Nashlly told him.

"Where is he?"

She looked across the room. "In the closet."

When Trevon tried to release LaToria, she clung to him tighter. Nashlly brushed by them and then yanked the closet door open. Swagga was naked and secured with wide strips of duct tape. His nose was bloody, and he had a seeping gash along his hairline.

"I exist now, huh!" Nashlly kicked Swagga on his knee. She stared down at him with raw disgust clouding her eyes. "Jamilah said she wished she could be here, but she'll settle for the life insurance when we body your ass!"

Swagga strained against the tape. When Trevon stepped up next to Nashlly, he stopped struggling. Swagga stared at Trevon, knowing the outcome wouldn't be in his favor. He recoiled when Trevon squatted near him. Trevon had no pity for Swagga. He slowly pulled the duct tape off his mouth. Swagga dropped his head on the dirty floor, breathing hard.

"Why we have to go through this shit again?" Trevon wanted an explanation. "You risked everything you got . . . for what?"

Swagga ignored Trevon. If Rick had told him the truth about the Fritz issue, he knew a murder case was over his head. So what, Frank Ocean came out of the closet. Swagga couldn't do it. He couldn't face the shame.

Trevon stood back up just as Art reentered the room with a red gasoline jug.

"Nooo, nooo, nooo, please!" Swagga moaned. "Nashlly, baby, I'll make it up—"

"Save it!" Nashlly shouted. "You're worth more to me dead!"

Trevon didn't feel right with what was about to go down. He tried to build off his dislike toward Swagga, but his conscience returned. When LaToria squeezed his waist, it was then the vision of Swagga's burning yacht popped back in his head.

"You were right 'bout this night being like last year," Trevon said as Art opened the jug of gasoline. "Only this time it's your ass that's getting burned!"

Gasoline fumes filled the bedroom as Art began sloshing it around the room.

"FUCK YOU!" Swagga screamed. "Fuck all of y'all."

Trevon turned with LaToria in his arms and left the room. Swagga's screams and loud cursing followed them down the hall.

Nashlly moved aside as Art poured the remaining gasoline on Swagga. His anger was now reduced to pleading tears and choking sobs. When Art pulled out a lighter, he looked at Nashlly.

"G'head and—"

"No." She took the lighter. "I'll do it. Go and get the van started."

"You sure?"

She nodded. Once she was alone, she wiped a tear from her eye.

"It didn't have to be like this, Swagga. I *tried* to save your ass from Jamilah, but you didn't want me, so—"

"Please shoot me, Nashlly! Please, yo! Don't let me burn alive . .

." he cried, banging his head on the floor. "I'm begging . . . please don't make me suffer like this."

Trevon was backing out the yard just as a single gunshot ripped the silence of the night. Three seconds later, Nashlly ran out of the trap house as flames engulfed the bedroom. He watched it burn for a few seconds before he left it all in the rearview mirror. He sped off in silence, with LaToria curled up in the passenger seat. His night wasn't over, Jurnee. Was she dead or alive? He drove directly back to the hospital as his heart stirred for LaToria.

Tahkiyah was minutes from going to bed when her cell phone rang. She intended to ignore it until she saw it was her private investigator calling.

"Hello," she answered.

"Ah, I know it's late, but I don't think you'll mind this call."

"What do you have for me?"

"My guy in Atlanta that works at that credit card company. He just sent me an e-mail. LaToria's name popped up when she used her credit card. She's back in Miami."

"I'm aware of that," she said. "I just don't know—"

"She has a room at the Mondrian," he told her. "She checked in on Thursday."

"Are you sure!"

"Positive. I went ahead and called down there to see if she's still checked in and she is. She's in room 214."

She thanked him, then sat down to calm herself. Her mind was made up a few moments later when she rushed to get dressed. Again, she left the room with the 9-millimeter concealed in her purse.

LaToria experienced a numbness toward reality as she rode the elevator up to her floor at the Mondrian. She had convinced Trevon that she was okay. She left him at the hospital with a promise to return after she showered and got herself together. As for the bullshit Swagga had forced her to do, she kept it from him. Her feelings of Swagga's murder was blank. She was neither happy nor sad. Stepping off the elevator with her head down, she wondered if Trevon would give her a second chance. Would he accept her child? All she wanted in life was to be happy.

"Excuse me."

LaToria lifted her head and saw a beautiful woman standing across the hall. What struck LaToria as odd were the tears welling in the woman's eyes behind her glasses.

"Are you LaToria Nicole Frost?" Tahkiyah dropped her hand inside her purse.

LaToria had been through too much shit tonight to be scared anymore.

"Yeah. And who are you?"

Tahkiyah closed her eyes. *I have to do it! I have to do it!* she chanted in her head. Opening her eyes, she took the first step in reaching peace and that sentiment of closure that left her heart torn. "LaToria," she said. "I'm . . . Tahkiyah Bradford. I'm your mother."

34

A NIGHT TO REMEMBER

February 10
Friday, 2:58 P.M. - Miami, Florida

The burning trap house in Carol City had burned to its foundation by the time the police and fire department arrived. An APB was already out for Swagga's Flyer Spur. As soon as the Feds received word of its location, they rushed to the scene. Many weren't surprised when a charred body was found in the closet. The county coroner pointed out the single bullet hole in front of the skull.

Swagga's life came to an end due to his jealousy and fear of how others viewed him. His demise also centered on him being enthralled with things he didn't have while ignoring the items he possessed.

LaToria had to practice what she wanted to preach to Trevon. She had to give Tahkiyah a chance to speak the truth. Tahkiyah tearfully told LaToria how she had cheated on her husband and gave birth behind her husband's back. She pleaded for LaToria to forgive her for putting her up for adoption. Tahkiyah sobbed deeply, asking for forgiveness and a chance to make things right.

LaToria had known of Tahkiyah by her first name only since she was ten. She cried with her mom, choosing forgiveness over hate. She told Tahkiyah of her unfair past and what pushed her to do porn. Together, they cried for both hurt and joy. LaToria knew she wouldn't be alone anymore when her mom promised to never leave her again. As for Trevon, Tahkiyah had sent him a text message before she returned to the hospital with LaToria.

I hope you will take this with an understanding that even I myself find hard to grasp. Our night. Let it stay between us. I was wrong to let it happen and had you known who I was, I doubt it would've happened. I'm sorry, but building my bond with my daughter is all I live for now. TTYL
Tahkiyah, LaToria's mom.

TREVON HAD READ Tahkiyah's text message twice, but emotionally he didn't have the strength to deal with it. With his head back against the wall and his eyes shut, a Black female surgeon entered the waiting room.

"Is there a Mr. Trevon Harrison here?" she asked softly.

Trevon shot to his feet. "How is she?" he asked, full of concern.

AT THE SAME TIME, LaToria and Tahkiyah walked up on Trevon and the surgeon. LaToria watched closely as the surgeon spoke quietly with Trevon. *Please God. Let it be good news.*

35

THINGS DONE CHANGED

May 25

Friday, 3:45 P.M. – North Miami, Florida

Three months later . . .

Trevon's career had rocketed past the moon and rose to a status of A-list stardom. With a new manager at his side and two new films on the market, his life was nothing like he dreamed of. He was talked about favorably from New York to Hollywood, California, with rumors trending left and right about who he was dating. He made a second interracial film with Chelsea that turned into an instant hit! Porn was his true hustle. He earned appearance fees to show up at clubs, and a buzz grew instantly when *TMZ LIVE* broke the news about him being seen in VIP at Club Honesty with Amara Lanegra.

Because of his hustle and the team behind him, Trevon became a star. *Any* woman he was seen with, the media speculated he was sexually involved. In most cases, they were correct, but in truth, he was 100% single and focused on his career.

The sun had its chest out today with a high of 92 degrees. Trevon slowed his brand-new Fuji white Mercedes-Benz S580 then into the horseshoe driveway of a modest two-story house. With the

496-hp engine quietly running, he tapped twice on the horn. Pulling out his iPhone, he sent a text message to Kendra.

Hey u! Hope all is well wit u and lil one. Just had u on my mind. Be sure to call me as soon as you have the time. Take care.

Trevon's conscience troubled him over Kendra's daughter having to grow up without a father. The day it was proven that it was Swagga that was shot and burned, Kendra and her daughter moved up to Raleigh, North Carolina. With the money left to her from Swagga's estate, she had no reason to ever work again. Trevon would never tell her of the role he played in Swagga's death. When a shadow moved over him, he looked up from his phone.

"Y'all ready?" he said, getting out of the sedan to help Ariana with the bag she carried.

"You're the one that's late," Jurnee said as she stepped off the porch. Trevon smiled at his best friend. The car accident had resulted in her left leg being amputated from the knee down. Though her walk was slow in the prosthetic limb, she was alive and deeply in love with Ariana. He tried to help Jurnee inside the car, and naturally she frowned and slapped his hands away.

"How y'all queens feelin'?" he asked as he backed out of the driveway. Ariana chimed from the back seat that she was fine as Jurnee leaned across the center console to kiss him on the lips.

Jurnee no longer dealt with any regret over being afraid to deal with concerns of her heart when it pertained to Trevon. The accident was a turning point in her life. She had woken up on the hospital bed to see Trevon at her side. He had held her hand, supporting her as the doctor told her about her loss and gain. During the amputation of her leg, her loss, her blood work made a discovery. Jurnee was a few days pregnant. Her gain.

"I can't believe Janelle is getting married today!" Jurnee said.

"And she's two months pregnant," Trevon added.

"Hey," Ariana said as she leaned up between the seats. "Y'all come up with a name for the baby yet?"

Jurnee smiled. "Not yet. But I've agreed to let my baby daddy come up with a name."

Nashlly was still in Miami and living off those five minutes of social media fame she had by dating Swagga. She flawlessly played the role of a brokenhearted lover. It was *rumored* that she was dating/fucking a rookie in the NBA, but he remained nameless.

Jamilah collected a check for $7.5 million, only half of what Kendra received. Jamilah knew Kendra was always number one out of Swagga's three baby mommas. Reluctantly, she gave Nashlly $1.5 million just to keep her out of her face. As for Art, he was back up in New Bern, North Carolina, thinking of ways to triple the $500,000 Jamilah had dropped in his lap.

LaToria and Tahkiyah had stayed true to their word. They gave each other a chance, and through time they became inseparable. They lived together in a five-star condo on Miami Beach and became what many people took for granted, a family.

"This doctor needs to hurry his tail up!" Tahkiyah said, losing her patience while she sat in the obstetrician office with LaToria.

"Something's wrong," LaToria whined from the examination table.

"Hush, girl, and stop all that worrying. He's just running some tests and—"

"My baby is too late. I shoulda had her two weeks ago!" LaToria calculated the facts in her head. *I was fourteen weeks pregnant back in November, so my nine months is . . . now! Please God. Let my baby be okay.* Lying on her back, she caressed her swollen belly with fresh tears pooling in her eyes. She *knew* something wasn't right. Her soul told her so.

To avoid worrying herself to death, she thought of Trevon. She was still in love with him, but she understood his choice to take things slow. He showed his genuine concern for her and the baby by attending a few doctor appointments with her. Back in February, she had visited him on Valentine's Day. Emotions that were once hidden were shown openly. They had sex twice that day, but a wall still stood between them. They spoke daily, for neither could go on and ignore the feelings they still shared for each other.

Now, in truth, LaToria was happy that Jurnee had pulled through. But in secret, she had cried her eyes out when she learned that Jurnee was pregnant by Trevon. There was no hate, only a sadness that left an aching pain on her heart. With her effort to gain Trevon's love back, his connection with Jurnee would forever be unique and special. Jurnee would give Trevon his firstborn.

LaToria needed to know what was wrong with her baby. A call suddenly came through on her cell phone that her mom answered.

"Hi, Trevon."

LaToria wanted to hear his voice, but she didn't think she could hold herself together. Instead, she motioned to her mom that she didn't want to talk.

"Yeah, we're still at the doctor's office—okay—well, we shouldn't be here much longer and no, we won't miss the wedding and—" She paused when the doctor walked back in. "Trevon, let me call you back. The doctor just got back in. Okay . . . bye-bye."

The doctor stood by the examination table with an iPad. "We have a problem here, Ms. Frost."

LaToria moaned, causing Tahkiyah to come to her side.

"Relax, baby." Tahkiyah rubbed LaToria's face, praying that everything was fine with the baby. "Please tell us what's going on," Tahkiyah said.

The doctor sat down. "The baby is in great shape. All of the tests are fine."

"But . . . you said there's a problem," LaToria cried.

"Ms. Frost, when you went to see that *other* doctor back in November, he made a mistake."

"What kind of *mistake*?" Tahkiyah asked sharply.

"Ma'am, your daughter isn't late at all. The mistake came in the form of your daughter being told she was fourteen weeks pregnant. The truth is, she was only eight and a half weeks pregnant. You're only eight months pregnant, Ms. Frost. Your baby isn't due until June."

Only the sound of the air conditioner filled the office. Kandi couldn't believe what the doctor said.

"Baby," Tahkiyah cried. "You hear that? That means...oh, my God! Trevon is the father."

It was true. A small mistake had sent LaToria on a path of destruction that tore up her happy home. She had no doubt who the father was. Trevon Harrison! Her smooch.

"You...have to let him know," Tahkiyah said. "Do you want me to call him back?"

TO BE CONTINUED

ABOUT THE AUTHOR

Victor L. Martin began his writing career back in 2003. His path to earning the title "author" was achieved while he was incarcerated. Born in Richmond, Virginia and raised in Selma, North Carolina and Miami, Florida, Victor used his life events to mix with fiction with the dose of reality to write his unique tales. Single, with no kids and set to make Atlanta, Georgia his new home will launch Victor to the pinnacle of his career in writing and his journey into filmmaking.

Photo by Dominique A. Covington

ALSO BY VICTOR L. MARTIN

The Game of Deception

Miami Nights

Miami Nights 2: Still Naked

Miami Nights 3: The Climax

Pretty Boy Hustlerz

Pretty Boy Hustlerz 2

CLASSIC STREET LIT SERIES

FROM WAHIDA CLARK PRESENTS INNOVATIVE PUBLISHING

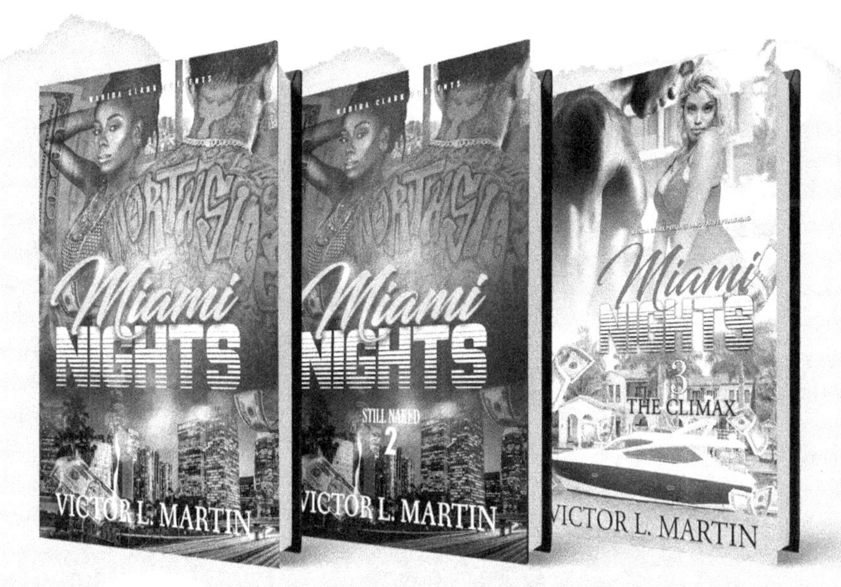

CLASSIC STREET LIT
S-E-R-I-E-S

FROM WAHIDA CLARK PRESENTS INNOVATIVE PUBLISHING

NEW SCI-FI FANTASY
FROM WAHIDA CLARK PRESENTS
INNOVATIVE PUBLISHING
LONERS
DB BRAY & WAHIDA CLARK
EMPERORS ASSASSINS
WAHIDA CLARK
RESURRECTION
BOOK ONE IN THE KINDRED SERIES
ZED AMADEO
Fractured Princess
DEBRA RENEE BYRD
THE ROAD TO RESISTANCE
FIRST BOOK OF THE VANGUARD I
CHASE BOLLING
THE ROAD TO RESISTANCE
FIRST BOOK OF THE VANGUARD I
CHASE BOLLING
THE WAR WE MAKE
FIRST BOOK OF THE VANGUARD II
CHASE BOLLING

SCIENCE FICTION FANTASY
FOR THE CULTURE
W. CLARK PUBLISHING

WAHIDA CLARK
PRESENTS
INNOVATIVE PUBLISHING

CLASSIC STREET LIT
—S—E—R—I—E—S—

FROM WAHIDA CLARK PRESENTS INNOVATIVE PUBLISHING

9 781954 161436